Black Cat Blues

by

Jo-Ann Carson

Black Cat Blues is a work of fiction. Although it takes place in Vancouver, which is a real city on the west coast of Canada, all names, characters, places and incidents are the products of the my imagination or are used fictitiously. Any resemblance to actual events, locales, or persons, living or dead, is entirely coincidental.

©2016 Jo-Ann Carson Terpstra
ISBN –9780994955609
Cover design by **Steven Novak**

Dedication

To my father, Max Carson, who loved the blues.
I miss you, Dad. This one's for you.

Acknowledgements

This story has been sleeping under the bed for two years. Part of me hoped it would age like fine wine, while another part wanted to think about the characters a little bit longer. Now, I'm bringing it to life.

I have many people to thank for helping me in this process.

First, I'd like to thank my husband, Piet, who encourages my passion for writing. He's been my rock through the tumultuous journey of becoming a published writer. I'd also like to thank my daughters Hannah and Jasmin for their love and support. I am truly blessed to have such a wonderful family. My deepest gratitude goes to urban fantasy writer JC McKenzie for being my kick-ass critique partner, and Hannah Myles and Judy Hudson for being my first beta-readers. I used their suggestions to revise the story.

Then there's my professional team:

Thanks go to my editor, Dr. Philip Newey who helps me clean up my language.

And thanks go to my cover designer Steven Novak. He nailed the urban noir feel of the story.

And lastly, I'd like to thank you, my reader. Without you, there would be no story.

All errors are my own.

Also by Jo-Ann Carson

The Mata Hari Series

#1 - *Covert Danger*

#2 - *Born of Magic*

#3 - *Ancient Danger*

#4 – *Loving Danger*

Vancouver Blues Series

#1 - *Black Cat Blues*

#2 – *Ain't Misbehavin'*

Black Cat Blues - Awards

- First, 2013 Southern Heat (contemporary series)
- Third, 2013, Lone Star contest (Romantic Suspense)
- Finalist, 2013 Romancing the Lake (Romantic Suspense)

Early Reviews

***** "Maggy Malone sings the blues, plays guitar, and finds dead bodies but she avoids police. She attracts men, murderers, bad luck, & cops. Each chapter begins with a musical quote which is quite fun. The Vancouver setting is a wonderful change. Add in a tale of treasure, cults, premonitions, bad marriages gone awry, a blind man, hunky suitors, witty RMCP, & a Marlin spike-wielding killer & you have a fascinating mystery with a little romance tossed in for good measure. I think I'll become a Maggy Malone fan. My first Jo-Ann Carson book, but it won't be my last. I won this book in a contest & the review is my own." Kay Lib, 5 star review on Amazon

***** "Holy hell this is a dang good book! Fast pace that will keep you turning the pages! Not an easy book to put down nor walk away from when

you started! Sure found myself reading all night and losing track of time. There's so much that lays behind the cover that you don't won't to miss!"
Peggy Salkill, 5 stars Amazon

***** "Black Cat Blues, is a heart-stopping non-stop thrilling suspense. I could not put it down! It kept me reading until late into the night. I devoured it to find out who was the murderer! Exciting till the very last page. Amazing debut, for Jo-Ann Carson's new series Vancouver Blues Suspense. A must to read if you love thriller suspense with a romantic touch! Excellent writing, a very fast-paced thriller that you won't want to put down.

CHAPTER 1

Music washes away from the soul the dust of everyday life. ~ Berthold Auerbach

Walking through a dark alley at three-thirty in the morning wasn't smart, but Maggy Malone didn't have a choice, or at least not one she liked. A bone-numbing, cold wind off the Salish Sea hit her face as she opened the back door of the Black Cat Blues Bar. Pulling her jacket close to her body with one hand, and holding her guitar case in the other, she descended the stairs into the inky darkness of the night. But after her first step, she checked over her shoulder.

Vancouver in November—endless gray skies and drizzle. The waning moon slipped behind layers of dark clouds, leaving little light to help her on her way. She quickened her pace. A warm glow beckoned from the street lamp, just a hundred yards away. Her scalp tingled as if a dozen spiders slipped across it. She took a deep breath of the salty night air.

What the hell. She could handle a few minutes of fear. Singing in the best blues bar on the coast had been her life dream. If it meant getting up close and personal with the creepy, back alley on occasion, then so be it. Her shoulders tightened.

Stepping over dirty needles, used condoms and Micky D wrappers left behind by the people who shared the alley—the prostitutes, the addicts and the homeless—she tried not to let the sadness of their lives reach inside her. But the stagnant stench of rotting garbage and urine turned her stomach. If only it would really rain, then the city would be washed clean.

Where are the street people? Usually there'd be one or two around at this time of night, huddled against the cold, brick walls with only a blanket to keep out the cold and misfortunes of the night. Something felt wrong. She couldn't put her finger on it . . . but something. She looked over her shoulder again. No one.

A chill crawled slowly up her spine. She adjusted the weight of her canvas guitar case into her other hand and prepared to run. She wasn't sure what she would be running from, but just in case. A woman in an alley has to be ready.

It had been a long night. She should never have descended into this God forsaken alley. Friggin Frank. It was his fault. She took a deep breath as her eyes darted in every direction. The feeling of darkness, much darker than the night around her, picked at her senses. Her throat tightened and she couldn't swallow.

I'm just scaring myself. The lights of the street were only a few yards away. *Everything will be fine.*

Then she saw the body lying still in a pool of blood. A silvery spike protruded from his chest. Her breath stopped. It was the handsome stranger she had seen in the bar an hour ago. Maggy ran to him.

She checked his breathing. It was shallow, but he was still alive.

She punched 911 into her cell phone.

Waiting for the connection, she yelled into the dark night, "Help." But no one came running.

Alone with a dying man. Was his murderer close by? No one gets a spike in their chest by accident. Was the murderer watching her? Tiny hairs rose on the back of her neck.

"Nine-one-one. State your emergency." The operator's toneless voice cut into the night.

"There's a man. He's been stabbed . . ." Maggy took off her scarf and pressed it to his wound around the spike. Could she stop the flow of blood? "Hurry."

"Where are you, ma'am?"

"In the alley behind the . . ." Her own voice sounded dry and robotic. She needed to get the words out. "The Black Cat Blues Bar on Fifth."

"An ambulance is on the way."

Maggy looked at the man. Would they make it in time?

"You need to apply pressure to the

wound. . ."

I'm friggen doing that. Bright red blood oozed through the scarf and onto her hand. The man's face paled as his life force drained from him. She put down the phone, swallowed hard, and used both hands to apply steady pressure to her scarf. "Hang in there, buddy. Don't die on me."

His eyelids moved just a fraction. But they moved.

Swollen and cut, his face looked as if it had taken a beating. She leaned down to listen at his mouth. His breathing was faint and ragged. Seconds ticked by slowly.

Then his lips moved. She strained to hear him.

"Tell Logan," he rasped. She waited for him to say more. Pain flooded his eyes. His lips trembled, but no sound came out.

She could barely breathe herself. The man's life was sliding away in front of her, and there was nothing she could damn well do to stop it. She pressed down anyway, and his blood seeped through her fingers.

"Tell Logan," he repeated. She bent closer. "The Emer . . . old . . ."

He made a horrid gurgling sound and a gush of blood flowed from his mouth. His muscles jerked and quivered. He was fighting to live, as his organs shut down.

As the sound of sirens pierced the night, Maggy sat up and met his dead eyes. Shivers ran through her body. Tears streamed down her face.

"May you find peace," she said. She closed his eyes and waited.

***

"And he said nothing?" Inspector Peterson from the Vancouver Police Department asked in a low, gravelly voice that raked her senses.

Maggy tried to tell her body to stop trembling, but it wouldn't. A tiny stream of blood flowed dangerously close to where they stood a couple yards from the body. A policewoman snapped pictures of the dead man. A medical examiner directed two assistants to take evidence. The paramedics waited for orders. It was like standing in the middle of a CSI set, only it was real, all too real.

Maggy took a long, shaky breath and looked at the policeman. "I don't know him."

He gave her a hard-ass cop look that could peel paint off a wall.

The dead man's blood, now dry on her hands, tightened the surface of her skin. At least her tears had stopped. She focused on taking deeper breaths and wished the annoying cop would leave her alone.

"I asked you if he said anything." Gravel Voice towered above her. He stood at least six foot to her five foot three. A jagged scar ran across his square jaw. He had the broad kind of shoulders she always noticed. No doubt he would look good in a uniform, but tonight he wore jeans, a Gore-Tex jacket and a navy-blue toque and looked like any middle-class man in the city, except that his hard-ass eyes screamed, "*Cop!*" A light rain started to fall. He continued to stare at her.

"Nothing," she said. "The man said nothing."

"You don't know anything about the victim? He has no wallet, or identification. Nothing. If there's anything you can tell us about him . . ."

"No. I never met him, but . . ." Her throat felt dry like worn sandpaper. "He was at the Black Cat, down the alley, earlier tonight. That's where I work. I saw him when I was singing. He stood at the end of the bar. I noticed him because his eyes . . ." She hesitated, not wanting to put words to her thoughts. The stranger's eyes had vibrated with a feral wildness, as though the devil had stolen his life. But she couldn't say that. She cleared her throat. "His eyes were intense. I don't know if that helps you. Just a feeling I had. I don't know his name." She left out the part about how sexy he made her feel when he watched her sing.

The detective's silence was more disturbing than any words.

She shifted her feet. "Look, I feel real sorry for the man, but there's nothing I can do for him now. Nothing any of us can do. I need to get some sleep."

"You're tired?"

"Worn out. It's been one hell of a day and now this . . ." She stopped, not finding the words she wanted. How could she complain about her day, when a man had been murdered? With another breath she continued, "I've got day jobs that start at the crack of dawn." That was only five hours away. "Can I just go? I don't know anything about the murder."

She wanted to fade into the night and be forgotten. No, it was more than that. Like a bad nightmare, she wanted her experience in the alley to end so she could get on with her life. She wanted to close the door on her memory of the stranger who had died in her arms.

The inspector gave a solid nod of his head. His brow wrinkled. "Before you go, just tell me one more thing. Why were you in a dark alley in the middle of the night?"

She exhaled slowly and looked once more at the puddle of blood near the dead man.

"We can talk in my car if you prefer, or back at headquarters."

"No, no, I just want to get this over with." She shook back her hair. "When I finished my last set at the Black Cat, I headed out the back door to go home. My car's parked on the street. It's the black Honda. I can give you the license plate number if you want."

"No," he said, tapping his pen on his notepad. "But I still don't get it. Why didn't you go out the front door? It would have been safer. Were you meeting someone in the alley?"

Maggy shook her head. "I was avoiding a drunk named Frank. He keeps asking me out. When I wanted to leave, he was leaning on the wall beside the front door waiting for me. I knew he'd ask me out again and rake his eyes all over me. I didn't want to end my night like that, so I went out the back door. It should have taken five minutes for me to get to my car. I've done it before."

"So tell me again your story of what happened in the alley."

"It's not a story," she said, and repeated the details of how she'd tripped over the man's dead body in the alley.

His right eyebrow rose. Did he know she was holding out on him, or was he a control jerk getting his thrills grilling her?

His hard mouth turned downwards. "You look like you do need sleep," he said. Was that compassion in his voice? A compassionate cop? Maybe he thought she was crazy, or too exhausted to be of much help. Whatever.

"I'll walk you to your car," he said as he fell into step beside her. "What do you have against cops?"

Her shoulders tightened. This guy was good. "Not much." *Just everything.*

The look in his eyes said he didn't believe her, but that was his problem. No doubt he would check her out and find his own answer. All she wanted to do was wash the dead man's dried blood off her body and out of her mind.

They reached her car. She put her guitar case in the back seat and then got in the front. After she closed the door, the inspector tapped on her window. She rolled it down.

"If you remember anything else tonight that may help us learn more about the victim, or the murderer, call me. Otherwise, I want to see you in my office tomorrow morning at nine to make a formal statement." He handed her his card.

"But I can't."

"You will," he said. "Your memoires will come back a piece at a time. Traumatic events steal them for a while." He grimaced. "But they have a nasty way of coming back to haunt you."

"Bloody cops," she muttered just loud enough for him to hear. He stepped back as her old engine sputtered into life.

***

With a trembling hand, she unlocked the door to her houseboat in the Shady Lane Marina at Granville Island. The memory of the dead man in the alley wouldn't leave her. His eyes had touched her in an unsettling way. Had she done right by him? Should she tell the cop his dying words? *Hell no.* The last thing she needed was to get involved. Especially with the police.

After toying with the inspector's card for an hour, she threw it in her recycling bin and went to bed. She'd see Gravel Cop tomorrow. Dead tired, she fell into a restless sleep. The memory of the dead man's blood, pooling in the dark night, kept calling to her.

CHAPTER 2

Music in the soul can be heard by the universe.
~ Lao Tzu

L ogan Daniel's gut wrenched. What kind of mess had his brother Jimmy gotten into this time? He paced the floor of his ex-wife's Kitsilano condo.

Sasha, his five-year-old daughter had a cough that sounded worse than anything he'd ever heard. Her doctor said to do the usual: have her drink lots of fluids and rest. Logan had added ice-cream to list, but she still hacked away, a sound so deep and hoarse it worried him. She sat on the couch eating a bowl full of her favorite ice-cream, Rocky Road with a little spoon. Watching her suffer sucked.

Where the hell is Kate? His bitch of an ex-wife promised to return an hour ago. He put his hand to Sasha's feverish head. *Still hot as hell.*

Knowing Jimmy waited for him at the Black Cat Blues Bar made the time pass more slowly. He had no idea why his brother wanted to meet with him, or why he picked a dangerous part of town, but the edgy sound of his voice told him it was urgent.

Logan opened the window two inches for fresh air and a damp chill flowed into the room, biting into his bones. He began to pace back and forth. There was nothing else he could do.

"Daddy." Her voice cut through his worry. "Come sit with me, Daddy."

An hour later Sasha fell asleep, nestled in his arms watching a princess movie. With his free hand he checked messages on his mobile phone.

What's going on? Why did Jimmy want to meet at the Black Cat? Why the cloak-and-dagger crap? And where the hell was The Bitch?

Logan had never been to the Black Cat, but he'd heard the music was good if you liked Chicago-styled blues, the food okay and the clientele eclectic. *A good place for secrets in the shadowy side of town.* Worry gnawed at his gut. But Jimmy was a grown man who could take care of himself.

Sasha coughed and he rubbed her back. Bundled up in his arms, so perfect, so vulnerable, he felt almost swallowed up by how much he loved her. The world was too imperfect for her. He kissed the top of her head and rocked her in his arms.

Jimmy had stopped answering text messages at three in the morning. It wasn't like him to not respond. Logan tried calling, but his calls went through to voice-mail. A cold lump settled in his chest. He shook his head. This was no time to let his imagination take over. Jimmy probably got lucky and busy and, well . . . lucky.

But that heavy sense of foreboding wouldn't leave Logan. Jimmy could be reckless. He was the one who was always looking for "The Big Break," the one that would give him enough money to go away and leave the drudgery of a regular job. Logan knew it was just a matter of time before he split.

Maybe he had been a fool to bring him into the security business to start with, but his little brother rocked at being a PI, and Logan liked having him around, covering his back and sharing the load. They'd always been close. His gut churned.

Where the hell is Jimmy? Why didn't he call?

When Kate finally came home, he shot past her without a word.

***

The sign said, "Closed," on the door of The Black Cat Blues Bar. The flashing lights which came from behind the building called to him and in a couple of minutes he found the alley. Two cop cars and an ambulance blocked the end where it met the road. The whole area was lit up with police lights. Forcing himself to breathe, he walked closer. Crime scene tape surrounded a large area. *No. No . . . it can't be.* A body lay on the ground behind the tape. Logan's stomach fell like a rock into a deep, fathomless well. With a certainty he didn't want, he knew what lay behind the tape . . . a scene that would haunt him forever.

CHAPTER 3

Without music, life would be a mistake. Friedrich
Nietzsche

"I killed a man . . . I killed a man." Gilbert Harris stumbled through the deserted back alleys towards the docks. Bile rose in his throat. As he swallowed it down it burned the lining of his esophagus. The dying man's face stuck in his mind. The metallic smell of his blood lingered in his nostrils. No one had told him what it would be like after the kill.

Should he have stayed and made sure the asshole was dead? With all that blood he had to be dead by now. Had to be.

And who was that figure coming toward him. It looked like a woman. Did she see him? The moment he struck the fatal blow he had the eerie sense he was being watched. But then again, it felt like the whole fucking universe was watching him. Gil shook his head. It had to be his imagination. He had cased out the alley ahead of time. It had been empty.

His heart raced. His breathing was erratic. *I'm in shock. That's all.* He would feel better soon. But with every step his feet grew heavier and more awkward, as if they didn't belong to him. His hands trembled and his muscles twitched. Would he be able to get away?

Gilbert pushed on. Escape. He had to escape. Sweat poured down his face. Sirens blared in the distance. He gasped for air.

The horror of what he'd done pushed in on his mind. Daniels's face contorted with pain would not leave him. If only the asshole had cooperated, told him what he knew. The man would still be alive. Gil didn't want to be a murderer.

The asshole's laughter had really done it. It made him feel two inches tall. Daniels shouldn't have called him a foolish old man. Gil had had enough of people sneering at him.

But now, on top of all his other failures, he'd taken a life.

Gil reached his destination, his fishing boat at the docks. It felt as thought hours had passed, but his watch told him it had taken twenty minutes. He jumped on board and unlocked the cabin door. How could he ever right this wrong? Was there such a thing as redemption? *Shit, that only happens in the movies.*

Once inside the cabin he went straight to the

head and puked his guts out, feeling the weight of the cross he wore on a chain around his neck. It hit his chin as he leaned forward. "Fucking hell."

When he finished upchucking, he poured a glass of water. Time. All he needed was time. He lifted the glass to his mouth, but his hand shook so violently the liquid splashed over the sides and covered his blood-soaked hands. "God dammit." Focusing on his breathing, he willed it to slow down, but it would only work for a breath and then it would speed up again. He had lost control of his body, his mind . . . his fucking life.

His cell phone rang. Cops? His system went into overdrive.

The screen display said: Mother. *Oh fuck.* That was all he needed. He'd been late with her money. She'd yell and insult him. He snickered. What would she think if she knew her only child had become a murderer?

CHAPTER 4

*Music can change the world because it can change
people.* ~ Bono

Maggy groaned as the first streaks of light filtered through the window above her bed. *Coffee.* She shook her head as if that would rid her of the memories of the night before. Today had to be a better day. Her mouth tasted like a compost bin. It felt as though a metronome swung back and forth inside her skull. And her feet ached from stupid, new shoes that pinched her toes. *Coffee.* She had to get moving. *At least as far as her coffee pot.*

A big cup of java would help her pull herself together. Peterson, the detective with the gravel voice, expected her in his office in a few hours and she had to fit in her dog walking job first.

Coffee . . . her elixir for dealing with all of life's crap. Well, that and red wine. She wanted to be clearer when she dealt with the cop this time. Otherwise he'd keep pestering her, thinking she knew something, which she didn't. Well, almost didn't. She grumbled.

She dragged herself out of bed and descended the ladder to the main floor of her houseboat. The kitchen area was in the right corner. She ground a cup of beans, poured the grinds into her filter machine and hit the "on" button. When the familiar swooshing started, and the smell of fresh coffee intensified, an expectant feeling of calm flooded her senses. It was the best part of the morning.

While she waited for the pot to fill, she hooked up her phone to speakers. A moment later Diana Krall's voice filled the room. *"The boy from Ipanema walked slowly . . ."* Good music, coffee and . . . hope. The day was improving already.

A familiar tapping came from the door. Joe. Rather than knock, he used his white cane to tap a rhythm to identify himself. She smiled as tension drained from her shoulders. She hadn't realized how hunched up she'd become.

Opening the door wide she waited until he crossed the threshold and then gave the old man a long hug. They had grown close in the year they had known each other. Joe lived in a room above the Black Cat Blues Bar. He was her boss's cousin and her mentor in all things to do with the blues.

He sniffed the air. "Coffee, cinnamon and oranges." His warm baritone voice reverberated through her heart. Last month he had turned seventy, but his mind was sharp and his ear even sharper. He used his cane to walk to her kitchen table. She cleared a few sheets of music out of his way and waited for him to speak.

"Your voice dripped honey in your last song." Joe raised his chin. "Stirred my soul."

That was a high compliment coming from Joe. He knew the blues better than anyone she'd ever met. Listening to his feedback was like mining gold.

"It felt right," she said. She had emptied herself into that last song, the old classic, "I Just Want to Make Love to You." "Maybe I should finish every night with it."

A smile slid across his narrow face. "I tell ya, it would keep a lot of men warm for the night." He sat back with a bawdy laugh only he could get away with.

She eyed him. Joe liked her singing, but he hadn't come all the way here to talk about that.

"You just keep getting better every night, baby," he said.

She gritted her teeth. No matter how many times she complained about him calling her "baby", it kept falling out of his mouth. Time to change the topic and get down to what he really came for. "I'm okay Joe."

He nodded slowly, as if in disbelief. "It was one hell of a night." Reaching across the table he touched her face. His fingers traced her features slowly, leaving a trail of warmth behind.

When he finished she said, "Today's another day. I'm fine—really."

"You found the man. I heard there was a lot of blood." Joe lowered his voice. "That's gotta mess with your head."

Yeah it did, but talking about it with Joe wouldn't help. He had enough problems of his own. She touched his arm. "I'm okay."

"Something you'll remember till the end of your life."

Oh dear. Here he goes again. "I hate it when you talk about the end of life, Joe. Let's talk about the weather."

"Nothing much to say. It's November—all it does is rain."

Joe's fingers tapped with the beat of Diana's song, "Peel Me a Grape," playing in the background. Maggy placed her hand over his. His skin had an alligator roughness. It probably had something to do with his meds. "Did you see the doc yesterday? It was so busy at the bar last night I didn't get a chance to talk to you about that."

His lips compressed into a thin line.

"Joe?"

"Doesn't matter what he says. I'm doin' fine."

"Stubborn old goat."

"Hush, child. You worry about other people too much." He removed his hand from her grasp. "I've lived longer than you. I know what I'm doing."

"You need medical help."

"I'm doin' fine, Maggy." But his glassy-blue eyes looked more fragile than a thin sheet of ice on top of a spring pond, cracking and melting in the morning sun. And the trembling in his hands told another story.

"Joe . . . "

"Don't waste your time worrying about an old music man. Get out there and live your life. Sing. Have some fun. Find a good man to love. Have a family. In the end that's the only treasure worth having."

Talking about love again. He sounded lonelier and older every day. She took a deep breath and leaned towards him. "Tell me about the meds."

"Diana's voice is sexy," he said in that low, bedroom voice of his. His chin moved with the beat.

Another day, another impasse with Joe. How could she get him to take better care of himself? She got up and poured them each a mug of coffee. Placing his mug in front of him with a thud she leaned towards him and said, "You're impossible."

He laughed. "You're not the first woman to tell me that. Don't worry, Maggy. Everything will work out—always does."

Platitudes from a sick man. She ran a hand through her hair and looked at the clock on her microwave. She had to get moving. "Whatever you say, Joe."

"Oh, before you rush away, I have a message for you."

"What?"

"A man phoned the Black Cat. He said he wants to meet with you at the library at ten. Said it has to do with the murder. He said he thinks you're in danger."

"Me? In danger?"

Joe drank down his coffee. "I'm just the messenger, and I sure as hell don't like that role. I don't like you messed up with murder. But that was what the man said. Maybe you should tell the police."

She shrugged. "Don't worry, Joe. I can handle a librarian."

CHAPTER 5

Music is the divine way to tell beautiful, poetic things to the heart. ~ Pablo Casals

Rain dripped off the edges of Maggy's umbrella, dampness seeped into her bones and she shivered. Shrouded in clouds, the coastal mountains hid their beauty. Hell, everything hid its beauty on a rainy Vancouver morning in November.

As she walked along the city street, the eyes of the dead man nudged at her conscience. She couldn't get him out of her mind. Adjusting her ear buds, she turned up the volume on Janis Joplin. But it didn't work. Music usually made her feel better, but not today. The dead man's eyes stayed with her, her own version of a tell-tale heart, every step of her journey. Maybe, she should tell the cop, exactly what had happened in the alley. And then maybe the image of the corpse would pass on.

She squeezed her right hand into a fist, the one that had held his. There were no traces of his blood left on her skin, only the tingling sensation of a connection remained. Shit. She hadn't asked to be a witness to his death, and didn't want to be burdened with his spirit.

Meandering through the crowds on the sidewalk, she decided to focus her mind on the living. She had just finished her second interview with the cop. Good lord, that man knew how to interrogate. His questions seemed endless, designed to trip her up. The last thing she wanted was to get tied up in the middle of a murder investigation. She didn't even know the dead guy. He wasn't her problem. At least, she didn't want him to be.

Although Maggy had thought she would tell Peterson that the guy wasn't actually dead when she found him and that he spoke to her, she changed her mind when she was in the police office. The detective would not stop badgering her. She figured the less she said, the better. The guy was dead and there was nothing she could do about that.

Maggy looked up for the sun, but it wasn't there. All she wanted to do was get on with her life. Was that asking too much? For as long as she could remember, she'd wanted to sing. And after her marriage fell apart, she had decided to go for it. She deserved some good fortune. And the clock was ticking. If she didn't grab some of it soon, she'd be an old lady with broken dreams and no voice left in her. She was thirty-five.

A shudder rippled through her body, a certainty that someone was watching her. *What the hell?* She looked over her shoulder. No one. Why did she even look? There was nothing to be scared of, in the middle of the day, on one of the busiest streets in downtown Vancouver. Besides, Inspector

Peterson would find the killer. He looked capable in a policeman kind of way.

The dead man's eyes nudged her again. Okay, she could phone the cop and say she forgot to tell him the whole story. He might think her a complete idiot, but in the big picture that didn't matter. She could still tell him all the truth. Taking a deep breath, she shook her head. *But I don't want to get involved.* And the few words the dying guy said didn't make sense anyway. Emer-Old? Better to stay out of it.

What about the dead man's family? Her stomach cringed. Didn't they deserve more? At the very least, the knowledge that he wasn't alone at the end might bring them some peace. Can anyone find consolation when someone they loved, in the prime of their life, is stabbed in a dark alley? She winced.

Maggy looked over her shoulder again. A sea of commuters floated along with black umbrellas and briefcases. A few homeless people wove between them, looking dirty and desperate. All zombies shuffling to their destinations. *I really have to stop drinking the cheap wine.* The horror of last night clung to her like a second skin.

She turned up the volume on her music. The cold wind gripped her as she turned onto Georgia Street. Menacing, black clouds swirled in the sky. She could taste a storm coming. At ten o'clock, she pushed open the heavy doors to the library and entered for her mysterious meeting.

Standing between rows of bookshelves in the reference section, a wiry man waved her over with a *Georgia Straight* magazine. As she approached, he scanned her closely, and she did the same to him. He'd be easy to remember: middle aged and bald with beady black eyes and rectangular, tortoise-shell, reading glasses perched on the end of a long narrow nose. He looked like a human Minion.

He motioned for her to sit at the table. After looking around, she complied. It was a public place. What could happen here?

"My name is Edgar," he said in a hushed voice. Her eyebrows rose. *This guy watches too many spy movies.*

"Edgar?" she prompted.

"You're in danger—grave danger."

She gritted her teeth. There was no reason for her to be in danger. No reason. She swallowed.

"Not me," Edgar said, shaking his head. "I won't hurt you. But the murderer—"

Her mouth dropped despite her effort to keep a poker face.

"What did Jimmy tell you?"

"Jimmy?"

"The man who was murdered in the alley behind the Black Cat."

She nodded reluctantly.

"Jimmy Daniels was killed because he knew too much."

"Look," Maggy said. "I appreciate your concern for my safety. But I don't know anything about Jimmy. I found his body in the alley, his dead body. That's all." The way Edgar kept looking over his shoulder made her skin crawl.

His eyes returned to her. "Jimmy told you

something."

"He was dead," she said. How could he possibly know?

Edgar's eyes narrowed. "He said something to you."

"Listen, man. Dead men don't talk."

"I was there."

She leaned back. It was dark that night. He could have been in the alley. And that meant he may have seen the murder.

Edgar's beady eyes bulged as he motioned for her to lean in. A few yards away a young child laughed and his mother shushed him. Normal, everyday library sounds, were oddly comforting. Her mind spun.

Edgar continued in his fidgety voice. "I was following him. I wanted to see who he met."

She let out her breath slowly. "Why?"

"Because, I want the gold."

"Okay," she said, standing. "If you know anything about the murder you should talk to the police. The inspector in charge is Peterson."

"You have to listen to me. You're in danger."

She froze. "Why would I be in danger?"

He looked around the room with a nervous twitch in his shoulders. He grabbed her hand. His felt cold and clammy.

"You have to listen to me. Your life depends on it."

She pulled her hand away, but sat back down.

"I heard Jimmy was good at doing

investigations, so I went to him for help. See, I needed help to find the treasure. He did some snooping around for me and the next thing I know, he's dead." Edgar's face went white.

"I don't get it. You don't make any sense. If Jimmy was working for you, why were you following him?"

A fat tear slid down his left cheek. "I told him the work was dangerous. He just smiled. Jimmy didn't take me seriously and now he's dead. Cuz of me."

"What treasure?" She had to ask.

"Brother XII's"

Her back straightened. "The Brother XII?" This was too strange.

He nodded.

"The cult leader who scammed people in the early twentieth century?" Edgar sure dreamed in Technicolor. The story of Brother XII was legendary on the west coast and Maggy knew all the sordid details. Memories of stories told around campfires late at night, about buried gold, black magic and wild sex, sped through her mind.

"Yeah." He leaned back and held her stare with bloodshot eyes.

"People searched all over the islands for his treasure for over a century." She leaned in. "What is it you know that they didn't?"

"I came upon some new information. My great-grandmother Rita worshipped Brother XII." His left eye twitched. "She was one of his lovers. I didn't know anything about their affair, but when my mother passed last month, I sorted through her things and found Rita's diary. That's when I learned about their relationship and the gold."

"Brother XII's followers left him before the end." Maggy had looked up the con man in the archives, when she was a teenager, to see how much of the legend was fact and how much was fiction.

"My great-grandma Rita left when Brother XII took up with the dominatrix Madame Z. In her journal she describes her as a sadistic, evil bitch with a whip. She made their lives unbearable and banished any female competition. But that doesn't matter. Rita knew Brother XII well enough before that. She knew where he hid the gold."

"So why didn't she go get it?"

"Rita didn't need money and she was a proper lady. She married a prominent business man less than a year after her affair. Ashamed of her relationship with a cult leader, she didn't tell anyone. The family thought she had toured Europe with a girlfriend, or at least that became the official story of where she had disappeared to. Her affair stayed hidden."

"I always thought someone had to know something."

"Brother XII's gold wasn't worth ruining her reputation for. Rita and the family didn't want anyone to connect her to him and his cult. She came from money and married money. She didn't need the treasure. She loved Brother XII because she believed in his prophecies of the future." Edgar's cheeks turned red. "The brother was a skilled lover who had little difficulty seducing a young, naïve virgin. She didn't want his gold."

"Okay, now I understand her. But what about you? Why don't you go get it?"

"I don't know where it is. I have a couple pieces of the puzzle, but not the whole picture. That's why I hired Jimmy. I need to know more. I . . ." Edgar stopped. His mouth fell ajar, his hands clenched into fists. He looked around, and then he got up and ran to the nearest exit.

Seconds later, a stocky man, dressed in a black hoody pulled low enough around his face to hide his features followed Edgar out the door. Medium height and wearing black jeans, he dressed like a teenager, but he moved like a middle-aged man.

Fear squeezed Maggy's stomach, real fear. Edgar was an odd guy, but he was in the alley and he could be telling the truth. She swallowed. Catching her eye, in front of her on the table, beside the *Georgia Strait* magazine, lay a blue sticky note. It read: "Trust no one."

CHAPTER 6

One good thing about music, when it hits you, you feel no pain. ~ Bob Marley

Maggy headed home. She couldn't help but check over her shoulder every few minutes for Edgar or the guy who was following him. *Sweet Jesus, my life is going crazy*

Vancouver's November gloom had gained a whole new dimension, one of strange men. It didn't matter how many times she told herself she couldn't be in danger, her body physically disagreed. The goosebumps that rose when the name Brother XII was spoken had not gone down.

As she reached an intersection, a white delivery van rushed by and brushed the side of her umbrella. It knocked her off-balance and she fell to the ground. Maggy drew a quick breath, and picked herself up off the dirty, wet road. You don't stay down in a big city. Her jeans were soaked and gravel stuck to her hands. *Just great!*

After brushing herself off, she carried on, promising she would only look behind her every ten paces. Counting would slow her down and make her feel in control. But her pulse raced and the short walk home seemed endless.

Edgar's story sounded so strange it was hard to believe, but his fear and the hooded man were real. As real as the murder.

When she walked down the entrance to Granville Island she finally exhaled all the air she'd been holding in her lungs. She'd made it home.

Maggy loved it here on the man-made island. To her mind it was the best place to live in Vancouver. She'd been born in Burnaby, one of the suburbs, and in her twenties she had lived in different areas of town. When she got married they moved into a sterile, cement high-rise in North Vancouver. Her husband liked it there. After their final fight, six months ago, she chose to live in a houseboat on the docks. It was her place.

The culture of the island rocked. Always had. Situated in the middle of an inlet, it had a history as a meeting place. It collected people, all sorts of people. Filled with an eclectic mix of nationalities and personalities it had become her sanctuary.

Granville Island had started out as a sandbar in the middle of a tidal flat in False Creek and was used by the First Nations people during low tide. Every high tide it was totally submerged and washed clean. Members of the Squamish Nation called it "Snauq." They used it to corral fish and harvest a wide variety of shellfish. Some nights she swore she could hear their songs in the wind, but she didn't tell anyone that.

Back in the late eighteen hundreds the harbor commission took it over and reclaimed it from the sea by driving piles around the perimeter and adding fill. They called it "Industrial Island" to start with, but later changed it to Granville Island because it lay directly under the Granville Street Bridge.

The island had been transformed many times over, with different industries, a shanty town, a grisly murder, typhoid, and Second World War saboteurs. Many ghosts hid in that dark past and she liked the texture they added to the culture. The island's history lived alongside its present, in the landscape and in people's minds, giving it a special aura. To her mind, it was a sacred place.

Thinking about the island and all it meant to her brought comfort. Then she reached her houseboat. In front of her door stood a man who looked identical to the man who had died in her arms. Tall, lean and gorgeous.

Maggy walked up to him. "What do you want?"

"Were you with Jimmy Daniels when he died?" His voice sounded controlled.

She looked closer. Dark circles ringed his eyes, but there was no mistaking how much he looked like the victim. He had to be a relative. "Come on in," she said.

The man followed her into her home and as he scanned it, she imagined seeing it through his eyes. On the lower floor was a couch handed down from her mother, a comfy chair from the thrift shop, and a basic kitchen and bathroom. Guitar music lay strewn over every surface. It smelled of coffee and orange peels. The bedroom was in the loft above the main room and could only be accessed by a ladder.

"Sorry about the mess." But she wasn't. She ran a hand through her hair and motioned the man to the chair by the window. He walked past her, moved some music sheets out of his way and sat. He smelled of expensive cologne.

"My name is Logan Daniels." A buttoned down baritone. The smoothness of his voice almost hid his grief. He wore well-pressed, brown khakis and a cotton shirt, under a sports coat.

She nodded. "Are you the dead man's brother?"

"Yes."

"I'm sorry for your loss."

Their eyes locked. His held the kind of depth a woman could get lost in. She looked away. "Can I get you a coffee?"

He cleared his throat. "Just tell me what happened."

She sat on the edge of the couch near him and stared over his shoulder as she spoke, not wanting to be distracted. "I was walking through the alley and I saw his body. I screamed for help, but there was nobody around. I dialed 911 and waited for the police." The parts she left out wouldn't hurt anyone.

"He was dead?"

"Dead."

He shifted in his seat, as if the act of sitting was uncomfortable. "I thought maybe he said something."

Damn, she was a lousy liar. Always had been. A prickly sensation ran up her spine. Jimmy had wanted her to tell Logan. It had been his last wish—a dead man's last wish.

He raised an eyebrow.

"No, nothing," she mumbled, looking at her feet.

He stared at her.

"Dead men don't talk." She couldn't tell him. What good would it do him to know what his brother said? It didn't make sense, anyway. Emer-Old? "I tried to stop his bleeding." She hesitated. "It felt like the right thing to do."

He nodded, but the fine muscles around his eyes twitched. She really shouldn't look at those eyes. He looked away. "I was supposed to meet him. He said it was important. I thought maybe he said something about that."

"I'm sorry," she said, shaking her head.

Logan sat in silence. Grief hung around him like a thick cloud. She wanted to help him, but if she told him what Jimmy said, the cop would be down her throat for lying. It would be far better if she stuck to her story and got on with her life.

But if she didn't tell Logan the truth, she was lying to a grieving man who deserved to know what happened to his brother. Her gut twisted. That wasn't right. And, to top it all off, according to

Edgar, she was in danger for knowing the truth. So was it safer to tell, or not to? *Sweet Jesus . . . how did I get into such a mess?*

"You sure you wouldn't like a cup of coffee?"

"Okay." He studied her face as if the answers he sought were there.

As she brewed a pot, he found his voice. "What were you doing in a dark alley at that time of night? I saw the alley. A beautiful woman like you shouldn't be walking there at any time of day. It doesn't make sense to me."

Maggy went back to sit on the couch. "I sing at the Black Cat. I was on my way home. And I may look small to you, but I can handle myself." She did her best to sound cool, but her body purred from his compliment. It wasn't often a woman heard the word "beautiful" from a handsome man. Maybe she should open a window to cool the room.

Logan's eyes narrowed. "Did you see Jimmy earlier in the bar? I thought the inspector said something about that."

"Yeah, actually I did."

"Did you talk to him?"

"No. But I wanted to." Her cheeks burned.

Logan laughed. "Yeah, Jimmy was always the charming one."

He was leaning close enough to her that his fancy cologne made her nose itchy. She smiled, "Oh I think you caught enough of the family charm, Logan."

Their eyes locked.

He grimaced. "But Jimmy said nothing?"

"Sorry."

Logan stood and headed for the door. "Can I take a rain check on the coffee? I'm going to go down to the Black Cat to see if he talked with anyone."

She wanted to blurt our Jimmy's message, but she didn't. Instead, she nodded. "Good luck," she said.

Maybe she should have said more, but she had her afternoon job to go to and . . . she really didn't want to be involved.

Or in danger.

CHAPTER 7

*Music is a moral law. It gives soul to the universe, wings
to the mind, flight to the imagination, and charm and
gaiety to life and to everything.* ~ Plato

Gilbert's chair creaked under his
weight as he leaned back and swore
at the roof of his cabin. *Fucking
hell.* I missed the idiot again. He wanted to strangle
more information out of Edgar Whitley. Gil looked
out of the port hole of his fishing boat. The day
wasn't over yet. If he could just corner the guy.

The weasel had to know more than he was
saying. Had to.

Gilbert scratched his grizzly jaw. It had been
almost two days since he'd killed Jimmy Daniels.
After Gilbert's body stopped shaking and he'd
puked out his insides, a coldness had taken over him
and it hadn't left.

It was a darkness sent by the devil himself.
He hadn't meant to kill the guy. He didn't want to
be a murderer. At first the weight of his guilt made
him contemplate suicide. He didn't deserve to live.
That he knew.

But then something happened inside him. It
was as if a switch was toggled and he stopped
thinking about what he had done. He pulled himself

together. After all, the murder had not been his fault. Jimmy was the one to blame.

His mouth tasted bitter. How long had it been since he ate?

If he was going to find the gold, he needed to take care of himself.

Find the gold . . . Then everything else will fall into place.

What about the blond Edgar met with in the library? What was that about? Was she the shadowy figure in the alley? Damn it to hell. She was the right size and shape. He drummed his fingers on the arm of the chair.

Time to move.

CHAPTER 8

*Beautiful music is the art of the prophets that can calm
the agitations of the soul; it is one of the most
magnificent and delightful presents God has given us.*
~ Martin Luther

"When they weigh my soul at the pearly gates, I'm going straight to hell."
Maggy said to the dog.

Eager to hump the next available leg Napoleon pulled her along the sidewalk on English Bay, until her wrist hurt. There were so many other things she could be doing, like fixing the broken string on her guitar, or listening to some cool blues. But walking Mrs. Randolph's miniature poodle helped pay her bills.

But the dog wasn't great at giving advice, so she pulled out her cell phone and dialed her best friend Mei.

"Morning, Sunshine," answered her friend. The light hint of laughter in her voice warmed Maggy's heart. She wasn't a morning person at all and the sunshine comment was a reference to that.

Mei had a wicked sense of humor and a mind as sharp and deadly as an executioner's blade. They had bonded when they joined forces to sabotage a chemistry experiment in the eighth grade, because the teacher had a bad habit of groping the girls. It was a damn good bomb and the memory made her smile whenever she saw blue smoke. They had been as thick as thieves ever since.

Maggy cleared her throat. "Remember the guy I found dead in the alley on Tuesday night?" She had already told Mei the police version. "Well, he was actually still alive when I found him and he spoke to me."

She imagined Mei blinking. "Have you been smoking weed?"

"I'm serious. Listen to me. The guy talked to me." Beads of sweat formed on her upper lip.

"Sounds intense."

"That's not even half of it. Now there's a guy called Edgar who says I'm in danger because the dead man knew where Brother XII's gold . . ."

"Wait. Stop right there. Brother XII?" Mei had also grown up on the coast, been at the same camp fires—knew the same stories.

"Yeah, I know. It's all bizarre. Anyway, he says I'm in danger because Jimmy, the dead guy, spoke to me. And now his brother Logan wants me to tell him everything I know about the murder."

"So tell him."

Napoleon yanked her to the right towards a tree. Her body jerked as she followed along on the lead. "It's not that simple. I didn't tell the police, so I can't tell him."

"You lied to the police. What were you thinking?"

"I told them I found him dead. It was kinda true."

"Are you stupid?"

"Yeah, well." Maggy took a deep breath. "You know I don't trust cops. And you know why."

"And now you feel bad because you think the brother deserves to know everything about Jimmy's death?"

"Yeah."

"Is he hot?"

She hesitated. "That's not the point."

"Uh-huh. What did Jimmy say?"

Maggy leaned over and scratched Napoleon's head. "I'm going to tell Logan. It's only right." Saying it out loud eased her squeamish stomach.

"What did Jimmy say?"

Maggy opened her mouth to answer, and froze. The hair on the back of her neck rose. She had that feeling, that unmistakable feeling that someone was watching her.

Her eyes couldn't scan the area fast enough. People filled the wide, paved path about five yards across. Some were walking. Others were running and cycling. The seawall was always busy. "I think someone's following me" She pocketed the phone and quickened her pace. Napoleon lived about a half mile away.

She couldn't let her imagination get the better of her. Just because Edgar said she was in danger, didn't mean she was . . . . And yet, that man a few yards behind her wore a black hoody. *Ah. There's lots of black hoodies in town.* She started to jog. Looking over her shoulder, she saw him jogging too. Increasing her speed, she considered all the places along the path she could stop. Her breathing became labored. It had been a while since she had run.

Her phone rang. "Mei, what is it?" She slowed her pace.

"Listen to me, Maggy. The lying is eating away at you. It's going to drive you crazy. Just tell someone. Logan, the cop . . . whoever. Tell someone."

Maggy came to a stop and looked around. Everything seemed perfectly normal. The man in the black hoody was gone. Maybe Mei was right. The only thing chasing her was her own conscience.

CHAPTER 9

E dgar sat on his bed staring at his great-grandmother's worn leather-bound journal. So many secrets kept for so many years. He'd reread the special pages again, just as he had every day for the last two months. All he needed was a few more details to find the gold. He was so close.

Rita's Journal
Cedar-by-the-Sea, June 4, 1927

I lost my virginity.

Brother XII is a great prophet and a wonderful man and I will follow him to the end of my days. Truly, he is an extraordinary individual. He sees things and hears things the rest of us don't. In touch with the spiritual world, he lives to give us guidance.

Tonight he drew a symbol in the sand that looked like a giant "T." He explained it was the 'Tau," an ancient cross the Egyptians used to initiate their kings into the mysteries of existence. Brother sees it floating above his head before his visions. It is a sign that his spiritual leader has a message for him. He is the chosen one.

Brother spoke about his leader tonight, under the moss covered maple tree in Cedar we call the Tree of Wisdom. His master is the twelfth brother of the "Great White Lodge," a group of advanced spiritual beings who direct the world from a spiritual plane. The spirit leader uses him to tell us how we should live. That's why we call him Brother XII. He is a prophet who channels the great spiritual leader.

I finished reading Brother's first book this afternoon. "*The Three Truths,*" is a clear explanation of what he learned from his spiritual guide. The words resounded in my heart like bells in a chapel. Finally, I understand the meaning of life. I realize, now, following Brother is my true calling.

There are three basic truths: the unity of all life, the immortality of the soul, and the law of karma. Brother says the world is ignoring these truths, and we are all going to suffer for it. There is going to be chaos and destruction, an Armageddon, if we don't mend our ways. And I believe him.

At the end of his talk he slid into a trance, communing directly with the spirits on the other plane. I will never forget his words. They reached deep inside me and took hold: "*Hear ye the words I speak, and fear not, for though destruction cometh upon many, yet for you it is the Day of Redemption. Ye shall come out of the House of Bondage, that House which is Egypt which is even the body-consciousness . . . I am the Messenger of the Fire, the Messenger of the Whirlwind, the Messenger of the Day of Adjustment. The fire burneth but dross, that the silver and the gold may remain. By the Wind ye shall mount to the heavens—if ye be the children of discernment."[i]*

Sweat poured down his face and he began uttering hideous sounds—other-worldly sounds. Truly his spirit was in another place. Then, as quickly as the trance came, it went and he was himself again. People applauded and everyone shook his hand.

Several people offered him money right there and then, but he told them to see him in the morning. His smile, peaceful and all-knowing, captured my heart. I knew I had witnessed a true prophet.

Later in the evening, when the crowd finally dispersed, I walked with him down to the beach. I was so excited to be alone with him. My heart thudded loud enough to wake the killer whales. When he said he wanted to get to know me better, I felt my life explode with delicious possibilities.

We lay in the sand looking up at the stars. Brother told me how much his mission means to him. He wants to help people see that the way they're living is wrong. My heart filled with joy that he, a man of vision, was spending time with me. He took my hand in his. I felt like a queen.

Then he leaned over me and I could feel his soft breath on my skin. I've been kissed before, but it never felt like it did when his lips met mine. It was a spiritual awakening.

And when he reached beneath my skirt with his strong hand, I filled with joy at the thought of being his chosen woman. He stroked my inner thigh as we shared kisses, innocent at first, but then deeper and deeper. Such exquisite passion. His hand slid higher and higher up my leg. A lady should not allow a man to touch her like this. She really shouldn't. Not until marriage, or at least an agreement to marry. She shouldn't. But I couldn't think to stop him.

I gasped as he pulled down my knickers and explored my body with his hands. I kept thinking I would stop him in another minute, but he stroked me so expertly with his gentle fingers until I had no resistance left.

The next thing I knew his pants were down. He whispered, "Sweet, sweet Rita," as he entered me. My virginity was ripped apart and my world exploded.

We are creating a new world order in the Aquarian Foundation, one in which old rules do not apply. I do not need a marriage certificate to justify making love. Losing my virginity to him felt right, and I know by the look in his eye that he loves me.

I never knew *it* would be like that. I had been taught to keep my knees together until my wedding night. But sex is not an ugly duty for a wife. It is a pleasure for a woman. A pleasure I will not deny myself.

The old Rita would be ashamed, but I am not. I know something that feels so good, can't be wrong. It is my destiny to be by his side. Imagine, me, the lady of a great leader, the man who will change the world.

My friend Roger went to the meeting with me and left early, warning me to be careful. He saw how I looked at Brother and how he looked at me. Roger labeled him a master in black magic, told me there are many stories about what Brother XII does to people who cross him. Roger's just jealous.

There are 2,000 of us now in the following. Brother's working with a few other men, making plans so we can all live together here, in British Columbia. It's a rugged, beautiful place on the shores of the ocean, with mountains and forests. A place that holds a lot of promise they say. We are going to build an "Ark of Refuge," to prepare for a better time, the Age of Aquarius.

Tomorrow, I will read his second book and attend another lecture. I hope he takes me to the beach again.

Am I a wicked woman?

Quite possibly.

CHAPTER 10

Music is love in search of a word. ~ Sidney Lanier

Sitting alone in his office, Logan scrunched a piece of paper into a tight ball and lobbed it towards the wastepaper basket on the other side of the room. He missed and balled up another. Shooting two out of five was low for him on a bad day. He had been at it for an hour. His average was four, and on a good day he could ace five. But there was nothing good about today.

Ripping another page out of his latest business plan, he made a tight ball, sighted his throw and launched it into the air. He missed again. Tearing another piece of paper, he decided to scrunch it harder, as if the act of squeezing it could somehow fix it and everything else in his world.

He'd find his rhythm. Always did. He'd move his average back up to four. And dream again of five.

If he could ever dream again.

Scrunching the tenth page into a tight ball in his hand, the size of a ping pong ball, he stopped. What the hell was he doing? It felt good to take control of something, but he needed to be doing something more useful than playing paper basketball. His business may be collapsing, but he could and would fix it.

Why couldn't it have been him in the alley?

He threw his last projectile and aced it. *Yay!* He threw his hands in the air.

They looked alike, Jimmy and him. A lot people said they were alike, but they weren't. Not really. Jimmy was the one with character and charm. He had a love for life that oozed out of him. When he entered a room heads turned. Men wanted to be his best friend, and women wanted him, all of him. Logan chuckled out loud. Women swarmed him from the time he turned ten.

Granted, Jimmy's enthusiasm for life didn't fit well in a suit, but they were working around that. Logan made the business deals and Jimmy did most of the snooping.

"Who would want to kill Jimmy?" He'd never thought of what life would be like without his brother. It had never crossed his mind, because Jimmy had always been there. So full of life. They were tight like friends, but the bond went much deeper. It ran in their blood.

He balled up another sheet of paper and stopped. He had aced the last one. Why tempt fate?

He picked up the phone and dialed. He couldn't put off the call any longer.

It seemed to ring forever, and then his father picked up.

"Logan, so glad you called."

He cleared his throat. "Dad."

"Son, we just got in from the airport." He paused, and when Logan didn't say anything he continued, "I see you've been leaving me messages. What's up?" His familiar voice, suddenly deepened with concern, hit Logan hard. His chest tightened.

"Dad . . . " How could he tell him? How could he tell his father Jimmy was dead?

Jimmy had been a pain in the ass kinda kid to raise, but everyone loved him. Dad especially. He'd ream him out for every rule he broke. He even used a strap on him once, but as they grew older it became clear that their dad was secretly proud of Jimmy's fun loving wild streak. "That's my boy," he would say.

What could Logan say now to make the grim news easier?

"Speak to me, son." His father's voice became taut like a fragile wire about to break. "Just say it. What's wrong?"

Logan pictured his strong father trembling, knowing it was bad news.

"He's dead, Dad. Jimmy's dead."

***

As the night turned cold and lonelier than he could ever have imagined, Logan decided to go to the Black Cat Blues Bar. He knew he would never be able to find his brother again, but maybe, he could find some connection to him. Make some sense of what happened.

Maggy Malone stood on the stage with her guitar. Her blond hair tumbled over her shoulders in waves. Almost every eye in the run-down bar looked her way.

Had the curvy lady been Jimmy's last lover? He always did have good taste. Two inches of cleavage peaked from the top of her tight black lace top. The come-hither look in her eyes added heat to the room. Her sultry voice made his pulse quicken. Yeah, he hoped she had been Jimmy's last. Every man deserves a woman like that in his life, at least once.

Maggy looked his way and smiled. The connection made him instantly hard. What a time to get the hots for a woman. A singer no less. But then why not? Maybe, she needed consoling too. He smiled back at her.

Her soul-stirring blues flowed through the room like a panacea for all of God's forgotten people. She started a new song, the classic, "I Put a Spell on You." The audience went silent, mesmerized by her performance. Her sea-green eyes held his for a brief moment and he felt bewitched. Damn she was good. He could blame it on the beer, but he knew it wasn't alcohol messing with his system, it was Maggy Malone.

After she finished her set he waited for her. She went back-stage, but he figured she'd return his way sooner or later. It no longer mattered if she'd been Jimmy's last woman. He knocked back another beer.

His worries could wait until tomorrow.

Ten minutes passed slowly. Had she not felt the connection when they shared that look? He checked his watch again.

"Logan?"

"Maggy." Good line, buddy.

"I'm surprised to see you here. But I guess it makes sense."

His mouth went dry. She smelled of cinnamon and vanilla and woman. "That isn't exactly what's on my mind right now." He moved a lock of her unruly hair away from her face. Soft skin and full lips.

"I lied," she said

"Excuse me?" He was imagining what it would be like to taste those ruby-red lips.

"I have to tell you. I lied."

Earth to Logan. She's trying to tell you something. "Uh . . . about what?"

"About how Jimmy died. It wasn't exactly the way I said it was."

Fuck. He exhaled noisily and leaned back.

Maggy swallowed. "When I found him, he was still alive, barely, but still alive." She touched Logan's arm.

All his blood ran south. He took a deep breath. Talk about feeling hot and cold in one single moment. "Maggy . . ." was all he managed to say.

"Your brother was lying in the alley, like I said. I recognized him, because I saw him in the bar earlier, standing exactly where you're standing now. You're not the kind of men a woman forgets."

"He was alive?"

"Barely. There was blood everywhere," she continued. "I mean everywhere, all over him, all over the ground. And he was ghastly white and still. You know." She bit her lower lip. "A silver spike was sticking out of his chest. I knew he didn't have a chance. I screamed for help, but no one came. I dialed 911 and put pressure on his wound until the ambulance and police arrived. That was all I could do." Her voice rang true.

"Was he in a lot of pain?" Logan had to know.

"I think he was beyond that, if that makes sense. He was unconscious at first. Then he opened his eyes. I did my best, but there was no way anyone could have saved him. He was too far gone."

"You stayed with him till the end?"

She gave him a small smile. "I held his hand."

Logan nodded. At least Jimmy wasn't alone.

They looked at each other and a warmth flowed between them. Logan looked away, trying to gather his thoughts.

"He spoke to me," she said.

"Sounds like Jimmy. He always wanted the last word." Why was he trying to make light of it? "What'd he say?"

"He said, 'Tell Logan, "Emer-Old."'" I don't know if that makes any sense to you, but that's what he said, and then he died. He used all his strength to get those words out."

The message made sense to Logan; crazy sense, but sense all the same. He nodded, not wanting to share his thoughts.

"I'm so sorry for your loss."

The lines around Logan's eyes crinkled. "Why didn't you tell the police?"

She shook her head. "The message was for you." She turned and looked towards the stage.

He took her arm. "Maggy, were you and Jimmy lovers?"

"No." The look she gave him was like a shot of good cognac, filled with heat and complexity. And hot . . . so hot it burned. The woman knew how to use words, but she knew even better— how not to.

She nodded towards the stage. "I have to go."

"Last set?"

She nodded, while her eyes still played with his.

"I'll stay."

She gave him a promising smile, then turned and walked away. Long, blond curls bounced down her back to her waist, and below that her wide hips and round ass swayed its way to the stage.

"Emer-Old?" What had Jimmy gotten into?

CHAPTER 11

The world's most famous and popular language is music. ~Psy

Many of the regulars at the Black Cat made a point of staying to the end of the night to hear Maggy sing her last song. With her sultry, honey-dipped voice she put everything she had left into it. Joe said her finales kept the men warm for the night, and then some. Tonight Maggy planned to sing the classic, "I Just Want to Make Love to You."

She waited for the room to hush and then she said, "This song's for Jimmy Daniels."

Looking over at Joe to steady her nerves, she saw his weathered face break into a wide smile that warmed her from the outside in, like a tropical wave. Despite all his health problems Joe never complained, never weighed anyone down. Seeing him in the audience eased her nerves and brought out the best in her voice.

Waiting for the growing expectation of the crowd to hit its peak, she took a sip of water. She could feel a different kind of hunger from Logan. Each fueled her in its own way.

Logan Daniels looked like a good port in a storm: strong, confident, and commanding. Good for a one-night stand. His eyes slid over her body warming every dirty thought crossing her mind. The last thing she needed was a broken man. She had trouble enough piecing together her own fragments. Still, something about Logan pulled her. She gave Logan a nod.

Tossing her mane of thick curls behind her, she started to sing. Her voice pulled the audience with its trembling longing. It was everything they expected and more. Putting her soul into her voice had become easy, thanks to Joe's coaching.

The image of Jimmy bleeding to his death in the alley grabbed her, but she didn't push it away; she used it, holding nothing back. The crowd went silent.

By the end she'd emptied herself, exhausted by the experience of channeling all her feelings into her voice. She lived for the experience. Some people have religion, some people politics . . . she had music. It was all about the music. The crowd cheered their appreciation.

As she packed up her guitar she wondered if Logan would understand her. But did it matter, when she only wanted a hook-up? Nothing more.

She gave him her 'come hither' look, a look as old as time. And he came to her.

***

At her place, she locked the door behind them and leaned her guitar against the wall. After lighting the candle on her kitchen table she turned to face him and started unbuttoning her blouse.

He took her into his arms, and pulled her close. His five o'clock shadow brushed against her cheek, lighting every nerve ending in her body. Heat flowed through her system pooling in lower belly. He even smelled sexy.

Gently he kissed her mouth, igniting a flame of desire. It had been so long since she had been with a man. Too long. She opened her mouth to his and he deepened their kiss.

His large hands roamed over her and he pulled her even closer. She moaned as his hardness pushed against her.

This was what she needed. Oh, hell, yeah. Exactly what she needed. Simple sex. Fast and hard and easy. A horizontal mambo with no strings attached.

No strings? Wait. Who was she kidding? Sex always came with strings. Sometimes they were visible and sometimes they weren't, but they were always there. She pulled away from him.

His eyes met hers. "What's wrong?" he asked with a voice husky and rough with need. "I thought you wanted . . . "

Heat coursed through her body, a primal heat that said, *Oh yeah baby, you are exactly what I want*. She straightened her blouse and started doing up the buttons from the top.

"I don't know you." She cleared her throat, attempting to gather her thoughts from a desire-riddled brain. The air between them, electric with currents of passion, nudged at her resolve.

He grumbled and leaned towards her. "I can fix that," he whispered in her ear.

"No." She did up another couple buttons. "I thought I wanted this, but I don't." Their combustible chemistry was unsettling.

She put her hand on his chest and pushed him back a bit. "Neither of us needs this tonight." Yes, the sex would be a good release, but the left over emotions would be messy. She held his stare in the flickering candlelight.

He tilted his head and gave her a killer smile that warmed her body right down to her pinky toes.

"Logan . . . " She meant to say, "Logan, no," but somehow the second part of the sentence didn't come out.

He touched his forehead with hers. His fingers settled on her hips and they felt like fire. Lust, pure, potent lust, surged inside her, urging her on like an animal in heat. It was just biology. She needed to ignore it.

But why ignore it? A simple night of sex. Why the hell not? They could figure out the consequences later. Nah, that was just her libido talking. She knew better.

Maggy took a step back wanting control, but his hands stayed on her body. Two adults enjoying each other's company. She swallowed. All she had to do was say yes.

They stood looking at one another, a momentary impasse of unresolved passion, locked in an awareness of each other's needs.

"Maggy . . . "

The neediness of his voice, a desperation born of more than passion, re-triggered a wave of caution as cold as ice in her mind, cooling her overheated body. What was she doing? She hardly knew this man. Her life was a mess. His life was a mess. She took a quick breath and pulled back. "It's time for you to go." She folded her arms around herself. "I'm sorry. This just doesn't feel right."

It would have been easier if Logan had said something nasty to her before he left, but he didn't. Grabbing his jacket, he left without a word, closing the door quietly behind him.

***

She threw her pillow at the wall for the fourth time. Her body wanted him. But it wasn't right. You'd think she'd have more sense. The last thing she needed right now was a fling with a needy man. But wasn't she equally needy? What a time to be out of batteries.

Damn, the craving for sex reared itself at the worst times. Her love of men would be the death of her yet. She retrieved the pillow and tossed it onto her couch.

He was hot, so hot . . . in so many ways. The visceral memory of his hands on her body burned. Damn he was good. She ached for him in every way a woman can ache—and then some.

CHAPTER 12

Music is a higher revelation than all wisdom and philosophy. ~Ludwig van Beethoven

The noise that woke Maggy wasn't loud, just out of place. Way out of place. She rolled over and checked her clock: 8:00 a.m., too early for any of her friends to visit. They knew she worked late. They knew she hated mornings. Who else would step on her barge without permission? The small sound seemed to ricochet in her tiny home. Footsteps?

She sat up. Daylight peaked through the edges of her blinds. Did she lock the door when Logan left? She couldn't remember.

Reaching for her cell phone, she cursed her stupidity a second time. It was dead. How could she be so dumb? She had forgotten to plug it in. Now what? A shuffling sound. Her pulse quickened. She strained to hear more as she plugged in her phone.

Nothing.

If she ran, she'd make it down the ladder and to the door to lock it in a minute. But how much good would that do? It would be easy for someone to break through the window beside the door. If only she'd listened to Mei and put up strong, wooden shutters last month, she wouldn't be in this predicament. And she had called her friend paranoid. She hated it, when Mei was right.

If she screamed someone might hear. But it could make the intruder more aggressive.

The distinct sound of light footsteps on her barge came to her door and stopped outside. She gulped.

Three knocks. "Maggy? You awake?" Mei's voice.

"Yeah," Maggy called out as she ran a shaking hand through her tangled hair.

"You better come out."

Maggy opened the door and squinted as sunlight flooded into the room. "What's wrong?"

Mei smelled of jasmine. She had pulled her long, shiny black hair into a high pony tail, which would look casual on ordinary women, but looked stunning on her. She had perfect skin, a tiny nose and dark eyes that always held mischief. But at the moment they also looked pissed off. "We're having a dock meeting at The Skuttlebut. There's been some weird stuff happening on the docks. I've been texting and phoning you, but you didn't answer."

"When's the meeting?"

"In ten minutes."

"Ten?" Maggy groaned. "I'll get dressed. Thanks."

"Sure." But Mei didn't leave.

"What?"

"Who was that guy hanging around your barge?"

A tingling sensation crawled across Maggy's skull. "When?"

"Just now. I thought he might be a friend of yours and would have introduced myself, but he flew out of here as soon as I walked up."

"What did he look like?"

Mei scrunched up her mouth. "Like a regular dock guy: jeans a hoody and a black toque. I didn't see his face."

Maggy shrugged, but she could feel Mei's eyes staring her down. "Honestly, I don't know. A noise woke me up and I was about to come to the door to check it out."

Mei tilted her head. "Maybe you got a stalker from the bar."

A stalker? That was more than possible. It could even have been Frank with his beer breath. Maggy shivered. But Frank would never blend with the locals. No matter which way she turned this puzzle it came out wrong. Was Edgar right? Was she in danger? A single drop of cold sweat trickled down her back. "Who knows? Some creepy fan could be checking me out."

Mei wrinkled her nose. "The glamour of being a star, eh." She shrugged. "See ya at the café." She walked away with the grace of a ballerina, and Maggy had to stop herself from asking her to stay to keep her company. Really, she needed to get a grip. Too many late nights was playing on her nerves. The guy could be a salesman, or someone with the wrong address. Just because he came to her door. . . didn't mean he was a murderer.

Still, she wondered. On her way to the meeting Maggy stopped at a pay phone and dialed Inspector Peterson's number. She hated cops with a passion, and for good reason, but it was time she talked to him. The beginning of a serious migraine sat in the spot between her eyes. Damn that alley.

"Peterson," he said.

"This is an anonymous caller," she said, muffling her voice.

"I don't like anonymous." His voice sounded like gravel being kicked around, just the way she remembered it.

"The Black Cat murder's linked to Brother XII's buried treasure."

"And I'm a Martian with two dicks." He hung up.

That didn't go well. Why the hell can't cops listen?

***

Smokey, an old hippy who'd lived on Granville Island since its latest rebirth in the 70s owned and operated The Skuttlebut Café. Set a couple hundred yards in from the docks in the lower floor of a century-old, red-brick warehouse, her diner had become a gathering place for locals. It had a down-home granola feel to it, wooden tables covered in blue and white gingham table clothes and decent coffee. Not great coffee, but drinkable.

Unless there was a hockey game on, her sound system played classic rock and roll in the afternoon, but Gordon Lightfoot dominated her morning playlist. Smokey got her name from the days when she sang with a rock band. No one knew her birth name and given her personality, no one asked.

It was hard for Maggy to believe her community was holding a formal meeting. Dock people rarely gathered for such things. They drank beer together on occasion, and when any excuse came along for a celebration, they'd hold wild parties, that no one talked about afterwards, but they weren't the "let's have an agenda" kind of gang. They were great neighbors and interesting people, but definitely not committee types.

She had lived in her houseboat at the Shady Lane Marina for six months. No one seemed to know the official origin of its name, but there were lots of stories. It had twenty houseboats at the moment. Some city planners called it the Dogpatch Everyone knew everyone else and secrets were rare. But the laid-back attitude of the community made it comfortable to live in and it fit her like a well-worn, leather mukluk. Without anyone saying it, everyone knew the cardinal rule: "live and let live."

Beside her houseboat community was the Blue Heron Marina, a private docking area for thirty upscale yachts and sailboats. She knew a few people from over there, but most of them only came to their boats when the weather and stock market were good.

Catching up on her text messages, she gathered this meeting would involve all the people from both marinas, because some idiot had been messing with property in both locations. It had started with minor stuff and escalated to a fire set on one boat this week. The worst fear of anyone on boats, if you ignored mythical squid legends, is fire. There would be a good turnout.

When she opened the door of the café Maggy almost fell over. At least thirty people crammed into the small space. It looked like almost every house from 'Shady Lane' was represented, and at least half the boats from the Blue Heron. Mei sat near the front.

Maggy chose to sit near the door. If her headache worsened, she could slip out. Smokey wearing her blue *Go Canucks* apron plunked a big mug of coffee in front of her. It was her favorite cup. On the side there was one line, "Don't mess with me." Black fluid rippled over the edges of the cup and onto the table. Maggy used a napkin to clean the mess and took a long drink. Yup, good enough and just what her headache needed. For good measure she knocked back a couple pain killers from her purse.

Loud, anxious chatter filled the room; conversations laced with anger and fear. She didn't need to hear every word spoken to gauge the worry in the crowd. It showed in their drawn faces and the way they leaned towards each other, as if proximity could keep out the darkness of the world.

Hunter stood up, and the crowd hushed, stopping their conversations in mid-sentence. She'd never thought of Hunter as a leader; a protector yes—he loved his boating community—but not a leader. But this crowd gave him credence.

Hunter ran a successful sailing charter from a thirty six foot sailboat docked at the Blue Heron marina. Besides that, the man was a bit of a puzzle. One, she had often dreamed about unraveling. Six foot, well-built and with a wide smile, he had to be the hottest single man on the docks. He had honest, dark blue eyes that could heat an igloo for a month, cocoa colored skin and wavy black hair. He got his eyes from his Irish father and his skin color from his Haida mother, but there was that missing piece of the puzzle she wondered about. Hunter had an aloofness that went beyond being cool and into the zone of scary. Clearly he had a past.

Hunter started talking. "Just to bring everyone up to speed there have been four events now. Last Monday two kayaks were stolen from Huey's yacht. Tuesday, Lopez's houseboat at the Shady Lane marina was set on fire. We got the fire out before it hit the gas tanks. Two hundred dollars was taken." The crowd grumbled. "Last Wednesday, the Franklyn's twenty-four-foot sloop was cast adrift in the middle of the night." The grumbling grew louder. "And Thursday, Elena's yacht had a galley fire."

"What the fuck is going on?" called out one person in the crowd.

"We have to get to the bottom of this," said another.

The crowd's response had escalated as Hunter detailed the catastrophes. Concern swelled like a tsunami. Maggy's head pounded.

Hunter raised his hand and once again they went quiet. "Someone is sabotaging our community. And each time they strike, they hit harder."

"You're makin' too much of it," yelled Smokey by the counter. "Each incident is different. They're not the same."

"They're escalating." Hunter stared her down.

"Bullshit." Smokey rolled her eyes. "I betcha a loony Elena the nymphet over there set her boat on fire to get your sweet ass on her boat."

A buck! Only Smokey would place such a bet.

The crowd went silent, looking back and forth between Smokey, Hunter and Elena.

Elena stood up and shifted her shoulders, drawing everyone's eyes to her over-flowing bikini top, peeking through her open sailing jacket. Maggy blinked. *Does the bitch ever give it a rest? A bikini top in November?*

"I don't know how you can say a nasty thing like that," Elena's Swedish accent weakened on the word *that*. She pulled her jacket closed, but didn't zip it up, so it fell apart again a second later.

Maggy could tell by the steel in Hunter's eyes that the poor dear man hadn't considered himself prey. But he got it now and his jaw went rigid.

"Told you," said Smokey. People snickered in the crowd.

Hunter shook his head and looked around making eye contact with everyone. "Even if Elena lit her own fire, that still leaves three incidents." He raised his arms in supplication. "Let's cut the gossip and get to the facts. Someone is out to get us."

Maggy looked at her empty cup and decided to leave. The headache wasn't getting any better. Politics take time and as usual, she didn't have any to spare. She needed to walk Napoleon if she wanted to eat this week and then there was her afternoon job. She stood up and quietly slipped through the crowd.

Hunter called her name as the screen door of The Skuttlebut slammed shut behind her.

***

Napoleon, the neurotic poodle, looked more pathetic than ever. He had a bald patch the size of a hockey puck on his back. "What happened?" asked Maggy.

"I'm not sure, dear." Mrs. Randolph adjusted her pearls which hung over her classically cut, navy-blue linen suit. "He scratched all night long, and his hair keeps falling out. Something is bothering him. We're going to the vet later today."

"I'm sure he'll feel better after his walk," Maggy said in a soothing tone reserved for Mrs. R.

With a poop bag in hand, Maggy hit the road. The poor mutt looked sad with his drooping ears. She'd give him an extra good walk. She rubbed between her eyes. The pain had dulled a bit. Putting on her sunglasses to block the light that made her migraines worse, she gritted her teeth. She could do this.

Once she and Napoleon hit their stride, stopping every few feet, so that he could mark his territory like the big, mean alpha he'd never be, she pulled out her cell and called Mei.

"Why didn't you sit with me at the meeting?"

"I have a killer headache. I sat at the back near the door, so I could leave."

Silence for a moment. "So tell me about your night."

"Logan came to the Black Cat. You know, the dead guy's brother."

"Did you tell him?"

"Yeah, and you were right. It did make me feel better." Maggy told her what had happened between them.

"And you pushed him out the door?" Mei's voice rose.

"It seemed the wise thing to do at the time." Napoleon pulled her to a grungy looking fire hydrant covered in graffiti.

"Sometimes," Mei said, "it's better *not* to think, honey. Twisting the sheets with a hot guy might take care of your migraine."

"It's the murder that's got me edgy."

"Did you call the police, yet?"

"Yeah."

"Wow. I'm impressed."

"I phoned Peterson and told him there's a relationship between Jimmy's murder and Brother XII's buried gold."

Mei cracked up. "Did he laugh?"

"No. He hung up."

"At least you tried."

The phone was quiet for a minute. Then Mei

said, "I got to go. A kid just knocked over a can of paint. Take care." Mei ran an artist's co-op on Granville Island.

Maggy pulled on Napoleon's lead. He really liked this particular hydrant for some reason. Picky poodle.

"Here, I'll take care of him," said a man whose familiar voice made her blood run cold.

She turned to see Edgar. His face, whiter than yesterday, looked longer. She threw him her "don't-fuck-with-me I-gotta-migraine'" look: crossed eyes, glazed with a threatening layer of vengeance.

Edgar picked up the dog and gave him an affectionate squeeze. Napoleon nuzzled his chin. "I'm good with dogs. This one's upset. You need to be extra kind to him." His voice dripped syrupy sweet, like the voice people use with newborn babies. Why do adults do that when they talk to pets? With luck Napoleon would give him a good nip. Surely he'd see through the human syrup.

Maggy continued to stare at Edgar.

"I'm sorry about running out on you at the library. I got spooked. This man . . ." Edgar stroked the dog.

"I know. I saw the man with a black hoody following you. What the hell, Edgar?"

"I'm sorry. It's all my fault. Jimmy was taking so long to get back to me I decided to get more help. I wanted answers, so I hired another man to get information for me."

"Okay. You lost me." Was it the headache or the goofy story? *Please let it make sense.*

"I hired Jimmy to locate an area on the coast that fit a physical description my great-grandmother left in her memoir."

"Got it.

"But Jimmy was taking too damn long, so I hired another guy to go looking."

"The man in the library?"

"Yeah. Well maybe. I'm not sure. I never met the man."

"How could that be?"

Edgar winced. "I hired a Decourcy Island fisherman over the phone, to study the local charts and locate caves. I didn't tell him why."

Maggy shook her head. How stupid could he be? "You know people on that island are used to gold hunters."

"Yeah, tell me about it. Anyway, a couple days later the library guy turned up at my door. He said he knew what I was after and wanted to know everything I knew about the location of the treasure. I told him I didn't know what he was talking about. He pushed me back into my house and threatened me." Edgar looked over at the street. Maggy didn't need to see the fear in his eyes; she could feel it.

"So what happened?"

"I was lucky. My housekeeper arrived, and he fled."

"And since then?"

"That happened last week. I phoned Jimmy to warn him. But he wouldn't listen to me. He told me not to worry; he could take care of himself. He said he was still looking. But he had been looking for a month and I got suspicious. I got to thinking that he'd figured out the location of the gold and planned to get it himself." Edgar stopped for a breath and scratched Naploleon behind the ears. Maggy waited.

"I decided to follow Jimmy to see what he was up to. But I didn't catch up to him until Tuesday night in the alley. He lay there covered in blood talking to you. I got out of the alley as quickly as I could. The next thing I know that man from the library started tailing me." His had lowered his voice.

"Did you talk to the police?"

"No."

"You don't want to share the gold. Is that it?"

His shoulders sank a fraction. "I saw you in the alley. You said he didn't say anything, but I saw you lean down and put your ear to his mouth. He told you something."

"I was checking to see if he was breathing. He wasn't."

Edgar narrowed his eyes. "Listen, lady, even if he didn't tell you anything, you're in danger. The murderer probably saw you too."

"Phone the police. You're scared. They can protect you." Did those words really come from her mouth?

Edgar looked deeply into her eyes as if he was about to do surgery on the back of them. "Why won't you tell me what he said?"

"Do you think it was the man in the hoody who killed him?" she asked.

He let out a breath slowly. "I didn't get there

in time to see who stabbed Jimmy. When I arrived he lay on the ground and you were with him."

She nodded. "Yeah, I confess. I talked. I said a prayer for him. It seemed like the right thing to do. He was dead."

Edgar's face dropped. Without another word, he handed Napoleon back to her, like a moldy bag of potatoes, and wandered off towards the city center, slumped under the weight of his quest for gold.

CHAPTER 13

E dgar shifted his reading glasses. There had to be something in this damn journal that would get him to the gold. He read his great-grandmother's second entry:

Cedar-by-the-Sea,
October 30, 1927

I never dreamed life could be so exciting. Brother XII is becoming famous and our colony in Cedar-by-the-Sea is growing every day. He now has eight thousand followers contributing to our Foundation! Money is pouring in for our community, the Arc of Refuge. People are hearing the truth.

The brother is brilliant. *The Chalice*, his monthly magazine, reaches thousands all over

North America. He has pamphlets too. But his speeches are my favorite. When he preaches to us about working together to build a better world, I know I am listening to the words of a prophet. Anyone who hears him knows he's telling the truth given to him from beyond this world. His words echo in my being. He is lighting our way.

But, greatness draws evil. Scandal follows the good brother. People say the most wicked things about him. Any action he takes is misinterpreted and marked with a malevolent slant, painted by the devil himself. Evil is everywhere.

I watched him hypnotize a man at the Orpheum theatre in Nanaimo. Once in a trance, the man went down on all fours and barked like a dog. He actually barked. Completely in the brother's control, he followed his commands. I couldn't believe my eyes. And before us all stood Brother XII, small in stature, but large in power, with his signature red rosebud in the lapel of his black suit jacket.

My old friend Roger called the brother's powers black magic, but he only uses his gift for good. I would call it—white magic. Or, better yet, not magic at all. It is the power from beyond, a spiritual gift given to the chosen ones. That's how the brother explains it.

Tonight, he proved his capabilities to the gathering. I believe he can control us all, but he lets us find our own way. He harnesses his great powers for our own good, lets us choose between right and wrong. My path is to follow him.

I finished reading his second book, *A Message from the Masters of Wisdom*, and I have to say it gives me nightmares. The corrupt outside world is heading for destruction. People are living their lives without thought for the greater good. That situation cannot continue forever. I wish more people would listen.

We need to put all our energy into building our community, the Arc of Refuge, where we can stand by each other. There we will attain spiritual enlightenment. There we will be saved from the coming chaos. When he talks about the darkness ahead, I can feel it coming like a big, dark shadow growing in strength.

Brother XII refers to himself as the "Messenger of the Fire," "The Whirlwind" and "The Day of Adjustment." He is all those things.

But to me, at night he is simply my lover. Sometimes I call him Eddie. When he takes me in his arms the troubles of the world melt away and the looming shadow vanishes.

He does things to me, I would never write down. He says he learned how to please women in the Far East. Lately, he's been asking me to do strange things. Things I never imagined. . . But, I will do anything for him. More about that later.

Tomorrow night he promised me a boat ride.

CHAPTER 14

Music is the mediator between the spiritual and the sensual life. Ludwig van Beethoven

Logan kept thinking about Jimmy's last message. What was he trying to tell him? Waiting for his father to join him at the funeral home to make the final arrangements, he shuffled the two words in his mind. "Tell Logan—the Emer-Old." Hmmm. He had to be referring to the *Emerald Empress*. But what about it?

The cleanliness of the waiting room irked him. Its sterility left no space for life. Jimmy didn't belong here. The lump that had been in his throat since he saw his brother's dead body thickened.

He tried to think of ways to make this easier for himself and his family, figuring that was his job as the oldest son. Strange thoughts crossed his mind. He wished he had a sacred talisman to remind them all of the joy his brother brought into this world. But this institution offered instead the faint smell of lavender, emanating from of a wall socket gadget. He hated lavender, had always hated lavender and from now on would really hate lavender.

Logan shook his head. It just wasn't fair. What the hell did Jimmy get into?

His father, who was usually more punctual than Big Ben, was twenty minutes late for their appointment. Logan got up and paced the small area.

His lawyer told him this morning that his ex, Kate, wanted an enormous amount of child support. As if he had money. How could he keep his business going without Jimmy?

Sasha kept losing weight and still had that horrible cough.

It seemed as though the walls of his life, that he had so carefully constructed were falling in on him from all sides. This was not his life plan. Everything was fucked up.

But there was Maggy Malone. A stirring of hope warmed him. She wasn't his type at all. But she had to be the most provocative woman he'd ever met. Remembering the taste of her lips and the feel of her curves under his hands hardened his mast. He exhaled slowly. He'd like to tell Jimmy all of this. He had a way of laughing at the ups and downs of life that eased the soul.

Wonder what Jimmy would say about Maggy? He smiled. He knew what he would say:

when life offers you something good, take it, especially when it's in the form of a woman.

One hell of a woman that Maggy Malone— full of life and music that made him feel different, as if his senses were all on hyper-drive. And she was so damn sexy with that wild mane of blond hair that fell in curls over her well-rounded breasts. A man could get lost in her. "I put a spell on you . . ." The memory of her sensuous voice pulled at him.

Slow down buddy. She pushed you away. But maybe, she'd give him another chance.

Aroused like a buck in season in a funeral parlor, no less. He laughed out loud. Talk about black humor.

Get back to Jimmy's dying words. "Emerald . . . Why say that with his last breath? Trust Jimmy to leave an enigmatic message.

Wanting a diversion, Logan picked up a magazine from the coffee table. On the table was a picture of a rose-covered arbor over a gate. On the first page he read: "Coffins: the best made products in America." Coffins. Shit. He threw it down. His stomach turned and he swallowed hard. Not fair, not fair at all. But he would get his life back together, piece by piece.

At least he had figured out the *where* of the message. the *Emerald Empress*, a small sailboat they had bought under their company's name five years ago, sat at the dock at the Kitsilano Marina.

The door opened and his father entered. His eyes were swollen and red, and his shoulders hunched. As they embraced, his father, a big burly man, did his characteristic three manly thumps on Logan's back. Time to bury Jimmy.

CHAPTER 15

"Music is the shorthand of emotion." ~ Leo Tolstoy

When Maggy climbed the steps to the stage of the Black Cat, the whole room hushed and Logan's chest tightened. He'd run a red light just to hear her sing one more time.

The bartender, a young, dark-haired man with a sparse goatee, plunked a beer down on the glazed wooden bar in front of him. "Like Maggy?" he asked.

Logan cleared his throat. "Her intensity," he said.

The kid laughed. "Yeah, right."

Maggy strummed her guitar and adjusted her stool.

"Seriously. It's like she pulls all of life's sorrows into her music and makes them better."

Logan took a swig of his cold beer. Something about being near death made him philosophical. Like talking such shit could alleviate his pain.

"And sings it with the voice of a vixen," said the bartender, studying him closely. "I saw you two together last night. Maggy could do with a good man."

"Yeah, her voice is something, isn't it."

"My name's Tommy, by the way. I'm always here." They shook hands and then the bartender moved away to help another customer.

As Maggy started singing, Logan gripped his beer with a sweaty hand. A sensual heat flooded his senses, like a fine cognac burning all the way through his system. When she looked his way and tilted her chin, he could barely swallow.

By the end of her first song, Maggy had made her mark with her sugary voice that could peel grapes. It spoke of life and pain and getting through it all. She melded with her music—with the blues. His fingers ached to touch her and he felt drunk, but it wasn't the beer.

After her last song she came to him.

"Hey." Her raspy voice licked at the edges of his aroused state.

"Hey." A bead of sweat rolled down the back of his neck.

"Found the treasure yet?"

"Found you." He moved closer to her and put his arm loosely around her waist. *Weak line, buddy.*

She stretched her soft, warm body against his and kissed him gently on the mouth. Then she whispered in his ear. "I have one more set tonight."

Pulling her closer, he caught her sea-green eyes. "I love your voice."

She moaned in a way that heated his blood to boiling point, and then she took a step away. "I don't like to be rushed." The way her eyes twinkled in the dark tavern lighting hinted that later she could change her mind. At least, that's what he wanted to believe.

He ran his hand through her curls. They felt like finely spun silk. "You're killing me."

"Hmmm."

"Excuse me," said a man's voice. They turned.

"Logan, this is Clarence, my boss. Clarence, I'd like you to meet one of our new patrons, Logan Daniels."

He shook Clarence's hand. The shake was weak and sweaty as if the man had just seen a ghost. He must have known Jimmy. People often did a double-take between them.

Clarence nodded his head towards the back of the bar where the rest rooms and office were. Maggy nodded and rolled her eyes. But after squeezing Logan's arm, she followed her boss to the back.

***

Pissed off, Maggy squared off in front of Clarence's desk with her hands on her hips. "What the hell?"

"Maggy, times are bad." His eyes were slits in swollen skin as if he'd not slept for ages. His slightly blue lips twitched. "I appreciate you filling in these nights. But we're paddling in shit around here."

"How deep?" She wanted to be nice and care about his business problems, but he had no right to interfere with her talking to a guy during her break. She hated it when men messed with her life.

"I should've told you sooner, but I kept hoping things would change.

"What?"

"The club's in bad shape financially. It's fucked. Been that way for a while."

"Tough times?" The economy had been in one long recession for a couple years, beating everyone up. She knew it had to have hurt the Black Cat as well. People stop going out when money gets scarce. Clarence's drinking habits had made her wonder. But this was the first time he had talked to her about it. "Fucked?"

"When I bought this bar forty years ago it sat in the middle of run-down warehouses. Now it's surrounded by upscale condos. My taxes are going through the roof. I've got inspectors looking for any sign of pests to shut me down, and developers beating down my door. Meanwhile the old building's falling apart and I can't afford to fix it."

This didn't make sense. "We're doing well in here," she said. The place is packed tonight."

"Not only do we need to keep it packed every night, we also have to raise our prices. There are people who want us out of here; because we don't look refined enough for the neighborhood and others who just want the land we stand on to turn it into another cement condominium."

"But if the Black Cat goes . . ."

"I know. It's the only true blues bar in the city, and the best on the coast."

"Can't you get them to back off?"

"I've tried." His head dipped.

A sense of dread settled into the room. There was something he wasn't saying. "What did you do?" She touched the cold brick wall behind her.

Clarence looked above her shoulder at the picture of Bob Dylan on the wall behind her for a moment and then returned his eyes to her. His face paled like a death mask. "I sold part of the business."

She worked at not gasping. Her career counted on the Black Cat. After a lifetime of dreams she had finally started to taste success, here at the Black Cat.

"And you don't want to know who bought it." He lowered his voice.

"Who?" Her stomach clenched.

"Three months ago to keep away the fucking vultures I sold one third to a man interested in keeping us going. He's a real blues guy, and it helped. But then the plumbing in the men's' washroom plugged up and more bills poured in. I was broke again.

"So, last month, I sold another third to the guy who was murdered in the alley, Jimmy Daniels." He grimaced.

The air rushed out of her lungs. "Does it get any worse?"

"Yes. Two days ago I found out that Jimmy had talked to the local developers, Smith & Sons, about selling his share."

She leaned closer to him. "You didn't?"

"Hell no." The smell of scotch hit her face with his breath. "I sure as hell felt like murdering the son of a bitch, but no, I didn't kill him. I yelled at him some. But that's all. I swear."

But something in his voice told her he was lying. A shudder ran through her body. "All?"

He grimaced. "And I punched him in the face. I probably left some DNA there. Ya know what I mean."

Maggy nodded.

"When the police find out they're going to want to talk to me."

An image of Jimmy's swollen, bloody lip slid through Maggy's mind. The pieces were beginning to fit together. "Why did Jimmy Daniels want a share in the bar?"

"Money. Plain and simple. When he told me it was a good investment, I thought he meant in the blues, but he meant in his pocket. He intended to flip it for big bucks. The asshole wasn't straight with me."

"And the third owner?"

"Let's keep him out of this for now. I may need your help with him later, but for now he's a silent, friendly partner."

She ran a hand through her hair. "So you want me to vouch for you with the cops?"

"Hell no woman. I told you I'm innocent." His eyes widened and he threw his hands in the air in defense. "I want you to be extra nice to all our customers. I need them coming back, every night, staying late and buying drinks. And . . ." He looked at his watch.

"And?"

He looked at his desk as if he couldn't look at her. "I feel bad asking you this, but you could talk to your friend Logan out there and find out what his family intends to do with their share of the bar now that Jimmy's gone."

"Let me get this straight. You want me to be your spy?"

"Babe, with the Black Cat's future at stake, your job's on the line."

"Can't imagine anyone wanting to sell the Black Cat."

Clarence looked at his watch again. "It's time for your last set."

With a pained smile Maggy headed for the door. Over her shoulder she said, "We're not going to lose the Black Cat, if I can help it."

***

Looking at Logan she grabbed the microphone and sang, "*I Just Want to Make Love to You.*"

CHAPTER 16

Edgar filled his mug with Earl Grey tea. He'd only met his great-grandmother Rita once, a fragile old woman with clear, blues eyes that seemed to look right through him. He'd been almost five. She died soon after that. He shuddered.

Hard to imagine the old woman had once been young and naughty. He continued reading:

Rita's Journal
Nanaimo, B.C.
October 31, 1928

Brother XII's trial was a debacle.

I stood outside the city council chambers in Nanaimo for an hour yesterday at the corner of Bastion and Skinner. I heard with my own ears the lawyer for the prosecution, Thomas Morton, say to

the crowd that he wasn't afraid of spirits or ghosts
or anything like that. As if we in the Aquarius group
believe in such things. Imagine "ghosts!" People
believe the silly stories about Brother XII and black
magic! They call him a cult leader. If they only
knew the real story they would understand. They
are blind to his virtues, to his vision of a new world.

The brother's been charged under his legal
name, Edward Arthur Wilson, with embezzling—
stealing thirteen thousand dollars from our Aquarian
Foundation to be exact. Several of the loyal
followers, including our good friend Robert
England claim this to be true, but I can't believe any
of it. It's all a misunderstanding.

And when the charges went to court the
strangest thing happened. The magistrate, a
conservative man in an old-fashioned suit by the
name of Beevor-Potts, brought the session to order
and stated the charges. Then Thomas Morton, the
man I'd just seen outside the building saying that
spirits don't exist, collapsed. He just fell down, and
others did too. At the same moment! About ten of
them were lying flat on the floor, out cold. It was
spooky. People were screaming and running around.

I held my breath, sure that the spirits had
visited us and cursed the men with evil in their
hearts.

The judge lowered his gavel and, with a
shaky voice, adjourned the court. Rumors ran
through the town like wild fire. Some said Brother
XII hypnotized the people and told them to
collapse. Others said it was his black magic. A few
believe it was food poisoning. But I believe in the

power of the spirits. I know they struck those men down. Goodness will always prevail.

That all happened yesterday. Today, the judge moved the trial to Vancouver. There are too many rumors on Vancouver Island to have a fair trial, he said. The town paper is talking about Brother XII on the front page calling the event a, "local sensation." The judge thinks the trial will be safer on the mainland. I'll follow the brother wherever he's sent, but I do think this silly nonsense is a waste of money.

And I could tell the judge a thing or two. No-where is a person safe from the spirits, especially if they cross the brother. He can move the trial to Vancouver, but it won't make anyone safer.

Brother XII was not at all dismayed by the events. He shrugged his shoulders when I asked him how he felt about it, said, "Fools. The world is full of fools." Then he kissed me, and the worry of the courts melted away.

Last night, Brother XII and I continued exploring the edges of Decourcy Island. I love our moonlit adventures. He rows a little skiff and we talk about the constellations. We stopped inside a cave for about twenty minutes. A couple bats flew near our heads. It was really creepy. One flew within an inch of my head, and I screamed. That made him laugh. He does not laugh often.

When I complained about the cave, he rowed out and we settled for a while on the shore. We made love under the stars. He was tender as he had been in the beginning. I like him that way. When he gets all angry with people, he forces me to do things I don't always enjoy. At least not as much.

I wonder what the spirits think of my lust. Brother XII says, it is right for men and women to couple. It strengthens the community. It's a part of the natural law.

People say the brother coupled with another woman in the House of Mystery last week. The young pretty one whose husband's been sent to the other island to work. That's supposed to be a sacred place. I can't believe he would violate it, let alone be with another woman. That's just another nasty rumor.

In his magazine, *The Chalice*, he's been writing about the American election. He's so knowledgeable. I guess he must get it from the spirits.

I still wonder what he sees in plain little old me.

CHAPTER 17

You are the music while the music lasts. ~T.S. Eliot

Hunter rubbed his hands together for warmth. The new moon slid behind a blanket of dark clouds. Only the warm glow coming from inside boats and float homes at the marina lit the night, the kind of hearth glow that warms the heart. Damn, he'd like to be inside with a woman and, if he had his way, with Maggy Malone.

At the meeting in the morning people signed up to patrol the docks. He'd taken the empty spot in the middle of the night. It seemed like a good idea at the time. An hour had passed, but so far he'd seen nothing unusual and gotten himself soaked in the unrelenting rain. Did the Dock Rat know about the security patrols? *Dock Rat.* That was the name Smokey gave the unknown asshole who messed with their stuff at the docks. It fit.

Hell, he could be in one of the patrols. Hunter shook his head, hoping the Rat wasn't an insider.

Mist formed above the water in swirls. Dampness seeped into his bones, chilling him to his core. Walking the docks seemed the only way to keep the community safe. He kept himself warm thinking of snuggling up with Maggy. He could almost feel her soft skin, smell her scent. He shook his head to clear it. If ever there was a time he needed to focus, it was now. He needed to protect his community, including Maggy, and that meant keeping his guard up. That's how he'd catch the Rat, with vigilance and determination.

The brisk breeze off the Salish Sea caught the ends of loosely stowed sails, making rustling sounds up and down the docks. Boats rocked by the wind and water bumped against the docks. Mast fittings clanged in the wind. A fog horn blasted in the distance. The dock sounds, so familiar to him, would have been comforting if he wasn't looking for the person trying to ruin it all. Why would anyone want to disturb such peace?

The sound of a delicate footfall made him turn around. There stood Elena in her rain gear. He immediately wondered what was under it. She wasn't what he needed right now, or ever for that matter.

"Hey," he said. "Sneaking up on me?"

"I thought you might like company." She sauntered toward him.

Yeah, like a hole in the head. The woman lived with a Mexican drug lord. He didn't need that kind of trouble. "Did you set the fire in your galley?"

She hesitated too long. In the faint light, her fine-boned face turned into a smile. "What if I did?"

"I'd be seriously pissed off."

She moved closer.

He was a man, and despite being angry, his body responded to her proximity. He tried narrowing his gaze.

"And what would you do to me if you were angry?" Her coy voice stopped him cold; too artificial for his tastes.

"If I weren't a gentleman?"

"Gentlemen are overrated. If you weren't a gentleman, what would you do?" She stood next to him now. Her warm breath touched his face and the heat of her body warmed him in a dangerous way.

"I'd throw you in the chuck." He put his hands on her shoulders and pushed her back.

Elena's baby blues popped. "Oh."

"We can't happen," he said.

"But, we'd be so good." She emphasized the "so" and inched closer. A piece of paper couldn't fit between them. This woman was persistent.

He stepped back. "First of all, you live with your boyfriend."

"He's away all the time and I get lonely. I need some toys to play with."

"He's a crook, Elena. Deal with it. And I'm not a toy."

"And if I wasn't with him?"

She'd moved in again, cunning like a cat slinking into warmth. He hesitated, probably too long. It was that disconnect thing. While his brain said, "No fucking way," his body said, "Oh yeah." The time it took him to think was all she needed. Her arms circled his body and pulled him to her with a strength he didn't know she possessed.

That's when he heard a strange noise.

His body froze. The hair on the back of his neck rose. It came from the end of the dock. He pushed Elena away and started running. It sounded like a hammer tapping. At three-thirty in the fucking morning? Who'd be building in the middle of the night?

Elena said something, but he didn't stop to listen. He wanted to get to the sound, fast, wanted to find out, once and for all, what was going on. Find the Dock Rat.

It felt like forever, but was more like two minutes, before he reached the end of the dock. Adrenaline rushed through his body, focusing his mind. He'd find the bastard who'd caused the trouble.

But there was no one in sight. He looked towards the sound and saw a hammer, tied to a thin rope, attached to the side of a sailboat. The rocking of the hull made it hit the side rhythmically. What the fuck?

He knew the boat. It belonged to Parker, a semi-retired lawyer who lived in North Vancouver. He hadn't been down to the docks for at least a week. Something about a conference in Vegas.

He reached down for the hammer and pulled it up. On the side of the wooden handle a message in black marker read: "Gotcha."

Using his flashlight Hunter scanned the dock, but he had just been here minutes before. The guy had to be on the water. He scanned the water. One boat, a small skiff headed towards Maggy's houseboat community. "Maggy."

Hunter started running. As he passed Elena she grabbed at his arm, but he pushed her away. He'd deal with her later, one way or another. Right now, he had to get to Maggy.

A metallic taste flooded his mouth. His muscles tensed but he ran full out. The Rat had a lot of explaining to do. He ran to her door. Candlelight flickered through her blinds. She must be meditating. Sometimes she got mystic-like after singing.

He reached for her door handle and didn't bother knocking. Too pumped. He opened the door wide and burst through. Maggy was in the arms of another man.

***

"Hunter," Maggy said.

She pushed Logan away and turned to face Hunter, watching his face pale at the sight of her naked breasts in front of him.

Logan turned also. "What the hell?" His voice growled at the edges. He reached for Maggy in a show of possession.

She moved away from him, grabbed her jacket off the floor, turned and put it on.

Hunter moved towards Logan. Not a good thing. Squeezing between them, she held them apart with her hands.

"Hunter, what's going on?" she asked.

He shifted his eyes away from Logan and locked with hers. It took him a minute to answer. "A guy. I saw a guy in a row boat heading this way." His steely blue eyes began to soften. "I'm sorry Maggy. I didn't mean to . . ."

Logan backed off. "You could have knocked, man." His voice sounded less ragged now. Maggy's pulse slowed.

"Look, buddy. I don't know who you are," said Logan. She kept her hand against Hunter to make sure he didn't lunge. This was insane.

"What did the guy look like?" she asked.

"It's pitch black on the water. A fog bank is moving in. All I could see—" he paused to breath, "—was a black shape rowing a boat this way. No one's going to be out in the rain and cold in the middle of the night unless they're up to no good." Hunter hesitated. "I figure he's The Rat."

"The Rat?" asked Logan, his face red.

Hunter looked at him. "An asshole sabotaging the docks, cutting boat lines, setting fires, crap like that. He left me a note a few minutes ago at my dock. It made sense that the guy in the boat was that man."

"The Rat?" Maggy tried to piece it together.

"Whatever—the bad guy." Hunter's body relaxed. "He's probably long gone now, but you're safe, so . . ."

A scream pierced the night. "Aaaaaaaaaaaah!. Help. Someone, help me! Heeeelp!" They ran out the door, Hunter first, followed by Maggy and then Logan.

Elena stood on the dock beside Maggy's place. With a shaking hand she pointed at the water and then her body collapsed onto the wooden boards.

A body floated face down in the water.

Maggy knelt down to take a look at Elena while Hunter jumped in and pulled the body to the dock. Logan helped him heave the body on top of the wooden dock, then he extended his hand to Hunter. Together they rolled the body over together.

Maggy screamed. "Edgar!" A long marlin spike protruded from his chest.

CHAPTER 18

Where words fail music speaks.
~ Hans Christian Anderson

Moored two hundred yards away from the floating, dead man, Gilbert Harrison's fishing boat rocked on the gentle waves. His body shook and his gut churned. *A second murder!* And what really bothered him was how badly he wanted to stick around to see Edgar's face as he died. He wanted to capture all his horror as he realized he was dying. He wanted to see that horror transform the man's features into an ugly mask of terror before death set in and he grabbed his last breath. Shit, he was turning into one sick bastard. But he couldn't deny that imagining it brought him pleasure. Having the power to kill someone gave him a rush of adrenaline and some sort of weird ego-mania.

How depraved he'd become.

As the tremors in his body calmed, a warm glow of satisfaction flowed through him like an electric current, moving him from fear to elation. He had felt the edge of this dark energy the first time, but pushed it away thinking it was wrong. But he had gone beyond wrong this time. This murder had been planned.

For the first time in his life he understood how warriors felt looking over a killing field. For a moment in time, he had reigned over the man's life and death—like a god. Shit, this was a weird high.

But he wasn't evil. No, he wasn't one of the crazies who skins small animals from the neighborhood. In fact, he liked cats and puppy dogs. Not children so much, but small pets were okay.

He'd never thought about killing before he met Jimmy. He wasn't evil—just determined to get what he wanted. There was nothing wrong with that.

Assholes just kept getting in his way. No one had the right to make fun of him, the way Jimmy did. No, he wasn't a bad guy, just a man, a real man, getting things done and taking care of himself.

Gilbert swallowed. His mouth was moist again. His body would be back to normal soon, as if nothing at all had happened.

But could he ever think of himself as normal again? Shit. What a mess. If only he'd controlled himself that first night in the alley. What's a man's pride worth anyway? Not the life of another man. There—that pang of conscience again, rising as regularly as the morning tide. He was over-thinking it. Sometimes a man has to act, and that's all there is to it.

He'd joined the devil's team. Switching jerseys hadn't been a conscious decision. It all happened in the instant when he pushed his marlin spike deep into Jimmy's chest. His hand trembled at the memory. It had played over in his mind a million times in the last two days. He hadn't planned to murder Jimmy, but when he had called him a "'joke" he wanted him to shut up. And when he had said, "You're just an old man on an idiot's quest," he thought he'd explode with anger. He told him not to say that, but Jimmy started laughing and something inside Gil broke. He lost control. The damn thing about it though was that even though he silenced Jimmy forever, he still heard his laughter in his head.

Expediency made the second murder necessary. When Edgar wouldn't tell him the location of the gold and accused him of murdering Jimmy, he had no choice. Edgar had to die. He knew too much. *The second time was easier and— more fun.* Shit, did he actually think that?

He turned on the radio, trying to settle into the rock music. An ugly little voice inside him wondered what the third time would be like. It was such an intense rush, he could imagine becoming addicted to it.

A woman would get his mind off this. Maybe the bitch at the local coffee shop, the hockey nut who swore at her customers. He knew by the way she'd stayed longer at his table than she had to that she was putting herself on the menu. Yeah, he could fuck her.

He scratched his chin, which he hadn't bothered to shave for a couple of days. It would take his mind off things. But women complicated things. They always did. It would be better if he kept to himself and got things done. That's what his grandfather would have wanted.

Gil got up and poured himself a glass of water. He took a sip and felt the coolness slide down his parched throat. The awful taste in his mouth could be washed away, but his sins were another matter. He lifted his glass to the sky, "To you, Gramps. To you."

Imagining the old man sitting with him relaxed him. The old gizzard loved the ocean. That was how Gilbert got into fishing. The old man had taught him everything he knew before he died and left him his boat.

The fishing was fun, but the times he liked best, were when Gramps would sit around the stove with a whiskey in his hand and shoot the shit. Gilbert's favorite stories were always about Brother XII. His grandfather had been there, way back in the 1920s and even talked to the man. He had listened to the cult leader's speeches, and watched him go into crazy trances. In his day Gramps believed in the man. Called him a prophet. Gil shook his head remembering the tales. His grandfather had got some bitter when the con man deserted them all and left them with nothing. He had given up all his savings to the cause. Gone in a flash. Gramps died believing that the Aquarian gold lay buried somewhere on the islands—his gold.

Over the years, Gilbert heard other stories about Brother XII and he'd filed them away in his mind. He told his grandfather that if ever he got a good clue as to the whereabouts of the treasure, he'd find it.

After the glass of water, Gil poured a shot of cheap whiskey to smooth out the last of his ragged nerves. His calico cat Sly jumped on his lap and nudged into his chest. Her breath smelled of salmon and her eyes closed half-way. She purred the instant Gil stroked her with his rough hands.

"It's adrenaline," he said out loud. His voice sounded different, kind of hollow. *Is that what voices sound like in hell?* "Nothing's wrong with me Sly, just adrenaline messing me up." He took a long slow breath, leaned back and closed his eyes. When would they find the body?

Light rain pitter-patted on the roof of his cabin. A scream of terror wrenched the stillness of the night. He smiled and waited. Five minutes later, a score of footfalls ran down the docks to where he'd left Edgar's body. People shouted at one another. The rain continued to fall. They must be gathering now, but he didn't dare look. In the distance the faint sound of sirens began. A slow smile spread across his face.

As the noise grew, Sly jumped off his lap and ran for cover under the bunk. "It's okay," Gil murmured. She hated commotion; liked it best when they were out at sea, far from land and unpredictable people.

But the commotion excited him. He rubbed the sweat beading on his brow. Had he lost all sense of right and wrong? Aw, fuck the conscience. What was done was done.

Scanning through the radio stations he listened for news. Maybe someone would be talking about him.

CHAPTER 19

"Ms. Malone." Peterson nailed her with his intense "don't-bullshit- me" cop look, "Tell me again, how you're not involved." The black pupils of his eyes, tough enough to penetrate steel, bounced off the back of hers. "Men keep turning up beside you dead—with spikes stuck in their bodies." His choice of words *almost* made the murders sound funny, but no humor lived in his demeanor. The cop was all business.

In the thickening fog, policemen in uniform held the gathering crowd of neighbors back from her home. She could hear them gasp and complain in the confusion. Hunter, Elena and Logan stood nearby, but not close enough to hear what Peterson said to her. Maggy looked over at them, not wanting to be alone. A second murder. She hadn't had time to fully comprehend the first.

She pulled the blanket one of the medics gave her close around her body, hoping it would stop her shivering. But it seemed nothing could keep the damp November cold out, not to mention the terror that flowed through her blood. What a night. She cleared her throat.

"His name is Edgar."

"No last name?" Peterson's left eyebrow rose.

"I don't know it." Her words started fine in her head, but when they came out of her mouth they sounded garbled and stilted. She swallowed. Her mouth tasted like dry dirt off a road on a sunny day. "He might have told me, but I just don't remember it."

"Take a deep breath." His hazel eyes softened microscopically, but not enough to be truly comforting.

The sound of a fog horn pierced the night. The salt air felt good in her lungs. She concentrated on slowing her breathing but her body fought back.

Peterson slid his eyes over her body and came back to her face.

"How do you know Edgar?"

"After Jimmy was murdered, I met him in the library and we talked."

"About?"

Now was the time to come clean, tell him all the truth. She opened her mouth, but the words would not come out. Sometimes she hated being herself. She ran a hand through her tangled hair and considered her options. She tried to keep her emotional response to cops buried deep in a jagged crevice of her heart saved just for them, but having to deal with old Gravel Voice shook her emotional baggage loose. No matter how professional the inspector appeared to be, she couldn't trust him. He was a cop and she had been screwed over way too many times by the men in uniform to trust him. She clenched her teeth and tried to swallow.

The damned murderer had left her a dead body. Some calling card. And someone, she was sure of it now— someone had followed her the other day. Would she be next on his list? Did he know Jimmy talked to her? She cleared her throat again, buying time.

"Ms. Malone?"

"He wanted to know what Jimmy said to me that night in the alley."

"You told me Jimmy was dead."

"That's what I told Edgar."

Peterson's eyes narrowed. She swore he smelled her lie.

"Edgar said someone had been following him, and I saw a stocky man with a hoody chase him out of the library. That was Wednesday."

"And?" Peterson's voice didn't hide his exasperation.

"On Thursday I saw Edgar down by English Bay. I walk a poodle there in the mornings. We talked about dogs and he asked me again about Jimmy. He said he knew he was being followed at the library."

"That's it?"

"Yes," she said. "That's it." But she didn't look him in the eye.

"And the next time you saw him, he was here in the water?"

"Yes."

"Here?" He motioned towards the patch of water where Edgar had been floating face down minutes ago.

"Yes, in the water." A shudder ran through her body.

"So, let me get this straight. Edgar met you at the library?"

"Yes."

"Why did you go?"

Shit, he was good. She coughed, to stall, hoping it sounded real. "He called my boss, Clarence. Told him I was in danger. Told him to get me to meet him. I guess you could say I was curious."

"Danger? No kidding." The inspector's mouth twisted. A minute of agonizing silence fell before he continued. "What kind of danger?"

"I asked him, but he was evasive. He said 'others' would want to know what Jimmy said to me, and they would be after me. He scared me." She hated how the words made her sound like a helpless female, but she couldn't deny what happened.

"Others?" His eyebrows twitched.

"Yup, others." She took a deep breath. At least breathing was getting easier.

Peterson stretched his back, cracking some bones. He looked over at the people gathering on the dock and then brought his face back into hers. The movement increased the intensity of his stare. She swallowed. His lips formed a firm line.

"Is this about Brother XII?"

"Who?"

"I got a call from a woman, from the pay phone on the corner of the docks earlier today. An anonymous caller with a muffled voice." He paused, letting another agonizing minute of silence fall while his eyes bore into hers. "She said Jimmy's murder had something to do with Brother XII's gold."

"Gold? Oh you mean that guy on the islands who buried his gold in mason jars?"

"Yeah, that guy."

"I grew up on the coast. I know the stories about Brother XII." As she pulled the blanket closer around her, it made a crackling sound. She worked hard to give him a helpless expression. "What would that guy have to do with Jimmy's murder?"

"That's what I'd like to know." His mouth turned down. Did he believe her? Silence again. The cop used it better than he used words. Maggy scratched her ear. If she just held to her story, he would get tired of asking the same questions and go away. Or so she hoped.

"Describe the man in the library following Edgar." He took out a pad of paper from his pocket.

"Stocky, medium height, black hoody pulled down hiding his face, black jeans, runners. Kind of like an old guy dressed up like a teenager." Peterson wrote down what she said and then let an uncomfortable quiet deepen between them, again.

He looked over his notes and tapped his pen on the pad. His forehead ceased as he stared at her again.

Her throat constricted. She wanted to go home.

"Well," Peterson said at last, "you can go for now. I'll call you tomorrow to ask more questions. We'll need you in to complete a report." He looked over at the others. "I'll be talking to your friends."

Maggy nodded. Gravel Cop reminded her of a dog with a carcass, scratching and eating away every morsel of meat, right down to the bone. Maybe she should tell him more. Glaring police lights flooded the area, cutting through the settling fog and illuminating not only the detective but also the grisly scene of death. Maggy stared him down.

"Nothing else you want to tell me?"

"No, Inspector."

"Nothing about why Edgar thought you talked to Jimmy at the murder scene?" A smirk glanced off his face as she passed him. He knew she knew more. But for now it was stalemate.

***

Maggy sat up in her bed with a steaming cup of chamomile tea and pulled her grandmother's blue cotton quilt tight to her chest. All she wanted to do was sing, but Jimmy's murder and now Edgar's had brought her life to a halt.

The image of the second marlin spike flickered through her mind. Who would want to kill Edgar? The library goon? A shiver ran down her spine.

The fog horn blasted in the distance. They were socked in. Light rain pattered on her metal roof.

She lifted her cup to her mouth with a trembling hand. How did she get in the middle of this? She turned on a classical radio station to soothe her nerves. A soprano singing an aria from Verde's opera *Aida* came through. But even her clear notes could not shut her mind off.

Too late to call Mei. Besides, too much crap had gone down to squish into a text. *Deal with it. Put your big girl panties on and deal with it.*

Trying to avoid being involved with the murder hadn't worked. Time to face it head on.

What did Jimmy say? "Tell Logan, the Emer-Old." It had to mean something. She'd talk to Logan and figure it out. She'd make him tell her what he knew. Then she'd figure out who the murderer was and tell the cops to pick him up. She finished the tea and lay down again.

Twenty minutes later, she jolted awake. Someone pounded on her door.

CHAPTER 20

Music is my religion.~ Jimi Hendrix

Hunter approached the cop slowly. He wanted to follow Maggy, but he knew the routine. Cop first, then the woman. There'd be questions and more questions to go through, before he'd be free again.

"Ernest Hunter." Peterson kept his tone polite but cool, and his eyes shot "don't-fuck-with-me" daggers directly into Hunter's head.

Hunter tilted his chin up, put his hands on his hips and waited. *Fuck you too.* He didn't bother offering him a hand. Surrounded by light from the floodlights they took their time looking at each other.

Logan and Elena stood behind yellow tape, watching from a distance. Other people were wandering down the dock towards the lights to check things out. Cops in uniform mulled around the corpse. Paramedics arrived. The onlookers watched each other, and took in the scene at the same time.

Compared to the noise of the activity around the murder, the two men's silence seemed obscene. Shouldn't they be doing something? A man was dead.

Peterson opened his notebook and flipped a few pages until he got to one he seemed to like. "After Jimmy Daniel's murder I investigated Maggy Malone and all her known associates. I pulled your file." He tapped his pen.

Hunter took a deep breath and let it out slowly. *Here we go again. There's no escaping the past.* "What do you want to know?"

"Murder reduced to manslaughter?"

Hunter staged a yawn. "I did my time."

"I made some phone calls."

"Shouldn't we be doing something for Maggy, or the dead guy?"

The inspector narrowed his cop eyes. "She's safe and he's dead."

A man of few words. Hunter liked that. "I didn't know the dead man. Never seen him before."

"My sources said most people thought you were wrongly accused of murder in Masset."

"What difference does that make?"

"They said you deserved a medal, not time in jail."

Hunter winced. *He didn't need a cop's pity. Learned the hard way not to trust it. Especially when it came from a white guy*. Would his fucking past ever be over? "Like I said, I did my time."

The asshole nodded.

"What more can I tell you Inspector?" Hunter stared him down.

"You got a marlin spike?"

"A couple. Most boat people do."

Peterson nodded and made a note in his book. "Look," he said, stepping closer, "I don't know if you were guilty of murder in the past. I don't really care. But if you know anything about these murders or Maggy Malone's involvement in them I need to know."

"Maggy's not involved."

"She keeps finding dead guys. She's involved."

He couldn't argue with that logic. Fuck. "What I mean, is she's no murderer."

Peterson stared at him for a minute. "What were you doing before you found the body?"

Hunter told him about walking the docks with Elena, about the safety patrols the community had organized because of the crap that had been happening. "And so when I saw a man in a row boat headed towards Maggy's place I ran. I went into her houseboat and was talking with her and her friend. We heard Elena scream. When we came out we saw the dead body floating in the water. Face down."

Peterson didn't flinch. No way to know what thoughts were going on in his mind. He tapped his notepad with his pen. "Lot of stuff going down."

Hunter tilted his head and nodded. Maybe, the cop did get it.

"I'm keeping my eye on you." Peterson closed his book.

Hunter laughed. "You can't seriously think that I would murder a guy and then be stupid enough to dump him where I live?"

"Stupid enough, or drunk enough. Doesn't matter. Both theories work for me." Peterson turned to watch the medical assistant zip up the body bag. The finality of the sound made Hunter's gut twist.

"It bothers me," he continued, "when a guy with a record is near two murders."

Wanting to tell the inspector where to stick his theory, Hunter pushed his hands deep into his pockets where they couldn't get him into trouble. He looked at the black sky and forced another yawn. "Believe what you want, but watching me is a waste of your time. There's a murderer running around."

Peterson's mask cracked. His nostrils flared. But he said nothing. "So your story is that someone is sabotaging your life down here on the Granville Island docks, so you and goldilocks over there were um patrolling in the middle of the night." His eyebrows lifted. "Like you couldn't think of better things to do with her."

Hunter pushed his hands further into his pockets.

"You saw a man in a rowboat, chased him and found a dead body."

"You left out the part where I went into Maggy's houseboat, but otherwise, yeah, that's what happened." The memory of finding her half naked crossed his mind. It wasn't a moment he wanted to relive.

"You don't know the dead man."

"No."

"And you didn't know Jimmy Daniels."

"No."

Peterson did his deep, cop scowl. He should be on TV. Hunter relaxed his hands.

"You're free to go, Mr. Hunter. I'll see you in my office at nine tomorrow morning. We can put your full statement on paper then."

Hunter turned to leave.

"But remember . . . "

"Yeah, yeah, you're watching me." *What an asshole.*

It was time to go home. The Rat wouldn't strike again tonight with so many around. Maggy had gone home. Logan would probably follow her after he was questioned and they'd be together again. Shit. Why did she want to be with Logan? The guy looked like a walking suit. The memory of her round breasts flickered through his mind.

A gust of wind moved the dock. Boats banged against it and the clanging of the masts became louder. Hunter looked up. A sliver of moon peaked through the fog sending a chill up his spine

As he passed Smokey she said, "There's strange things going on around here."

"Got that right." He climbed up onto the island and headed for his own marina. Got that right.

CHAPTER 21

For me, singing sad songs often has a way of healing a situation. It gets the hurt out in the open into the light, out of the darkness. ~Reba McEntire

"Maggy, let me in." It had to be Logan. His clipped vowels and deep voice made him sound like a lawyer at a trial. Nobody in her circles sounded like that.

Sliding out of bed naked, she donned a midnight-blue, silk robe, edged with delicate lace. She opened the door. Under the warm entrance light she watched him take a second look. This she didn't need right now. Edgar's murder had put her feet firmly back onto the ground.

She tried to stand taller, but still felt diminutive beside his height. "It's time to get serious."

"Serious?"

"Logan. I'm going to talk straight. I'm attracted to you."

His eyebrows rose.

"Okay, very attracted."

His arms reached towards her.

She stepped back. "But the timing's all wrong."

"I know it's awkward, but . . ."

"No buts." She ran a hand through her hair damp from the night air. "I can't handle buts right now. Not even a handsome one whose kisses drive me wild."

He rubbed his chin and looked genuinely confused. "Can I come in and we'll talk."

The rising heat inside her said, 'Oh yeah,' but her mind screamed, 'Hell no.' She hadn't been with a man since she left her husband Adriano six months ago. Six months is a long time to be without a man in your bed. She hesitated for a moment with her hand resting on the cold door handle, and then she turned and motioned him to follow her inside. With a wave of her hand she directed him to a chair.

Logan sat. She took the couch, leaving them a few feet of space, but that air between them flooded with desire.

He took her hand in his. "Okay. I agree. The timing is wrong." His molten, chocolate brown eyes melted her insides. "But I'm attracted to you, Maggy, and I'd like to think that when this is all over, you'll give me another chance."

Maggy nodded slowly.

"I'm not looking for a quick hook up. I'm strongly attracted to you. I think we could be more."

"You don't know me."

"I know that when I'm with you, I feel more myself than I have for years. There's a freedom about you that's contagious. Give me a chance."

His words sounded sincere, but so had her husband's, in the beginning. "Are you involved with anyone?"

"My wife left me a year ago. I'm more attracted to you than I've been to a woman for a long time." He stopped. "But right now is not our time. Jimmy comes first." His voice broke on his brother's name.

Definitely not the time for a roll in her loft. The rawness of his emotions pulled her. Their affair would not be one of bodies colliding for release. Damn. What happened to her dream of an uncomplicated one-night stand?

Maggy raised her chin. "So let's get the bastard who killed Jimmy." She pulled her robe tightly around herself.

"Shouldn't we leave the murderer to Peterson?"

"He's a cop."

"That's my point. They know what they're doing."

Maggy exhaled slowly. "Even the best cops are hampered by rules we can ignore. Trust me. I know. The way I see it, my life's in danger. I'll do whatever I have to, to stay alive. Screw the cops."

Logan nodded more slowly than she would have liked. "I'll do whatever I have to, to avenge my brother's death, but. . . . I want the cops to know everything we do."

Maggy snorted. What was it about this guy that made her want to be with him?

Leaning back in his chair with long legs, lean body and a chiseled face, he looked more handsome than a man had a right to be, but that's not what drew her to him. The longer she was with him, the more she liked him. Little things. The way he could be tough, yet sensitive and open about his feelings, blew her away. Adriano had been tough both physically and emotionally. Logan's complexity stirred her and scared her. Logan was steady and sweet. Hell—she needed to concentrate. "So tell me what Jimmy's message means."

"The *Emer-Old*? Easy." Studying his hand for a minute as if the answer was there, he slowly replied. "The *Emerald Empress* is our boat."

"Then let's check out the boat."

"Now? It's seven in the morning."

"I can't sleep." Maggy stood up.

"You might want to put some clothes on." He grinned. "Not that I mind seeing you in silk lingerie.

* * *

Pre-dawn light peaked above the horizon as they drove to the Kitsilano Marina, ten miles as the crow flies from Maggy's dock. A veil of mist blanketed the city. The autumn rain dribbled like a leaky faucet over everything. Sea gulls squawked and crows gathered on telephone lines to goissip. The pause before dawn held a palpable feeling of expectation.

It took twenty minutes to get there. Jimmy and Logan's boat, the *Emerald Empress*, was twenty-seven feet long and broad in the beam. Painted a dark green, its chrome-work shone brightly. All its ropes were coiled perfectly. It looked well-maintained and sea-worthy.

Logan jumped onto the mahogany deck first and offered his hand to help her aboard. She took hold of a stanchion and hopped up.

"Just trying to be polite."

The tiny cabin smelled of cedar. The charts and sailing gizmos were organized and neat. *Why do men keep their boats neat, but have difficulty putting their dirty underwear in the laundry?*

Logan scanned his cabin.

"Anything out of place?" she asked.

He grumbled and kept looking.

Maggy went to the wall of the cabin with lockers. She opened the first and found tools, the second held chart containers, the third, bottles of drinking water. "A place for everything and everything in its place." Sailing with Logan would be safe and predictable. *What would it be like to screw him?* Did she really think that? She looked at the back of his wide shoulders and a fleeting image of mounting his body crossed her mind. *Concentrate.*

Logan went on deck and stood at the bow. He looked back over the boat.

Continuing her search below, she opened a fourth locker and found board games and a Louis L'Amour western. She flipped through the yellowing paperback. No notes inside, or handwriting of any kind. It smelled of mould and she sneezed. Tossing it aside, she looked at the games. There were three: a Vancouver version of Monopoly, Scrabble and a Ouija board. She took a second look at the Ouija board. Her stomach clenched.

"Logan," she called.

In a flash, he came to her side, his face full of anticipation.

Holding up the Quija box, she lifted her left eyebrow.

"Oh my God." He grabbed the old box. "I haven't seen this since we were kids. I thought we got rid of it years ago."

"Why would you get rid of it?"

"Oh shit." Logan looked out the port-hole for a moment. He rubbed his chin."Not a great memory," he said after a moment.

"Tell me."

"We played it twice. We were just kids. Everything was a game back then, you know. I'd have been about ten. Jimmy was eight." Moisture beaded on his brow and he held the box as though it contained some horrible secret.

"Yeah?"

"The first time was fun. We laughed for hours. I thought I'd pee my pants at some of the crazy answers it gave us."

"And then?"

"The second time, a week later, we decided to have a full séance with two of our buddies, Alex and Stan. I remember wanting to do it up big."

"A full séance, eh?"

"I'll never forget that night. We gathered in a circle inside our family's dome ten in our backyard in Burnaby. We were all expecting to play a spooky game, something that would scare us a bit, but only in a fun way. We had bottles of Coke, and chips and my mom's double-chocolate brownies. It was supposed to be a blast."

"And . . ."

He swallowed. "And at first it was fun. But then . . ." More sweat on his brow.

"You got scared out of your minds?"

"Yeah, to put it mildly. A spirit or something warned us . . . " He looked out the port hole again, as if the answer hid outside the cabin. "This can't be. It just can't be." He shook his head.

"What?"

"It spelled out on the board. You know." His face paled.

"Logan, what? What did the spirit say? Just tell me."

"Murder."

Murder? Oh great. Her stomach did a few somersaults. He may not have believed in spirits, but she sure as hell did. "Did you ask the spirit who would be murdered?"

He nodded, "It said, 'One of you.'" Logan dropped the box as if it were alive.

His words echoed oddly in the small space and a shiver rose up her spine. She balled her hands and used the pain of her sharp nails cutting into her flesh to steady herself. She could almost feel the spirit in his story. As if he or she were present. *Get a grip Maggy.*

It was his fear and the story and the . . . She pulled her coat closer to her body. She could swear the cabin had grown colder. Her imagination must be getting the better of her. They were alone. Absolutely alone. All the rest had to be her imagination, mixed with a side of post-traumatic stress from finding dead bodies.

Logan picked up the Ouija box from the table. With great care he lifted the top as if it contained a wild beast.

Maggy watched.

Inside there were a playing board and a planchette, the heart- shaped wooden indicator the spirits use to spell messages. No beast. Just an inexpensive, children's version of a spirit board. *All the same, it could have the power to summon ghosts and their messages from beyond.*

"Look underneath," she said. She had a feeling. She closed her eyes.

Lifting the board, he found a folded piece of paper.

"How did you know?"

"What's on the paper?"

A sudden gust of wind rocked the boat and the Ouija board clamored to the ground. Maggy grabbed the locker door more tightly and held on. A flash of light cut through their space, like lightening. Had a storm brewed up that quickly?

Logan's eyes widened.

"I think we're disturbing things," she said.

"Disturbing what exactly?"

"Let's get out of here." She headed for the cabin door. "This place gives me the creeps."

Logan picked up the box.

"And leave that damn thing."

He put it down again and held up the piece of paper. "We need this."

On the way out Logan grabbed a tube of charts that lay on the table. As they sped away from the sailboat, Maggy began to relax.

She didn't understand the spirit world, but she respected it. Swirls of sensibility, feelings, anger, confusion . . . and, finally, a flash of light. It couldn't have all been in her head. But it happened so quickly part of her wanted to dismiss it. She wanted to ignore all the strangeness that entered her mind, but she couldn't do that.

Logan broke the silence. "So you felt a spirit?" Though his words sounded fantastical, he didn't seem to be making fun of her.

"Yes."

"You're psychic?"

"No, at least I don't think so. I haven't won a lottery yet, or found a missing child."

He nodded. "But you feel the undead?"

"Not usually."

They drove in silence for a few minutes.

"Sometimes I get déjà-vu moments, like everyone else." She rotated her shoulders, trying to loosen them. "Maybe a bit more than others. But that's all."

"Ghosts?"

"Never, but . . ."

"What?"

"You're going to think I'm crazy."

"Try me."

"On Tuesday night, when Jimmy looked at me, something happened. His eyes were kinda wild looking and they reached out to me. They pulled me in. I felt like something snapped inside my head, and nothing's been the same since."

"Like an attraction?"

"No, it was more than that. It was like a part of him entered my head."

Logan swallowed slowly. "Jimmy could do that or at least he said he could. He said if he concentrated hard he could connect with some people inside their heads. I never believed him."

"I believe him."

"So, you made a connection. This is weird stuff."

"I'm not a medium. But I'm beginning to think I'm linked somehow to Jimmy and maybe to his murderer too."

"Not a cool psychic power, like in the movies."

"Definitely not." A shudder ran down her spine. "I feel things more clearly than other people. Always have. It's like some people eat spaghetti and can tell you five spices in it, because they have a heightened sense of taste. I can eat the same spaghetti and only detect garlic. I believe people have different abilities to perceive reality. I'm hyper-sensitive to the world around me. I was just born that way, or at least that's what my grandma told me. I experience life so deeply that I catch an awareness of things around me that other people miss. Jimmy tapped into that."

"Did the spirit on the boat tell you anything?"

"I sensed it wanted to, but I just wanted to get out of there. I just wish we could find the murderer and all of this stuff would end." She didn't want to tell him about the dark sense of foreboding that was pooling in her stomach.

"I think having extra information about what's going on around you would give you an advantage over the rest of us."

"Nah uh. It's partly what drove my husband Adriano crazy. He's the sort of man who likes everything drawn in neat, straight lines, drawn in solid strokes. I'm not like that."

"That's why you sing the blues."

Logan not only *got* her, he didn't judge and make her feel like she lacked something vital. Cool.

Adriano had tried for five years to understand her; or, at least he put in the effort during commercials in televised soccer games It's powerful mojo when a man cares enough to look into the hidden corners of who you are and tries to understand what he finds between the cobwebs, and even more powerful when he accepts it.

"Yeah," she said, "that's part of it. The blues, well the blues are everything to me. But, enough about me and my *spirit-dar*. Where are we going?" His finely tuned car moved through the growing morning traffic as dawn broke on the horizon.

"We're here." He pointed to the right. "My place." They were in the west end. He turned into a parking lot beside a tall, gray cement apartment building with ivy growing up its sides. It fit him, tidy and expensive.

***

To call his apartment austere would be putting it mildly. An espresso-scented bachelor pad with no heart but lots of light. The living room flowed into the kitchen and dining area. On top of a navy-blue IKEA couch, *a Sports Illustrated* magazine lay open at a picture of a smiling football player. His bookshelf held an assortment of paperbacks and an old, hard copy of the *Oxford Dictionary*. Dominating the room a soft, brown-leather recliner faced a fifty-inch TV screen. In between sat a beat up metal trunk with three mugs and one beer bottle on top of it. The kitchen area, in contrast, looked barely used. The bedroom door stood ajar.

Following him into the kitchen area her mind struggled like a sumo wrestler with that door. Logan pulled out the sailing charts and unfurled them on the wooden table. He opened the piece of paper Jimmy hid under the Ouija board and placed it on top. "Here's our clue."

CHAPTER 22

Rita's Journal
Vancouver, November 22, 1928

Scandals keep piling up all around us like nasty weeds, choking us to death. Last month Brother XII stood trial in Nanaimo charged with stealing the Aquarian Foundation money. Now they are charging him with a long list of evils.

You would not believe what they are saying.

Rumors spread that when he brought in the new sailboat last week she was filled with opium, and that he sold the drugs to make money. They also say he has been having his way with many women and not always with their consent. They say he doesn't care how young they are. Why would he be with other women, young or old, when he has me? I think people make up stories because they are jealous of him. He is our spiritual guide and I will not believe the wicked tales.

I came here to Vancouver at the beginning of the week to watch his second trial. The judge's name is Aulay M. Morrison. It has only been one month since his last trial, but the charges have piled up, because of those wicked rumors and lies.

At the first trial he was charged with stealing money from our group. This time he is charged with rape, assault, perjury, opium smuggling and sexual abuse of a ten year-old girl. Lies! All lies!!!

It is ridiculous. But not everyone hates him. Brother XII has his supporters. A surprise witness, Mary Connally, traveled all the way from Reno, Nevada, to speak in Brother XII's defense. I am not sure I like that woman.

The attorney general asked that the charges against Brother XII be moved to the next session because the principal witness for the prosecution, our former dear friend, Robert England hadn't shown up. He disappeared. No one knows where he is. How silly is that? Make all these accusations about brother and then vanish. I used to like Robert, but not anymore. He has turned out to be an evil, malicious man.

England's disappearance, of course, started more rumors, vicious rumors. People even accused brother of murdering him. They talked as if he has henchmen at his beck and call. They say he gave them a death warrant for Robert. Imagine.

The case was postponed to the next day. Robert England still did not show up, so the case was dropped, and my Eddie is a free man again.

I wonder what happened to Robert. I always thought him a good man, and a strong supporter of our cause. Peculiar—that he should choose now to run away. I think his conscience got the better of him and rather than stand up in front of a court filled with people and say the truth—that Brother XII is a good leader and had done nothing wrong,—he chose to run away like a coward and hide his shamed face, and his lies. I bet the ancient spirits are not happy with him. I fear for his life

Tomorrow, our group will be going over to Decourcy Island, just off the big island. Mary Connally has generously donated the money we need to purchase land there for our new community. Brother XII says it is like paradise, even more beautiful than Cedar by the Sea.

But late tonight, I will have my lover all to myself. He promised me a walk on the beach, and I know what that means.

You may wonder, dear diary, how I can still be interested in a man who has been charged with rape, and sex with children. Children! But they were lies spread by people who want to bring him down. The spirits warn us about such people. They want to stop our righteous crusade and they will do anything to get in our way. They are evil people who want the world to fall into chaos.

I cannot say I like the way Mrs. Connally ogles him. But she is a dear, sweet old lady to me, at least twenty years my senior. He's nice to her, but I am sure she does not get the attention I get. I am even more sure she does not know how to please him the way I do. The brother has taught me so many things, earthly things.

Still, I have to admit, dear diary, it bothers me when women hover around him. I can almost see them drool when he speaks. He is not a particularly handsome man but he has his charms.

CHAPTER 23

Music is the soundtrack of your life. ~Dick Clark

"I've got to find Jimmy's murderer," Logan said. His eyes darkened with pain, anger and—something else. That something else worried her.

The secret message sure didn't look like a treasure map, or a note left by a leader of black magic. In no way did it have the majesty of a legend-making relic. It was just a scrap of paper. It looked like a note kids might pass at school, revealing who kissed Bobby behind the tree in the school yard.

Logan's face paled and he looked lost in a place she could only imagine, populated with grief and thoughts of revenge. He paced the room twice, like a caged animal. Frustration mixed with anger hung on him like a sour cologne.

"I have to find his murderer."

"We will."

"Maggy?" He stopped in front of her. "I'm not a violent man, but I have to find Jimmy's murderer." He paused and rubbed his chin, darkened with morning whiskers. "The treasure will lead me to him."

She looked over at the paper. "What's it say?"

"Two words: Gabriola Island."

"That's it?"

He nodded.

"Why did you bring all the charts?"

He rubbed his chin; his face had regained some color. "Sailors never go anywhere without charts. I thought they might help. And it wasn't like I had time to be picky."

"Jimmy died for two words?" It was hard to believe.

Logan nodded.

"Two."

"Life makes no sense."

"Death never does," she said.

He winced. "I've never heard of anyone looking on Gabriola for the gold. Have you?"

"No, but it's close to Decourcy Island where Brother XII spent most of his time; no more than a stone's throw away at low tide. She visualized the geography in her mind. "A good friend's family has a cabin on Gabe and I've spent some time there."

"I've sailed in the area, but I've never been on the land."

"On a stormy day when we were shut in the cabin, I read about Gabriola's history. The power went out. By candlelight the stories of Brother XII read better." She laughed. "But his link with Gabriola is really weak. The Gabriolans were a small, spread out community of farmers when Brother XII established his commune. I don't think they would have wanted anything to do with the likes of him. Although one or two of them might have taken supplies over to him. "

Logan studied the chart while he listened. "He would have to have been careful to go around the currents of the treacherous Gabriola Passage. It has a tidal current that runs up to nine knots. It's destroyed a lot of boats, and killed more than a few men."

She shrugged. "I never sailed there, but I have heard of that passage."

He looked at the paper as if a larger message hid beneath it in invisible ink. "The islands are close. On a good tide, Brother XII could have used one of his boats to take the gold over there and hide it."

"He had lots of boats and knew the coast well from the time he worked the merchant boats in the area," she added.

"You think someone would have noticed."

She nodded. "Maybe not. The population on Gabriola being so small at that time, it's conceivable that he came and went without anyone seeing him."

He pounded his fist on the table, shaking the charts. "I think we have a lead."

"Uh." How could she phrase it?

"What?"

"I'm no chart reader, but I know the island is ten miles long. So that's not much of a lead."

"Good enough to kill for." He straightened his body and looked down on her. "Twice."

She ran a hand through her hair. Murder. How did she get caught up in all of this?

"You okay?" he asked, reaching out to steady her.

"Not really," she admitted feeling her cheeks redden. "This PTSD is hell, but the medics said it will pass."

Logan put his hands on his hips. "I'm going to go over the charts for Gabriola. I've sailed near it several times and docked at Silva and Degnan Bays. I'll look over the coastline for all the places where it's easy to land a boat—big or small. When I've that figured that out, I'll try to narrow the list down to ones those that would also be good places to bury gold."

Edgar's face flashed in her mind. "He knew something," she said.

"Who?"

"Edgar knew something else. That's why he was killed. It makes sense."

"So you think he had another clue?"

"Yes." She closed her eyes and tried to remember everything he said to her in the library. "He told me that he had some details about where it was hidden, but he didn't . . . " She squeezed her eyes together trying to remember as much of their time closed, as she could, not just what he said, but what he didn't say, what she sensed—anything.

"Why did he hire Jimmy, if he knew where the gold was?"

Maggy opened her eyes. "He didn't know. He had some vague details about the location. He gave some of them to Jimmy, and I assume the same ones to the Decourcy fisherman. He wanted them to find a location on the coast that fit the description. But I think . . . " She took a deep breath. "No, I'm sure he held back information from them. He wasn't a trusting man."

Logan crossed his arms. "Like two steps north of the palm tree?"

"Yes," she said. "Exactly that. It made sense. He wanted the men he hired to find the general location and he held on to the last specific details they needed to get the treasure for themselves."

"So where can we find those details?"

She released her breath slowly. "In his great-grandmother Rita's journal."

"I wonder if the police have it."

"Maybe, but . . . " She lost her thought. Her head felt heavy, her shoulders ached and her eyes burned. "Logan, I'd like to help you, but I can't keep this up." She touched his hand and he looked into her eyes. "I have day jobs. Mrs. Randolph, a sweet little old lady with arthritis in her ankles, counts on me to walk her dog, and after that I'll be needed to do a shift at the dental office. I gotta work. People are counting on me and I need the money."

He pulled her close, warming her insides as

well as outsides. "The gold's been buried for over a century. It can wait. Do you want to crash here for a couple hours?"

"I don't think that's a good idea."

"I'll sleep on the couch."

"No." Pushing herself away she said, "I'm heading home." It was the hardest thing she'd done that night. "Alone."

"If we find the gold, we'll find the murderer," he said.

CHAPTER 24

Music happens to be an art form that transcends
language. ~ Herbie Hancock

Being at the dentist felt good. That's
how screwed up Maggy's life had
become. She never liked being there.
Who would? She had become a dental assistant to
please her mother initially, and stayed on to pay the
bills. Adriano had thought it a respectable job. But
it wasn't an occupation of her choosing. She liked
the helping people part, but it didn't feed her
creative impulses.

Maggy completed her assigned chart work,
lined up shiny instruments on the dentist tray and
smiled at everyone. But in her head, she sang the
blues. Routines, wonderfully mundane tasks, helped
her relax. She hadn't realized how screwed up her

breathing had become until now.

Her mind kept going back to Jimmy and the alley. She should scrub something, anything, to keep her mind occupied. As if trying to figure out two murders wasn't enough. Her jaw clenched at the thought. A little disinfectant would do the trick.

And what was she doing with Logan? He was so not her type. Yet their chemistry rocked. No denying that. Was it an opposites-attract thing, or an emotional reaction to being around dead bodies? She grinned. Did she have some sort of quirky PTSD thing mixed with her starving libido.

I seriously need to get a grip. If it was the opposites thing, it wouldn't last, and she, Rose Magnolia Malone, would move on.

Then why was her hand shaking? Grabbing a disinfected wipe from the counter she reached up and rubbed the TV screen. And what about Hunter? She couldn't lose his friendship, or whatever they had. She scrubbed harder. The look on his face when he found her with Logan spoke volumes. He liked her too. *Get a grip, Maggy, your love life is not important right now.* At least she was safe at work. The world outside the office may be filled with danger and confusion, but no one would reach her here.

The dentist, Doc Hetherington, was a bitch on heels who kept her staff under her thumb. Maggy didn't like the view from under anyone's thumb. The woman relished making others fear her. A tall, fierce-looking woman with angular features and a cold heart, she drove Maggy crazy. Still, she needed this job.

A half hour ago when Maggy entered the office, Doc Heatherington greeted her with a death stare. Maggy checked her hair. Her braids contained her curls. Everything seemed in place. Checked her blouse. It was tucked into her business pants and there was no toilet paper attached to her butt. What was she missing? "Good morning," she had said.

"Late night?"

Maggy took a deep breath. "Yes." She exhaled slowly with an assistant smile frozen in place. "Nothing a cup of coffee won't fix."

The dentist tilted her head to the right on her long, crane neck. "You're sure about that?"

"Yes," Maggy wondered if that were the right answer. Are peons supposed to be sure about anything in the presence of their master? An ache started between her eyes.

The receptionist saved her, calling the dentist to take a telephone call. Maggy settled into her routine. Her shoulders dropped an inch. She cleaned the already clean TV monitor.

The dentist reappeared, followed by a man in his nineties. Everyone smiled politely and the procedures began.

Over his body Heatherington eyed her every few moments. Maggy's mouth tasted mucky, like coffee and a late night. *What's with the H lady?* Could someone seriously be fired for bags under their eyes?

Or had she read about the Black Cat murder, and made a connection? She'd made it clear she didn't approve of Maggy moonlighting. Did she know something? Better check the papers and ask the receptionist at break.

Maggy chatted away to the gentleman, as they prepared to give him a root canal. She poured every ounce of charm she possessed into the conversation. He talked about his latest interest, the flight pattern of migrating mallard ducks. She talked about her yellow rubber ducky at home. They both laughed. The procedure went well.

After the man left, Dr. Heatherington snapped off her gloves and turned to face her. "Keep it up and you may keep your job."

***

Maggy didn't have a lot of rules, but those she had, she never broke. Near the top of the list was: never hurt a friend and, if you do, make it up to them. The hurt in Hunter's eyes last night gnawed at her. They had never been a real item, but she couldn't deny the chemistry between them.

She dialed his cell number. "I'm on my morning break and I thought I'd call." She made her voice sound casual.

"There's not much to say, is there?" The harshness of Hunter's words was softened by the honeysuckle warmth of his voice. Her throat went dry. Why couldn't she make herself immune to him? From the moment she met him, she had tried to ignore her attraction to him. It would make life so much easier. This crush thing between them, or whatever it was, had gone on for months.

"Hunter . . ."

"Maggy?"

His voice held a special music for her—always had. On the surface its familiarity held a sweet comfort like a soft quilt wrapped around her on a cold, winter night, and, below that, it rumbled with a raw sensuality that pulled her, like a lover's touch. Hot. Hunter was so hot. Damn hot. Her mind drifted and came back. He had made it clear that he was interested in her, and she had made it clear that she wasn't ready for a relationship.

"It's complicated," she said, drumming her fingers on the cold, plastic tablecloth.

"Everything that matters in life is," he said. "I got a charter leaving in a few minutes."

Silence.

"Logan is Jimmy Daniels brother. The guy I found dead in the alley."

Silence. She couldn't even hear him breath.

"He came to the club and . . ."

"Maggy, you don't owe me an explanation." He paused. "And, I really don't need the details."

"I know, but . . . " If only he hadn't walked in on her half naked with another man.

"But?"

"You matter to me. I don't want what's going on between me and Logan to change that."

Hunter groaned. "Nice to know you care. But I don't want leftovers."

Maggy felt her face flush with heat. "Hell, Hunter, I wish I knew what was going on. I'm up to my nose in murder, someone's lighting the docks on fire, I haven't had sex for six months—my life is in chaos."

"Maggy, your life *is chaos*."

She stopped drumming. He had a point. "Well, it's worse than usual this week."

He laughed. "Six months, eh?"

In the five minutes she had left, she told him about the *Emerald Empress* and the weirdness she experienced in Logan's boat.

"And that brings us back to sex," Hunter said.

"Gotta go," she said.

CHAPTER 25

Rita's Journal
Decourcy Island, September 1930

I am terrified. Brother XII tells us to be frightened of the outside world. People live unjust lives that torment their souls and make them do evil things. They would hurt us if they could.

But I am beginning to be more scared of him than anyone else.

When we first moved to Decourcy, life was perfect. The men built several buildings and while they were rustic, we were comfortable enough. And at night I spent time alone with Brother XII. Precious time filled with our love.

Women hover around him. I'd like to think he doesn't bed them, but dear diary, I am no longer sure. I know he does not tell me everything. I catch him in little lies, and I do not know how he spends all of his day.

Our life on the island has changed. We live in a fortress now. There are stone cairns all around the perimeter of our land, and it is protected by guards with guns. He told them to be ready for a fight. He warned them that the police or the government could come after us at any moment, and they must be ready to shoot.

Darkness is falling on the outside world. Countries have fallen into an economic depression. People are out of work and starving. To protect our money he turned it into twenty-dollar gold bars. He seals them inside mason jars with wax.

But make no mistake, dear diary, it worries me that he now calls our money *his gold*. He has boxes and boxes of jars and spends a good deal of his time burying them, digging them up and reburying them, over and over again. He says people want to steal from him.

The brother has two boats now: a sail boat called the *Lady Royal* and a speedboat called *Kleunaten* with a seven-cylinder engine. At times I feel as if I'm living in his kingdom with armed guards, and a fleet. Is he going crazy? Dare I say that of Eddie? My Eddie?

Should righteous people need to barricade themselves away from the world? I wonder.

There is something wrong about this colony. I can feel it in my bones, like the bitter morning fog. Meanwhile, the brother seems distracted when I am with him. I'm not sure if he is losing interest in me, or whether his security issues have grown so large he cannot relax. A gloom is settling into our little paradise.

Still, when he holds me in his arms, my worries float away like the tide and everything seems good again.

I do love Brother XII. I just fear he is more a man, than the god he pretends to be.

CHAPTER 26

Music is very spiritual, it has the power to bring people together. ~ Edgar Winter

Maggy headed to Aiko's, a popular Japanese restaurant that had become a favorite place for her to meet with Mei for lunch. It built its reputation on its Ishikari-nabi, salmon stew with sake, but she favored various kinds of sushi with lots of wasabi.

The owner told her Aiko means "love child" in Japanese. Its namesake lay outside the front door as usual, a beefy basset hound with attitude. When in the mood his howl could wake the dead. Maggy stepped over him with care. Watching his left eyelid quiver when she opened the door made her smile. Not disturbing the baby beast had to be a good omen.

The smell of fresh fish and rice made her mouth water. The long room was immaculate, as always. Words spoken in Japanese flew hard and fast from the kitchen. She took off her shoes before entering the eating room, to which the waitress led her. It was one of six attached to the main room. Mei sat inside. She greeted her friend with a hug and they closed the screen that separated them from the larger room.

"I only have thirty minutes," Maggy said.

Mei gave her a wide smile. "Always running."

"Yep. Gotta keep the murderers at bay." She laughed, but the pretense sounded hollow even to her own ears.

"Tell me," said Mei, fixing her ebony eyes on her.

And Maggy did. She caught her up with everything that had happened in what her ex called their girlfriend-talk, a rapid voice with lots of abbreviations and looks to fill in the blanks. Mei nodded repeatedly until the food appeared.

Mei popped a California roll into her mouth. "So let me get this straight. Hunter's running around looking for an arsonist. You and your new man-friend Logan are looking for buried gold—and a murderer who likes spikes. And Jimmy Daniel's ghost is lingering in your head or something like that." Her smile, more than a little sarcastic taunted her. "How did you get yourself into all of this?"

Maggy started laughing. What else could she do? The situation sounded so absurd. If it hadn't happened to *her*, she'd never have believed it. But it had happened, was happening and wouldn't go away. Thank

God for friends.

"Tell me: what's Logan like?" Mei lifted an eyebrow. That eyebrow. The one that rose whenever she smelled a whiff of pheromones in the air.

It figured Mei would pick up on her feelings. She took a deep breath and put down her chop sticks.

"Okay." Mei laughed. "I get the picture. She popped more sushi into her mouth and mumbled, "But I still think Hunter's the man for you."

"You always say that."

"Because it's true."

Maggy shook her head. "I didn't tell you about my mom." She picked up her chopsticks.

"Your mom?"

"I got an email from her five minutes ago. Her blood work isn't good and they want her to start a new cancer med with another long Latin name. Because it's so new its cost won't be covered. But the doctors told her it's her only hope."

"You're already paying her rent and food."

"She needs this med. I'll have to find more money."

Mei frowned. "How much?"

"She said about two hundred and fifty a month. But truthfully I can't afford even a penny more. I sold my good car and bought the run-down Honda which gives me nothing but more bills. I maxed my two credit cards, got to my limit on my line of credit, and I've taken the biggest loan the bank would give me on my houseboat. I've run out of things to hawk. My work at the dentist office is steady but it's not enough. I'll see if I can pick up some more dog walking and pray that Clarence can keep me singing."

Mei leaned back. "You have a full plate."

She nodded.

"You could ask Adriano . . . "

"No." Maggy clenched her teeth.

"Hear me out, Maggy. He likes your mother and for ten years she was his family. Family stands by family. You should ask him. If he doesn't have the cash, he can get a loan easier than you can, because he makes good money."

"I hate to ask him for anything." Her gut churned. Damn it.

"I know, but if you have to . . . "

"Let's hope I don't have to."

Mei pushed her plate away and reached down to her bag. "We're going to do a reading."

"Really?" Maggy groaned. "Now?"

"It's the best time," Mei replied. "The I Ching is all about change, the perfect divination tool when you're in the middle of a big storm and can't see the shore. Trust me. It'll help."

Maggy grimaced. Mei had proven over the years to be adept at interpreting the ancient Chinese text of wisdom. When Maggy looked at it, she saw poetry that made little sense, but Mei could make the connections. She could divine the present, past and future from a hexagram.

The book's accuracy scared Maggy and she avoided letting Mei do readings. The truth wasn't always something she wanted to hear. Who does? She took a deep breath. Maybe she needed it now.

The three-inch-thick, hard-cover book with a tattered gray and yellow cover landed on the table between them with a definitive thud, creating a rippling wave in the bottle of teriyaki sauce. Maggy released her breath. It couldn't hurt to listen. "I can't believe you carry that thing around with you."

"Only for you."

"Okay," Maggy said. "Okay."

Mei placed three quarters in Maggy's palm and

closed her fingers around them. "Think of the biggest question in your heart."

She'd heard Mei say those same words many times, but never had they echoed in her body as solemnly as they did now, like church bells ringing on a quiet, dark night. The quarters in her palm warmed quickly. There were so many things she wanted to know. She played with them in her hand. So many. Who murdered Jimmy? Who murdered Edgar? Were they going to murder her? She squeezed the coins, feeling how hard and small they were in her world. How could she help her mother? And what about Logan? Questions raced through her head, and then one floated above the others. Her body froze. "How can I keep singing?"

It was a selfish thought, but it was her question. Everything kept getting in her way. She wanted to sing. She inhaled the tangy smells of the kitchen like an elixir for a long life and crossed her fingers. Hell, why not.

The fact that a book, written two thousand years before Christ, might understand her life better than she did—might give her direction—rattled her sense of the here and now. It raised too many questions about what life is really about. But still—Mei believed in it and she believed in Mei. And it was damned accurate.

Mei watched her face. "You know, Maggy, that no matter what question you consciously choose the divination will answer the one you need to know."

"Yeah, yeah." Her heart sank like a rock into a pit of glacial fear. The day before her marriage fell apart, Mei had given her a reading. Maggy had asked about her sister's stomach ulcers and the book of knowledge warned her instead about a problem closer to home. The next day, Adriano broke her arm. They had once had a love so intense she thought it would last forever, but it fell apart. No hiding from the oracle. It saw everything. Which gave her the heebie-geebies.

But if it could help her . . .

She tossed the quarters. The first toss formed the bottom line: two heads one tail. Then again: three heads. Again: one head two tails. And so on six times. Mei interpreted the tosses as solid and broken lines which formed a hexagram.

When she was done she sat back and waited.

Mei drew the hexagram on a napkin and then consulted her book.

―― ――
――――――
―― ――
――――――
――――――
―― ――

"It's the forty-eighth hexagram, "Ching," The Well, with nuclear trigrams Li and Tui," she explained in a quiet, calm voice.

"The Well." That didn't sound so bad. Wells are solid. Maggy shook a strand of hair out of her face.

Mei thumbed through her book and stopped at the appropriate page. "The well means union." Her smile shrank.

Was that a bad sign? Maggy's gut tightened. Often words that sounded good in the Chinese script turned out to be bad, and vice versa. For example, dragons are a good thing in Chinese culture, whereas we tend to slaughter them in ours. She waited for Mei's explanation.

It was all about change. Yin to yang and back to yin. Mei had explained it to her a hundred times, but her rational mind still wanted to reject it. If it wasn't so damn accurate, she would. She straightened her blouse, and waited.

Mei began: "The judgment reads:

'The well shows the field of character. The well
abides in its place, yet has influence on other things.
The well brings about discrimination as to what is
right.'"ii

Mei's eyes rose from the page, softening like a warm spring morning. "It's not that bad, Maggy." She touched her hand. "You know there's no pure good or pure evil; no one moment in your life defines you. That's what the I Ching teaches."

Maggy tried to breathe.

"Life is about change," continued Mei. "Nothing lasts forever. We go from moment to moment through change. What is important is how we act through the change. How we act can influence the change."

Maggy had heard all this before. She agreed with the spiritual idea behind it—yada yada yada—but how could it help her now? "Give it to me in plain English."

Mei's eyes widened. She didn't like to be rushed when she gave readings, believed in honoring the book of wisdom with a solemn contemplation of its lines. She looked up at the ceiling and continued. "In answer to your question, I believe the I Ching is saying that like a well, you offer nourishment to others. I believe it's your big heart that is the well. You share it with everyone. I think that is your true music." She stopped and closed her eyes for a moment. "It comes from deep inside you, so deep." She hesitated again to take a breath that became ragged. "So deep."

"So deep what?"

"You're not ready for this."

"Tell me."

"You're going to think I'm silly." Mei raised her other brow.

"Just tell me."

Mei closed her eyes again. "So deep it merges with the well of life and brings others in touch with all humanity, with . . . eternity." She exhaled and opened her eyes.

"That's it? That's all it's got to say?"

"Well no, there's always more. Think of a well. It's got a strong foundation and holds water inside it, deep, tranquil and clear. You must try to be strong for yourself and others. You must offer them your purest voice, your link to life."

Maggy swallowed, feeling the after-burn of the wasabi in her throat. "I'm not that strong." No one is that strong.

"You're stronger than you think. You must be. Look here." She pointed to the first broken line between two dark ones. This is the ruler of the hexagram. She read, "It . . . " Mei mumbled on, but Maggy no longer listened to the individual words. The book confirmed what she always knew. She was meant to sing. A warm glow filled her body. Somehow all this crap would work itself out if she kept her focus.

"So, the answer to my question is to act like a well?" Maggy said with forced humor. It made sense to her, but she wasn't about to admit to buying into the spiritual stuff. After all, what would be next? Looking for prophecies in chicken bones?

"That's right. Remember, the Chinese symbol for crisis contains the symbol of danger and opportunity."

Yada yada. She'd heard that line before.

"In this crisis," Mei continued, "you can help ensure a good outcome by becoming a strong well."

A crazy idea from an old book, but what was even crazier was that Maggy believed it. Her phone buzzed. Shit, fifteen minutes late. "I gotta run."

Mei put the book down. "Be careful, Maggy. It's not anything I read in the book, but it's something I feel. You're treading in dangerous waters."

"Tell me about it." She kissed her friend's cheek and put fifteen dollars on the table. On her way out she nodded to the woman at the cash register and said "Domo," the only Japanese word she knew.

Maggy leaped back over Aiko and ran to her office, her jacket flapping in the wind and her mind a messy smorgasbord of thought. Crap. "The Well?" How could she be expected to be strong for others when her life kept falling apart at the seams? A leaky well. She smiled. *A leaky well in a tsunami. That's me.*

She really didn't want to ask Adriano for

money. But her mother needed meds. She kicked a stone on the street. Sweet Baby Jesus, she didn't want to talk to him. She slammed the door of the office without meaning to. Damn it, the witch dentist would kill her.

As she yanked on her white lab coat over her street clothes, it came to her. She'd beg Clarence for more work. And while she was at it, find out if he knew anything more about Jimmy Daniel's murder. Kill two birds with one stone. Her gut tightened. The "kill" word stuck in her throat. She'd never make it as a comedian. Good thing she could sing.

**

The dentist was already working on her first afternoon patient without her. With a professional smile, Maggy took her place. Minutes ticked slowly along while Doc Heatherington's icy stares assaulted her over the body of an innocent patient.

The next one, a five-year old girl named Sally, complained about her left, lower molar. Maggy handed her Fuzzy, the office stuffed toy, to hold. Fuzzy was a hippopotamus that had won the heart of many a young patient, but he may not have had enough voodoo left in him to impress this one. Sally frowned. "He's only got one eye."

"Makes him more lovable," Maggy said.

Jenny, the prim new receptionist who was one of those few women Maggy knew who could walk in high heels with grace, slid into the sterile cubicle. "Excuse me, Doc," she said.

Heatherington lifted her eyes. "Yes."

"There's a policeman here to talk with

Maggy."

Maggy's throat constricted. What, now?

"Maggy?" Doc Heatherington lifted her overly manicured brow.

Maggy shrugged as if she had no idea in the world what this could be about.

The witch dentist tilted her head and scowled. "You'd better go see the policeman." She put down her pick. "Me and Fuzzy will take over."

Sally giggled.

"Excuse me," Maggy said.

The doc exhaled noisily. "I hope he's not here to take you away." Her grimace said a whole mountain of things, Maggy didn't want to hear. Like maybe it soon would be time to find another job.

"I'm sure it won't take long," Maggy said over her shoulder as she left the room.

Inspector Peterson looked about as comfortable in a dentist office as Sally did holding a one eyed stuffy. Not that anyone ever looks at peace in such a place. Patients lined the reception room, a long laminated desk housed three receptionists, working hard to appear as if they weren't watching Maggy. She thought the one on the left was going to go bug-eyed. Maggy sighed.

"Miss Malone." Peterson's deep, gravel voice resonated inside her as well as in the room. The patients hushed. Even though he wasn't wearing a cop uniform, everything about him spoke authority.

"What can I do for you, Inspector?" She thought she'd throw that to the peeping receptionists, in case they didn't already know.

He looked around and then back at her, squinting. "We need to talk." Had he realized he was the center of attention? He was probably used to it. It would be really odd to go through life like that.

She grimaced as she weighed her options. "How about the stairwell?" It was the only place she could think of that would be at all private.

He nodded, and she walked out the door with him behind her.

Once on the landing, she spoke first. "I'm needed in the dentist office."

"I'll be brief."

She scrunched up her mouth.

"What aren't you telling me?" His gruff voice was so monotone it was difficult to read. She felt like a fish under a filleting knife.

She threw her hands in defence. "I told you everything you wanted to know." Her stomach cramped with the lie, and she feared her face showed it. Do they give courses on how to be a better liar? Her words sounded so lame.

"Maggy," he said. "Can I call you Maggy?"

She nodded, squeezing her lips together. What did she care? It was just a name after all. But it was bothersome that he thought it was a significant step in developing a closer relationship she didn't want. She wanted their discourse to be simple, brief and over.

"You're holding something back." His steely gaze held hers like a flashlight holds the eyes of a deer. Shit, he was good.

"Okay, I'll put my cards on the table."

He leaned in. His bald head glistened with sweat.

"What exactly do you want to know? I'll do my best to answer your questions."

"No bullshit?" A grin started to appear on the right side of his mouth and then stopped.

"Nope."

"Was Edgar in the alley the night of Jimmy Daniel's murder?"

"Yes."

His eyes shot wide. "You didn't tell me that before." His anger seeped into the air between them, icy-cold and heavy, making her want to shiver, but she didn't. She held his gaze.

"Inspector Peterson," she replied, hoping the sound of his name would calm him. "I didn't know that when I spoke with you. I met Edgar on Thursday in the library, like I said. That was when he told me he was in the alley Tuesday night. He saw me with Jimmy. I didn't see him, but I believed him when he told me he was there."

Peterson's eyes narrowed. His ebbing waves of anger were still strong enough to swamp her if she wasn't careful. "What was he doing in the alley? Did he tell you that?"

She gulped. How much should she tell him? Damn! She wasn't going to get caught up in her own web of lies. "He said he was following Jimmy, but he didn't get into the alley in time to witness the murder. When he got there Jimmy was on the ground and I was trying to stop his bleeding."

"Following? Why would a bank clerk want

to follow a PI? It makes no sense."

She took a deep breath. "You might want to get your notebook out for this."

He tilted his head and did as she asked.

"Edgar's great-grandmother Rita kept a diary. He found it in his late mother's things. When he read it, he learned that Rita had been one of Brother XII's mistresses."

Peterson scribbled something.

"Do you know who Brother XII is?" she asked.

He nodded. "Go on," he said, gruffly. "Rita—one of Brother XII's sex slaves."

"She left information in the diary, which Edgar believed would lead him to the gold. But it didn't make total sense; or if it did, it wasn't enough information to get him to the treasure. He said it was vague and he needed help figuring it out. It had to do with geographical markers. So he hired Jimmy an investigator with a sailing background to find the location, but when he was slow to respond, he hired a second man, a fisherman from Decourcy Island whose name I don't know."

Peterson kept writing.

"The second man," Maggy continued, "started threatening Edgar, demanding more information. Edgar got scared and warned Jimmy about him. But Jimmy stopped answering Edgar's calls and that really worried him. He figured that Jimmy had double crossed him, knew the location of the gold, and wanted it for himself. So Edgar went after Jimmy. He caught up with him in the alley, lying in a pool of blood."

Peterson scratched his head. "Let me get this straight. Two days after the murder Edgar meets with you."

"He was really spooked. He thought he was being followed, and he warned me that I was in danger."

"Okay. It sounds possible."

"It's true, Inspector." She took a normal breath.

"And what do you know about Clarence's involvement?"

"Clarence?" Her voice squeaked, despite her attempt to sound cool.

"I have reports from—," he hesitated, "—people—that Clarence and Jimmy were yelling at each other earlier in the evening."

"I know nothing about that." Her insides burned with the acid of her lie.

"You're lying."

She looked at him. Their eyes locked. Damn. He knew she was lying, and he knew she knew. Sweet Jesus. She wasn't going to incriminate the man who'd given her a chance in the music business—maybe her only chance.

"Just tell me—something, anything—you know about their relationship."

She swallowed. It wasn't fair. Clarence had nothing to do with the murder. He wasn't that kind of man. Sure he could yell and scream at his employees and was known for his big scowl. But he was no murderer, and what she knew would make him look like one.

"Tell me," Peterson demanded. His square

jaw rigid enough to cut rock.

Sweat trickled down the back of her neck. She tried to stare him down, but she knew that wouldn't work.

"Clarence told me . . . " she began and swallowed. "He told me that the club was in financial trouble. He'd sold a third of it to Jimmy to keep afloat. Then he heard Jimmy was talking to some condo developer who offered him big money for his share. Clarence was furious. The club means everything to him, but he didn't kill Jimmy. I know that."

Peterson didn't smile. "Clarence may not look like a murderer, but he's still near the top of our suspect list. I'm looking into the other owner too."

"Then why are you asking me?"

"Listen, I know all about Clarence and Jimmy fighting over the Black Cat. Clarence told me this morning." He gave her a small smile. "I wanted to make sure that you were ready to tell me the truth about things."

"Bastard." She didn't mean to swear. It just came out. He'd put her through hell for what—a test. Cops. Stupid friggin cops.

"Ouch," he said in a disinterested monotone. "It's my job to know the people I'm working with. Now I think I can trust you." He hesitated. "Maybe."

She growled. "Can I go back to work now?"
"One more question."
"Shoot."
"What did the dead man say?"

Her eyes widened. He knew. Now where could she hide? "He mumbled a message for his brother that makes no sense." There she'd said it.

"In words, or on a piece of paper?"

"He said it. As he was dying he said it."

Peterson's eyes narrowed to pin pricks. "So he was alive when you found him. The truth this time Maggy."

The way he said her name made her shiver, but his quest for the truth, determination to find the murderer, compelled her to keep talking. He did listen to her. It was like he was offering her a safe harbor in the middle of this mess. Someone who seemed to understand her. But still, he was a cop. And she had lied to him. She took a deep breath and let it out slowly studying the wall behind him for a minute. It needed a fresh coat of paint.

"Okay. This is the deal. I was tired the night you met me, tired and upset, and I didn't tell you the whole truth."

"Why? Most witnesses tell me everything they know."

She bit her bottom lip. "I have trouble talking to cops."

"Because you were married to one?"

"It's a long story." She grimaced. Of course, if he had looked into her background he would have found out some of it. "Anyway, I sort of lied to you."

Peterson nodded.

"Jimmy was still alive when I found him, and he gave me a message for Logan, his brother. I thought that was a personal thing that didn't have to go through a man in uniform. Did you get all of that down?"

"What did he say?"

Shit. She thought telling him this much would be enough. But no. The friggen police always wanted more. "He mumbled," she said after a moment. "Like I said, it was impossible to make sense of it."

He stared her down. "Tell me what you heard."

"Tell Logan, 'Emer-Old.'" She shrugged. "See it doesn't make sense."

"What does Logan think?"

Would this never end? "It's confusing." She paused. Time to take more control. "Jimmy was killed with a sailor's knife, right?"

"Yeah, sort of, a marlin spike."

"What's that?" She knew, but she wanted to make sure the inspector knew.

"It's a spike used for rope work aboard ships. They're usually six to twelve inches in length. Sailors, fishermen and most boat people carry a small one in their pocket. It's handy for the unlaying of rope, splicing and untying of knots. But it can also be a deadly weapon. You're changing the conversation. Ms. Malone, I'm the one asking the questions."

"That settles it. Clarence wouldn't have a marlin spike. It's the sort of tool mariners have and he gets sea sick when he takes a ferry to the island."

"Yeah, we know all that. It's one of the reasons he's not been charged with Jimmy's murder. But, while it's unlikely he'd have a marlin spike, it's not impossible. This is Vancouver, a port town. It's not hard to find a marlin spike.

"We also don't have a motive for Clarence to kill Edgar. So he doesn't fit the profile of a murderer. But he's not off the list yet." He smiled gently. "Nor are you. You're avoiding my question."

"I really should get back."

"We're not finished here." His voice held a hard edge, but not his body. He put his hand gently on her arm. The warmth of the gesture sent warning bells through her system. This guy's smoothness worked way too well.

"Tell me what 'Emer-Old' means"

She opened her mouth to speak and his phone buzzed. She took a step back.

"Peterson," he said into the cell phone. "Yup. . . yup. . . yup . . . on my way." The tone of his voice said he was one unhappy man in blue.

"I'll get back to work, now," she said, thanking the universe for her luck.

Maggy watched Peterson fly down the stairs.

Had she told him too much? Hopefully not. At least he hadn't charged her with interfering with a murder investigation. She'd probably end up telling him the rest later. Would he understand what happened on the boat? She looked at the ceiling for a moment. Nah, she would leave that out. He might refer to Martian genitalia again.

But she wouldn't tell him her other reasons for hating cops. Not a story she cared to share with anyone.

For now, she had to concentrate on doing her day jobs. Getting through the day. She could do that. One step at a time. Then she could sing.

***

The next patient, Long John Black, a biker from the east end with a badly abscessed tooth took up the whole chair and then some. He probably always looked scary with his black, leather clothes, scraggly beard that a rat could nest in, and eyes darker than the night. In pain he'd look a whole heap scarier. Not looking forward to this event, Maggy put the bib around his neck, and patted his shoulder reassure him. "Dr. Heatherington's the best. You'll feel better soon."

The man grunted. It wasn't a nice sound. Some male grunts sounded kinda nice, but not this one. Definitely not this one. He smelled of beer.

The dentist, delayed by yet another phone call, left her alone with Long John. Who would take a name that makes you think of underwear and cold weather? Weird.

Wait. She could take advantage of the situation. "Do you . . .?" she started and then took the deepest breath she could muster.

His eyes widened and he grunted a second time. Most foul.

"Do you know anything about marlin spikes?"

His mouth twisted. "Yeah," he spat out. "What about 'em."

"A friend got one in the heart," she blurted out. Was she crazy telling this guy?

"Nasty," he said in a deep voice.

"Well, how common are they?"

"All the boat people got 'em."

She was a dock person and she didn't have one, but she didn't feel like correcting him. "Well, what I mean . . . " How could she put this delicately? "How common is it for someone to use a marlin spike for murder?" There, she'd said it. She'd picked the first murderous looking person she could find and asked him. Talk about profiling. She folded her hands to settle herself. Long John smelled of weed, beer and something else. Dead bodies? A chill ran down her spine.

His eyes narrowed. "Listen, honey, I don't murder people . . . " he hesitated a second, a long second. ". . .with marlin spikes."

She gulped. Was he saying he preferred other instruments? "I . . . I . . . I didn't mean you. I'm sorry, I didn't mean to insult you. I just thought you might know. I mean do you know. . . Have you heard . . . of other people using them?" Sweet Jesus, she sounded lame, so lame that the dentist drill going full speed in the next room sounded oddly comforting.

He breathed through his nose, which had black hairs sticking out of it, and looked at the ceiling with its painted, pastel giraffes. Then he put his hand to his sore jaw and spoke. "Nope."

Air rushed out of her. So the murderer was a boater, but not a regular murderer. Guess that made sense. "Thanks," she said.

"Don't mean it isn't a good weapon though," he said in a slow, heavy voice. "It is sharp and all."

She nodded.

He tilted his head. "You could keep it in your pocket and pull it out quick like a knife, but . . ."

"But?" The short hairs on the back of her neck rose.

"Why wouldn't you just use a knife? A quick switchblade or even a pocket knife would be easier." His eyes rested on hers. "Personally, I prefer guns."

That was too much information. She tried to smile. "Here, let me put some numbing solution on your gums, to prepare you for the needle."

"Needle? Fuck you. I didn't say I wanted any mother-fucking needle. I just want the fucker yanked out. What kind of place is this? A torture hall?" He stood up, anger emanating from every pore of his sweaty body. His eyes narrowed. "And what's with all the questions, bitch." He tore off the paper bib on his chest and stood up. "Are you wired?" She didn't realize how tall he was.

Dr. Heatherington came running in—click-clack, click-clack—in her heels. Her Chanel scent rushed in with her. "What's wrong?"

Maggy lifted her arms helplessly and said, "I wanted to numb his gums."

The dentist shook her head. "We don't use needles on Long John Black. It's written on his charts in red. 'No needle.'" She shouted in a shrill voice.

The biker nodded and sat down. Doc Heatherington hovered over his mouth. Maggy forced herself to breathe. She touched him lightly on the shoulder to give him strength, but his volatility made her jumpy. As the dentist pulled on the tooth, Maggy heard a soft popping sound, as the tooth came out, and the smell of decay and infection swamped the room.

Long John gave Maggy a funny look, and as he passed her on his way out he said, in a low voice only she could hear, "If you need to get rid of someone, call me."

She nodded as if he'd said a lovely goodbye. Now she had a murderer with a nasty beard at her disposal. Not many women could say that.

CHAPTER 27

Rita's Diary:

I hate that vile woman.
The sadist. The bitch.
I Hate. Hate. Hate her. Her real name is Mabel Skottowe and she came with her husband from Florida. Somehow she lost him and has become Brother XII's woman. His second in command. That red-headed bitch has taken control. I swear she's the devil's sister.

She changed her name legally to Zura de Valdes and insists we all call her Madame Zee. Brother XII is totally taken with her and changed his name to Amiel de Valdes. Has everyone gone crazy? They are having a new community built on Valdes Island to the north.

It's not just me who hates her. Everyone does. She is a sadist, spends most of her days ordering people around with a black leather whip on her hip. There are rumors she locks some people away in small cabins in the bush. I hide from her as much as I can and hope Eddie will become his old self again.

Mary Connolly lost most of her money in the stock market crash, so the scrawny, red-headed bitch banished her from our headquarters along with twelve others who'd run out of money.

The rumors are terrifying. Madame Zee imprisoned and beat a man for not working hard enough on the buildings. He broke free, found a boat and rowed himself to Vancouver Island. He told the police and they made a record of it, but nothing was done. We're too far away for them to police. Madame Zee has to be stopped.

Our once peaceful community is falling apart, and it's all her fault. People want Madame Zee gone. They want the old Brother XII back. They also want to know what's happening to their life savings. They're tired of being put to hard labor and being yelled at. There's a lot of complaining. I don't know what to do.

Would my family take me back now? I'm no longer an innocent virgin.

I tried reading Eddie's third book, but I threw it in the fire before I finished it. I couldn't help my anger. If the spirits are guiding him why is he acting so strangely? This was supposed to be a loving home for us all, a place where we could develop spiritually, safe from the outside world, a refuge in an evil world. But it's turning into hell itself.

I had started packing my bag when I heard him at my door. He asked me to take a beach walk in the moonlight. I couldn't resist being in his arms again. And I thought maybe he would explain to me why he chose to spend time with such a vile woman, and I would ask him if he realized the community is falling apart.

We walked and talked on the beach and then took a boat ride. We went to what had become our favorite spot on the larger island. He tied up the boat near the entrance of the bay. We hiked up the hill past a stand of Garry oaks to a beautiful meadow that overlooks the water. We call it our secret meadow. No one bothers us there. We are far away and alone.

Eddie reassured me that everything would be all right, that Madame Zee had been chosen by the spirits to lead, but that she has to learn how to deal with people better. We could help her by complying with her demands.

Eddie told me he doesn't really love her. She is just his business partner. He said when she gets used to her role in this life it would be easier for us all. That is what the great white spirit told him.

Then he drew me close and with a tear in his eye told me his heart belongs to me—only me. We made love, long, passionate love, and I forgave him everything. Afterwards, we lay under the stars in our own little heaven.

But that was last night. This morning in the light of day I wonder. I wonder about a lot of things.

I packed my bag.

CHAPTER 28

. . .music is the most profound, magical form of
communication there is. ~Lesley Garrett

Cold, cluttered and dark, Clarence's office suited him. Sadly, he couldn't afford to pay for good lighting, or heat in the back rooms. On the walls, stained from years of cigarette smoke were yellowed photos, in dollar-store frames, of important people who'd passed through the Black Cat. Some of them were musicians, others patrons. In almost every picture Clarence, with his flowing, shoulder-length hair, stood in the middle with a cigarette. It was so much his room that Maggy felt the air sucked out of her lungs when she entered. Normally, she avoided going in there, but today she had no choice.

Clarence sat behind an old oak desk in a worn black leather chair, his expression locked in a scowl. His blue eyes watery and edged in red. He tilted his head to focus on her, while his thin lips held a firm line giving nothing of his emotions away.

Maggy sat opposite him in a spindly wooden chair that creaked when she sat down and wobbled under her weight. She vowed to go on a diet when her life settled down. Getting right to the point, she told him about her mother's cancer, and explained that her only hope was a new medicine that cost a lot of money. Maggy waited for his response.

He took off his reading glasses and put them down on his desk.

"Anything you can give me," she pleaded, hating having to beg. But what choice did she have? "Anything would help."

"Yeah, baby, I got that." All women were "baby" to him, a relic from a bygone era. He leaned back. His face relaxed. "I got that." But his road-weary face showed no sign of compassion.

Silence filled the room.

"Is there— " she began.

"Listen," he interrupted, "I was going to call you in to talk things."

She sat up, straining to catch his words as soon as they came out.

"I got bad news." He swallowed, like a man trying to push down something he didn't' want to say.

"Bad news?"

"Like I told you before, the club's not doing so well." He pulled out a half-smoked cigarette, put it in his mouth, and lit a match by striking it on his boot.

"If there's anything I can do. Anything?"

He shook out the flame on the match. "I like your voice and you're doing real good for a beginner, but I've got two more experienced singers to take care of."

"You mean?"

"Yeah, I was going to let you go."

The words hit her like a punch in the face. "I'm fired?" She'd never considered that. She'd been getting good reviews. The audience liked her. "I . . . I don't understand."

"Like I said, the club's not doing well." He sucked hard on his cigarette.

Her gut tightened into a hard fist. What the hell! "I need this job," she said, standing. She reached out to him and said more softly, "I need this job."

"I know," he said. He held her glare for a long minute and then shrugged. "The club has to survive so, like I said, I *planned* to cut you." He tapped his tobacco stained fingers on his desk.

Past tense? "But?"

His lips turned downward. "I have a third partner, like I told you, and he doesn't want you cut." He tossed his eyes to the wall for a moment. "He likes your voice. Said losing you would be a deal-breaker. In fact, he threatened to sell his share to a developer if I did."

Maggy released her breath and sat down. "So I'm not cut."

"No, but if the club closes it won't matter. We'll all go down." He folded his arms across his chest, leaned back and lifted his feet onto his desk with a clunk. "You need to sing your heart out, baby, and keep the people coming in."

"I can do that," she said. She felt her pulse slowing to normal. Why the drama? Why did he put her through that? He didn't have to. What was the point? She winced. "Who's the guy?" she asked. "The other owner."

"Like I said before, he wants to remain anonymous." Clarence blew smoke into the air in billowing clouds of toxic gray.

"About my hours."

Pulling his feet back to the ground with a shuffle, he grumbled. Sitting forward he drummed his fingers on the table again. "No promises, baby, no promises. But I'll do what I can. I'm truly sorry about your mother." He looked at his watch.

"Thanks." *I think.*

"What can you tell me about Logan's plan for his share of the bar?"

"We haven't talked about it, yet."

"Too busy, eh? Well, I guess that's okay. You let me know when you know."

She nodded. "And Joe?"

"Leave Joe to me. He's my family. You got enough to worry about."

"Is he okay?"

"As okay as you can be when you're on the slippery slope out of this world." He swallowed and his Adam's apple bobbed. "Don't worry. I'll make sure he gets the best of care."

Maggy nodded.

She couldn't leave. Too much had been said, and worse had not been said.

"What?" he grumbled. His eyes squinting as if he was trying to look inside her mind.

"What really happened between you and Jimmy the night of his murder?"

"Ha . . ." Clarence started laughing, and the more he laughed the deeper it became until it broke into his rough smoker's cough.

"I'm not trying to be funny."

"I know. I know. Sometimes all a man can do is laugh." He did a manly swipe at the tear that ran down his right cheek. "The cop, that Peterson guy, has been on my ass since the murder. I've gone over every detail again and again. And I already told you about our fight." He leaned forward, all laughter had gone from his face. "So what more do you want to know?"

"I'm in the middle of it. Peterson's been hounding me too. I don't know why the murders are happening. I can't get away from it. So I . . . "

"Want to make sense of it," he answered.

"Yeah."

"Well," he said, breathing out slowly. "This is how it went down. You know Albert, my poker buddy who comes in most nights and sits at the front table, wears a suit and drinks single malt scotch."

She nodded.

"He's an accountant. About three months ago I asked him to look over my books and he flipped out. Said I had to find some capital quick and suggested I sell shares of the business. To make a long story short, Jimmy bought one third of the club two months ago. It helped, but then the bills started piling up again, so I sold another third to another partner. A local guy who's really into music."

"The anonymous partner who likes my voice."

"Yeah. So I thought my troubles were over, and then this realty guy in a blue tie comes in and makes me an offer. I jump all over the asshole, but he tells me that Jimmy is selling his share and it would be wise for me to do the same." He stopped, fixing his eyes on the far wall for a moment as if he could see the whole scene on a giant TV screen. "He threatened me. Said he'd make sure the inspectors found stuff that would get the Black Cat closed down. 'Rats, bugs, whatever it takes,' he said, and then he laughed."

Clarence's face turned redder as he spoke and sweat formed on his brow. The acrid smell of his sweat tinged the room. "I'm sorry," she said.

He nodded. "So when Jimmy came in that night I wanted to rip him apart. I mean it. If I was a younger man I probably would have tried. But I'm not a young man. And violence wasn't going to fix anything, so I tried to reason with him."

"People said you were yelling."

"Yeah, well you know me. I tend to yell, and I was plenty upset. Had a right to be. He'd told me he wanted to be part of the blues business and then when he gets a piece of it he turns around and makes plans to sell it off and bring the place down. It's not right. That's not right on so many levels.

"I agree."

"The asshole lied to me. And his lie would have put a lot of us out of a job, and left a hole in the west coast music scene. Not right, I tell you. Not right. So yeah, I yelled loud and long."

"What did he say?"

Clarence paled. "I didn't give him much of a chance. He mumbled something about, 'That's business, old man.' It only made me madder."

"So then what happened?"

"I took a swing at him. I couldn't help it. I was so fucking angry, I went wild. And that's why there's some of my DNA's his body."

"And?"

"He swung back. I landed on the floor and he slammed the door behind him when he left. I was no match for him. I just couldn't help trying." His face turned crimson.

"And then?"

"Nothin. I went back into the bar. I listened to your set and started cleaning up for the night and then I heard the sirens." The redness in his face started to ebb and he shook himself. "I'm no killer, Maggy. I punched him. That's all. I swear on my mama's grave, that's all. Just like I told you before."

The phone rang. He looked at the call number display and let it ring. His sad eyes fixed once again on that spot on the wall.

When it stopped ringing she asked, "What did you see when you went out into the alley?"

Clarence drummed his fingers. She couldn't catch the tune. He shrugged. "I saw the ambulance arriving, followed by cop cars. And . . . "

"And?"

"I didn't tell Peterson. He'd get too excited if I told him."

She tried to stare him into speeding up.

"I saw Edgar Whitley. Of course I didn't know his name then, but I do now. I saw his picture on the news. He was there, skulking in the shadows."

"Edgar," said Maggy.

"Yeah. He disappeared real quick when the cops got out of their cars."

"So you saw Edgar. Did he see you?"

"He looked right at me."

"Anyone else?"

"Nah. At least not that I remember. It was really dark that night. There could have been someone else in the alley, but I didn't see them."

"But . . . " she hesitated. Should she say it? She had to say it. "But the murderer could have seen you."

"Yup." Clarence's face twitched. Obviously the possibility worried him.

The room fell silent again.

"What a mess," she said.

"Got that right." He tried his knowing grin, the one he used to establish authority, but it didn't work. Instead, his mouth hung open in a weary attempt. "So tell me what you think of Logan Daniels. Will he sell us out?"

"I'll talk to him."

There was banging on the door. Clarence sighed. "Come in."

The door opened and Peterson strode into the room. "Don't you answer your phone?"

The old barman shrugged. "Not when it's the police." He gave the inspector a wily side grin. "It's never good news."

CHAPTER 29

Rita's Diary:
Decourcy Island, 1933

He's gone. Brother XII and Madame Zee have vanished. Some say they went to England to gather more funds. But others think they took the money and fled. What am I to think?

Rumors of heinous horrors created by Madame Zee circulate. Everyone is leaving our community and taking things. Everyone is panicked.

I hold on to the memory of my last night with Eddie in the secret meadow. He had a clear vision of life, and our future. Now he's gone. I'll never forget how it felt to be in his arms.

I'll wait for as long as I can for him to return. And if I see that Madame Zee ever again in

my life, I'll skin her alive and feed her ugly hair to
the seagulls for them to make nests and defecate in.

My packed bag sits by the door.

CHAPTER 30

I see music as fluid architecture. ~Joni Mitchell

When Maggy returned to her float home there was a note on her window from Hunter. "Dock meeting at Smokey's. Important." Below the words he'd sketched a landscape with mountains in the background and her float home in the foreground. Smoke billowed from the chimney. It looked peaceful and idyllic. Not at all like her life right now, but it made her smiled.

Using extra shampoo on her hair she tried to make sense of what was happening, as if bubbles could solve murders. She emerged from the shower smelling like vanilla beans but as confused as ever. She had a long list of things she wanted to know, like the name of the mysterious third partner who'd saved her job. She owed him one.

But one thought bugged her like an out-of-tune note: if the murderer had seen Clarence, he was in danger. But what could she do? The image of Jimmy lying in his blood wouldn't leave her mind.

Options? She could phone Peterson again, but didn't want another Martian anatomy lesson. Shit. She had to act. Do something. So she wrapped her hair in a towel and sent Peterson a text: "Clarence is in danger."

A text came in from Hunter reminding her about the meeting.

With her mind swirling with worries she threw on her favorite jeans. She swore they fit better the last time she wore them.Men told her they liked her the way she was, but she didn't. Her BMI was way the hell beyond healthy, and after leaving Adriano six months ago she had stopped looking in full-length mirrors. Grabbing her bag she headed for the island. Six o'clock. Hopefully the meeting wouldn't take too long. She needed some alone time to figure things out. Being fried at the edges like an undercooked burger hiding food poisoning, sucked.

Packed with dock people, Smokey's place felt more like a sardine can than a cozy diner. The edgy tone of people's voices and the tightness of their facial muscles gave the room an angry feel. She sat at the back near the door. The purpose of the meeting had been to calm people down and get them working together, but it looked like it was having the opposite effect. They were getting riled up and hostile.

The threat of arson hit the easy-going boat

people hard and she could taste their growing fear. Tonight it truly kindled, like a forest fire on the verge of burning out of control.

"I say we double the number of patrols and carry guns," hollered Wayne, the seventy-year old Vietnam vet, known for his weapon collection, which he kept well hidden beneath the planks of his deck. She had always avoided him. A small, stocky man with a mean look imprinted on his face, he believed dangerous bastards lurked around every corner. Something had happened to him in the war and he'd been on government compensation ever since. No one asked the details. No one wanted to know. His anger said enough.

"More video surveillance. That's what we need," Smokey added from the sidelines, with her hands in the pockets of her new Canucks sweatshirt. It already had a coffee stain on it.

Hunter standing beside a chart paper stand made notes in alternating colored pens. It looked so out of character for him, like a warrior taking dictation. But the intensity of his determination was palpable. His jaw was set and his eyes had turned that steely blue that meant only one thing: he'd get even.

The group continued to brainstorm what they could do to catch the saboteur. Ideas flew. Hunter nodded to her when she moved forward into a chair near the front. She wanted to be able to see more of what was going down. Others turned to see who he was looking at. Great, now everyone watched her. Boy they were spooked.

"Sorry, I'm late," Maggy offered the crowd.

"Do we know anything new?"

Bad question. A roar of replies came in her direction. None of them good. Hunter summed it up. "No Maggy. We don't know who's behind the incidents and now we have a murder to consider."

My murder. Maggy frowned. Her neighbours had adopted it. It made sense in a way. After all he did die on the docks. But it didn't make her feel any better. Could the dock problem be linked to the Black Cat murder?

"What are the police saying?" Maggy asked through the chatter

"Fuck all," answered Smokey from the side in her raw nicotine addled voice. "All they do is ask us questions. If they know anything, they sure as hell aren't sharen it. Fuckin constipated assholes, the lot of them."

Maggy nodded. Go Smokey. She looked around for Elena. There must have been thirty people there, but she wasn't one of them. Guess she didn't want to be blamed this time.

"Okay," said Hunter. "We'll double the patrols starting now. I've made a sign-up sheet. We'll keep a copy on the outside of Smokey's door and you can add your name to it."

A thin, young, bald man she'd never met stood up. "My name's Trevor. I moved in last month. I'll put the schedule on-line. I've started a website for us cuz we need one. Granville Island People at www.GIP.ca. Go to the site and click on the page "Rat.""

Everyone laughed at the name. It was a good one.

"I've put up what we know so far. I'll add the roster," the young man said.

"When we post on the internet aren't we providing the Rat with information too?" The question came from the back. Hard to tell who had said it.

A murmur of voices swept the room.

"Well," said the young man. "We could make the site available only to people who live here." After watching everyone nod their approval, he added, "But who's to say it's not one of us?

A cool silence sliced through the room with the sharp edge of a guillotine blade.

"I think we're better off leaving it available to everyone," said Hunter. "We need to keep our communication clear and open. There's no harm in the Rat knowing we're on patrol. Each pair could do their search in a different way, not detailed on-line, so there'd be no way of predicting where they will be. And on top of that, we'll all be watching. Let's get this thing going. We'll all feel safer." Everyone nodded and the meeting was over. A good number of the group headed over to the bar across the street.

Maggy wanted to get out as quickly as she could. She needed air and was in no mood for small chat. Who would have thought they'd have a website to track this guy? But it made sense.

She'd joined this peaceful community because it was, well, peaceful, and now they were dealing with a murder and sabotage. Was she in some way responsible for the change?

Hunter, busy talking to people, caught her eye and lifted a finger, indicating he'd only be a minute and wanted to talk to her. Not wanting to talk to him she slipped out, noting his look of disappointment as she closed the door. *There's not enough time in life to please everyone.*

***

Back in her float home she decided she had to figure things out. Looking at her guitar case in the corner of the room, her heart did that rapid "pulsing thing" it always did when she thought about music. It would be so nice to spend the evening singing her songs. Just singing . . . becoming one with the music. But that wasn't going to happen.

The troubles at the dock worried her, no doubt about that. But the murders held her by the throat. Until she knew who was behind them she couldn't rest. She needed answers.

Grabbing a bunch of empty junk-mail envelopes from her recycling bin and a pen she sat down at her kitchen table, determined to sort through the mess. She wrote a question on the back of each envelope. Envelope One: Who killed Jimmy? Two: Why kill Jimmy? Three: Who killed Edgar? Four: Why kill Edgar? Five: Where on Gabriola Island is Brother XII's gold? Six: Edgar's grandmother's journal?

The process of distilling her worries into six questions calmed her.

There was a familiar knock on the door and Mei entered. "I thought you could use some company." Her black hair was pulled into a side braid, revealing her beautiful face, which looked drawn from a long day.

Maggy hugged her. "I'm trying to solve a couple murders. Want to help?" She smirked.

"Sure. Bring it on."

Maggy showed her the six envelopes.

"What can we do with question number one?" asked Mei.

"One: Who killed Jimmy?" She put the pen in her mouth. "The way I see it the suspect list could include…" She started writing and said the names out loud: "One: Clarence, Two: Edgar, Three: the Decourcey Island fisherman, Four: the third Black Cat partner…"

"Or," added Mei, "Five: an unknown stranger"

"Yes. There's always him."

Mei brushed a loose strand of hair away from her face. "Do you really think the old rocker Clarence could kill someone?"

"I don't think he has it in him. He was mad at the guy, but I don't think he could commit murder. Nah. The guy's a pussycat with a bark."

Mei nodded. "What about Edgar?"

"I don't know much about the guy, but I don't think he's the murdering type."

"Okay, but you might have to re-think those two later, even if you don't want to. No one is above suspicion on the back of junk-mail envelopes."

They laughed and Mei gave her lopsided smile. "I'll make some tea. Read to me as you write."

"Question Two: Why kill Jimmy? One: money (the Black Cat Blues real estate deal). I told you about that remember. Two: money (Brother XII's gold – worth at least a couple million now) and your favorite Three: unknown. How does that sound?"

"Could be more reasons." Mei plugged in the kettle.

"Yeah, but I didn't know Jimmy. To me, he was just a handsome man who'd been hanging out at the bar lately, and then a dying man in the alley. He could have a closet full of people who wanted to kill him for all sorts of reasons. I can get Logan to help me later on this one."

Mei poured the water into the tea pot. "Logical. But I'm not sure that thinking logical works when you're chasing a murderer. It's such a passionate and illogical crime."

"I don't need philosophy right now. Question Three," Maggy continued, "Who killed Edgar? Suspect list: One: the first murderer, Two: someone else after Brother XII's gold and Three: an unknown person. That's all I can think of."

Without talking Mei placed the tea pot on the table and then the cups. Her mouth twisted a little as she poured the tea and the pungent smell of Bengal spice filled the room. "I don't know enough about Edgar to know all the possible suspects. He could have a deranged former girlfriend who wants to cut off his balls for all I know."

Maggy nodded and picked up her tea cup. "There are so many unknown factors."

Mei took a sip of the sweet tea. "But then the fact that both men were murdered with a marlin spike would seem to indicate it was the same murderer. Don't you think?"

"Okay, Watson. The marlin spike should lead us somewhere."

"What about Clarence?" Mei asked.

"Nah, I can't put him on this list unless there's some connection between them that I don't know."

"Okay, next."

Maggy scribbled on the fourth envelope an old hydro bill. "Question Four: Why kill Edgar? One: money—Brother XII's gold, Two: reputation—did someone in Edgar's family not want Rita's secret life as Brother XII's sex slave revealed?"

"I like that one."

Maggy laughed. "Seriously, there could be siblings or cousins that wanted to shut Edgar up.Three: the Decourcy island fisherman; and your favorite, which I'll call the Watson choice Four: an unknown person."

"Edgar." Mei sipped her tea. "It's hard to figure out who'd want to murder him when we know so little about the man."

Maggy smiled. "Okay, envelope five: Where on Gabriola Island is the gold buried? Not a clue, but the answer could be in Rita's journal."

"Rita's journal. I bet it's spicy."

Maggy laughed. "She was a virgin, how spicy can it be?"

"Brother XII with his ability to control people, the sex secrets he learned in the orient, the sex slaves, the whips—come on, it could be quite the read."

"Do you think she'd write about all that?"

"Women like to journal. Now and back then. I think we could learn a thing or two." Mei lifted her brows.

"Seriously." Maggy tilted her head. Could the whole mess come down to pillow secrets? "Pillow talk and lovers secrets. Maybe Great Granny Whitley's journal holds the last clue."

"Hey, I still think it's worth a read for the juicy stuff. Do you think she wore a corset? It must have really slowed down foreplay."

Maggy thumped a rhythm with her pen on the table. "If I sweet-talked Peterson he might let me see it."

"You're talking about the guy who talked about Martian genitalia."

"Yeah, I know. I told him about the journal Edgar thought would lead him to gold, but I'm not sure he believes it exists. He does this funny thing with his face every time I say Brother XII's name. Kind of like a wince with a cherry on top." She sipped her tea. It tasted heavenly. Tea made by someone else always did.

"But it could hold the final answers. And does the murderer know this too? Oooh, don't like that thought." Mei's black eyes shone.

"Hell," Maggy said, "I don't like any of these thoughts."

Her stomach twisted. There had to be something in the journal that would help. Something felt wrong. Grabbing the table to steady herself she looked up at Mei and waited for the darkness to subside. But it didn't. She began to shake. And then it was over.

"Oh, you've got a bad feeling again," said Mei.

"I don't want it." *What's with these weird premonitions?* She looked at her pages. Paper with scribbles. Some help they were.

Someone knocking on her door startled her. She looked at her clock: midnight. Who could that be?

CHAPTER 31

Rita's Journal
Nanaimo, April 26, 1933

I have come back to Nanaimo to witness another trial. This one was before the Chief Justice, Aulay M. Morrison. Mary Connally and Alfred Barley have charged Brother XII and Madame Zee with misusing their money. Everyone in town wanted to see him and his famous mistress with the whip. But the famous couple have disappeared. Some say they made the perfect get away. Will the trial proceeded without them?

I did not think things could get worse, but when Brother XII and Madame Zee came back from England conditions in our spiritual community fell apart. The two of them were angry, downright cruel all the time. Everyone fought over money. No one blindly agreed with Brother XII anymore. He had gone too far. I was too sad to write about it.

Scandalous stories have spread about that bitch Madame Zee hurting people. I was ready to leave again two days ago. I had heard enough of the dark rumors, had enough of living under the terror reigned on us from that woman from hell.

Brother XII reassured me things would get better. He took me to our spot near the Garry oak trees and we made wild passionate love, made even hotter, knowing that we were doing it behind the witch's back.

But the next day things in our community were the same. Conditions are appalling. People are bullied and hit for not working hard enough, and food is becoming scarce. Whatever happened to the thousands of dollars I gave the brother?

Finally, the anger in our group boiled into two law suits.

The courtroom was full. Rumors about Brother XII's hidden gold and wild sex life drew crowds eager for salacious details. They said he'd driven female slaves to madness. And death was delivered by Madame Zee.

I had noticed a couple of young women missing, but the group has become so fragmented I assumed they left on their own accord. It is hard to tell what is true and what is not. I'd like to think those rumors were wrong. But I am no longer sure of anything. Maybe it's time to face the fact that I've been duped.

It was a long hearing. Member after member of our Aquarian Foundation came forward and told their personal story about cruelty and deprivation on the islands. They talked about his use of black magic and sorcery. They detailed how he fortified the islands. They even dared to speak about his buried and cursed gold. Wild stories were told about strange invocations the brother used, from the ruins of Egypt. The crowd fed on the details, like hungry sharks from hell.

I said nothing, could say nothing. If I am to go home to my family I cannot have my name in court records about the brother. If I am to stay, I cannot be seen as a traitor.

It was not easy for those who spoke up. I admire their courage and tenacity. Before the hearing no one other than the two claimants from the Foundation wanted to talk. I could not blame the others.

At the first trial several men were knocked out by Brother XII's black magic spells. I now truly believe it was his spells. The man is powerful and dangerous.

When the second trial started Bob England, the man accusing him of wrong doing vanished without a trace. No one has heard from him.

And we have been struggling under threats and cruelty for months. We are a peaceful group of people now terrified by our prophet and that bitch with the whip. Many fear that Brother XII can reach us with his spells and curses wherever we are and strike us dead. I don't want to believe he would ever hurt me.

As I said, no one was willing to talk. But when Bruce McKelvie the managing editor of the Victoria newspaper, *The Colonist* spoke with the group everything changed. He gained their confidence and trust. He made them believe they were safe from the brother.

McKelvie, I am told, gathered the group together and told them that about a magic stronger than Brother XII's. The local First Nation magic, he explained, came to this land first and so, he said, it was stronger. They listened to him.

Some trembled with fear, so he gave them further reassurance. He showed them a Haida ornament, said it belonged to a famous Haida medicine woman and as long as we had it near no power under heaven could hurt us. The Haida are well known and respected First Nations people who live on islands to the north. They were famous warriors. Everyone knows their magic is strong.

The group looked at it. It was a stone labret, a lip ornament worn by the holy woman. The newspaper reporter claimed it had power and they believed in it.

When it came time to speak in court, every member of that group went into the witness stand and told their part of the story, holding the Haida ornament of power for protection. I was proud of what they were doing, proud of their courage to stand up for themselves.

Still I remained silent. I have my future, and now the future of the baby growing inside me, to think about.

It was a long and emotional hearing, but Mary Connolly was awarded twenty-six thousand dollars for money she had advanced the Foundation, ten thousand dollars in damages and four hundred acres on Valdes Island. Barley who was with Brother XII from the beginning, was awarded fourteen thousand dollars.

Outside the courthouse, Mary told me she'd give all the money back to Brother XII if he'd just be his old self. I know what she means. I believed in him and his vision, but everything has gone wrong since Madame Zee got her claws into him.

***

I can't go back to my island home. The men burned all the buildings and the *Lady Royal* our sailboat has been sunk in the harbor. Nobody knows where Brother XII is. There literally isn't anything to go back to. I will go forward in my life and raise our love child.

I've heard people are looking for his gold, but they will never find it.

Luckily, I didn't give all my money to Brother XII. I can see this is the end of the Aquarian Foundation. I'll have to make amends with my family in Vancouver. They will be angry, but they are good people and will take me back. I'll make up some excuse for my absence and marry that old fuddy-duddy Franklyn Whitley. He is a drinking friend of my father's, so Papa will like that.

But when I turn the lights off at night, I'll always remember being in the arms of Brother XII. And when I look into my first born's eyes, I will know that they are the descendent of a messiah.

CHAPTER 32

Music gives a soul to the universe, wings to the mind,
flight to the imagination and life to everything. ~ Plato.

Hunter entered the houseboat and joined the women. *Shit, Mei's here. Can't I ever get Maggy alone?* Maggy looked like hell. Her blond curls were a tussled mess. A pen stuck out above her ear. Her eyes bloodshot looked up at him and then glanced away. That mixed feeling of deep attraction and then rejection hit him in the solar plexus, or maybe a bit lower.

Mei stood up. "I have to be going." She hugged Maggy and whispered something in her ear the way women do. As she headed for the door she nodded to Hunter.

When the door closed behind her, Hunter asked, "What's wrong?"

"What isn't?" Maggy muttered.

Without thinking, he strode over to her and pulled her out of her chair and into his arms. He wanted to hold her tight enough that all the sorrows of her life would be washed away. Maggy may be the strongest woman he'd ever met, and he admired the hell out of her, but life kept throwing crap at her.

She took in the hug for only a minute. Long enough for him to smell the vanilla scented shampoo in her hair and feel her large, firm breasts press into his body.

Maggy pushed him away gently. "I keep getting weird feelings."

"Weird?"

"Like a cold hand is gripping my neck and trying to choke me." Her face paled.

"Maggy. You've been through a lot."

"Who hasn't?"

"Not everyone finds two murder victims at their feet." He reached out to touch her hair, but she moved back.

A small smile appeared on her perfect lips.

"My grandmother was psychic," she continued. "I'm not, but I do get 'feelings' now and then. Like déjà vu kind of experiences. Not many, and not often. Until now. They're coming on strong and hard and I hate it."

He nodded.

"I'm getting more. They're dark and scary, like shadows of nightmares, and I'm awake." She paused and pushed her hair back. "I wouldn't mind knowing the winning numbers of the next lottery, but this seeing ability's not like that. I'm getting messages about murder."

Maggy a seer? Yeah, it fit.

"Just a minute ago," Maggy continued. "Just before you knocked I felt like . . . " She stopped suddenly as if robbed of her words. "Like I was dying inside."

"Maggy. You could do with a good night's sleep. I'll stay here, on your couch. I'll protect you. You won't have to worry about anything. Take some aspirin and sleep it out. It'll do you good."

"You don't believe me?"

Hunter stepped closer to her and put his hands on her shoulders. "I believe you. My great-grandmother had the sight, or at least that's what she called it. People used to visit her in her tiny village on the cliffs in Ireland and ask her about their future. She was born in the caul, she explained to me, and she had the sight from birth. I've watched her through the years. I know there are things that happen in this world that are not seen by everyone.

"Did the sight scare her?"

"At first, maybe. I don't know. She was comfortable with it by the time I came along. She called it a curse and a gift and took care to protect it. The family took care to protect her."

"I don't understand why I'm getting it now. People who are psychic say they've known it all their lives. I've had a few experiences that made me think that maybe I had some extra-sensitivity, but nothing like this." The color flowed back into her soft, ivory cheeks as she talked.

"Could be Jimmy Daniel's murder triggered it."

"Could be," she agreed. "Jimmy Daniel's calling card. Which makes me worried that. . ." She went quiet as if the murderer had snatched her tongue. "That someone else has been murdered. I feel it. No, I know it."

"A third murder?" Hunter's gut twisted. "Your imagination could be working overtime." He ran a finger down her right cheek. She had the softest skin. "Let me take care of you tonight."

She raised a brow.

"No, I'm not making a move on you, though we both know I want to. I'm here to protect you. You need to sleep."

"Don't you have patrols?"

"I've done mine. I don't have to go out again until dawn."

She nodded her head. "I'll get some bedding."

After she handed him a pillow, sheets and a blanket, Maggy kissed him on his cheek and climbed up to her loft. His eyes followed her rear all the way up.

***

Maggy couldn't sleep, so she decided to phone Joe. Just to make sure that he and Clarence were doing okay. Just to be sure.

"Joe?"

"Love the sound of your voice, Maggy. Sweet and thick like honey. Sexy as hell."

"How ya doing, you old goat?"

"All's fine at The Black Cat. "Don't you

worry."

Like hell. "Clarence okay?"

"Why wouldn't he be?"

"Joe, humor me."

"I like to keep the ladies happy." His smooth voice and typical comments calmed her nerves like warm water in a bubble bath.

"Any of them tell you that you're lethal?"

"A few." He laughed his bawdy laugh.

"Good night, Joe."

"What are you wearing?"

"Shut-up Joe." She clicked her cell off.

Rain beat steadily on her metal roof. The place smelled of cinnamon and nutmeg from the tea Mei had brewed. Hunter lay stretched out on her sofa. His long muscular body hers for the asking, but she couldn't think about that now. She nestled under her quilt. The last thing she thought before falling asleep was how good Hunter smelled, like salt and sea and freedom.

***

How long had her cell been ringing. It felt like hours, but no matter how much she ignored it, it kept going. She rolled over towards her bedside table and snatched it. "Hello."

"Maggy Malone?" It was Peterson's unmistakable gravel voice.

Hell. "Yeah."

"We need to talk."

"It's . . ." She looked at her clock, "Three-thirty in the friggin morning. I need sleep. I'm exhausted . . ."

"He's dead," Peterson interjected.

She stopped breathing.

"Clarence is dead." She dropped her cell phone. A shudder ran through her body and she began to tremble. Shit. Shit. Shit.

She forced herself to pick the cell back up. "How?"

"You have some explaining to do."

CHAPTER 33

*One good thing about music, when it hits you, you feel
no pain.* ~ Bob Marley

Logan flipped the cap off another bottle of a beer and handed it to his red-eyed father, who sat opposite him at the kitchen table. "Jimmy was too young to die," he said. "Guess it's true what they say: the good ones die young, eh?" How many beers had they drunk? What did it matter? Jimmy was dead. Gone forever. That's all that he could think about. Jimmy—murdered in an alley. He'd never see him again. "He was always getting into trouble," his dad continued. A glint of light passed through his eyes, ringed with darkness. "Always pushing the limits."

"I figured you and Mom laughed about his escapades when we weren't around." It was getting harder to articulate consonants. *Must be the brew.*

His father nodded. "Oh yeah. We laughed about you boys a lot. Remember the time Jimmy threw a paper airplane at Mrs. Riddley's fat ass as she wrote algebra equations on the board?"

"I remember." He snorted and wiped his mouth. "The whole school laughed when they heard."

A tear trickled down his father's right cheek. "The whole time . . ." He sniffed. "The whole time we sat in the principal's office your mother squeezed my knee." Tears streamed down both sides of his weathered face. "She squeezed me hard, so I wouldn't laugh. But when we got home we both roared. That Jimmy. He always made me smile." He swatted at his tears.

Logan's gut clenched, but he smiled at the memory. "Not Mrs. Riddley, so much."

His father took a deep breath. "Ah. He charmed her with a rose he picked out of the neighbor's yard. Jimmy told us, he didn't' like the way she made some kids feel stupid, but it wasn't her fault she had a fat ass. At the end of the term he got an A in the course and they respected each other. At least that was Jimmy's story."

"Jimmy."

"Remember the time," continued his father, "he stole a young girl's training bra from her locker and . . ."

Logan's phone rang. He looked at the call display. "Excuse me Dad. It's the cops. They could know something about the murder."

His father nodded.

Logan got up and moved a couple yards away to be polite. "Yes," he said into the phone, trying to keep all expectation out of his voice.

"Peterson here."

"Yes."

"There's been another murder."

The cop mumbled on, but his words didn't register too well. Another murder? Logan couldn't let it go on. He had to find out who was behind it all, before anyone else got hurt . . . before Maggy got hurt. Maggy? The image of her soft green eyes and mane of blond, wavy hair flashed at him. "I'll be right down," he said, interrupting whatever it was that Peterson was explaining about the media coverage.

"That's not really necessary," Peterson said.

Logan clicked the off button. It was necessary to him.

CHAPTER 34

I think often sadness is a great place to get songs from.
~ Sarah McLachlan

Maggy exhaled slowly and told herself not to say something stupid. Or scream it. *Did Hunter really need to call Logan a "fucking prick?"*

Sitting between Hunter and Logan in the cop shop was worse than wearing pantyhose. No room to breathe and painful. The men glared back and forth at each other with laser beam intensity.

The building looked efficient, with counters, computers and uniforms, but it smelled of dusty papers not filed and stale coffee not finished. Her stomach felt like a cauldron of acid soup.

Snarled words almost below the audible level, passed between the men. She clenched her teeth. Bad enough being called down to the police station, without having two men acting like hormonal teenagers sitting on either side of her. In some ways life would be so much easier without men. In some ways.

But in other ways? Only two days ago she'd lamented that her life had no action, and here she sat between two outrageously handsome men who cared about her. When she was a teenager she thought of herself as chubby, freckle-faced and boring. Her sense of self-worth had improved over the years, but she had never imagined having this much male attention. If she wasn't such an emotional mess she might enjoy it, at least the irony of it. But her tears wouldn't stop. Hunter handed her another Kleenex.

Clarence. Hard to believe the cantankerous, old blues man had passed on, and not gently. Her stomach hardened into a knot. She had actually considered that Clarence was the murderer.

The hands of the clock turned slowly. She'd been waiting ten minutes so far, but it felt like an hour. She pulled out her cell and sent a second text to Mei. The evil that was afoot moved fast, and she had no intention of being its next victim, or letting anyone she cared about be the next victim. There had to be some way to get ahead of it, anticipate it.

Only a few days ago her life had been simple. She focused on her music and caring for the people she loved. Then she tripped over a corpse and kept tripping. Was the universe trying to tell her something?

Hunter massaged her neck with his strong fingers. Logan held her hand and with that simple gesture made her feel wrapped in their . . . well, whatever it was they shared that was growing faster than a Canadian thistle, and was just as prickly. Would Peterson ever show up?

Finally the inspector appeared, in jeans, sweater and expensive Italian shoes. She looked him in the eye and opened her mouth, but closed it catching his cold stare. He waved them to follow him and he walked down a hallway to his office. The three took seats, Maggy sat in the middle.

Peterson sat in his chair behind a messy desk and straightened his back. "First of all, you need to listen to me." His a no-nonsense cop tone grated her ears.

The only sound she heard was the institution clock ticking on his wall.

"Clarence B. Snyder was found by his cousin Joe in the alley. He had a silver marlin in his heart, just like the other two. Again, no fingerprints."

"Uh," she began, but he put his hand up to stop her from speaking.

"It wasn't pretty," he added, looking her square in the eye. "A lot of blood."

More blood. Even though she was sitting, Maggy felt her knees giving out on her.

"We think he was murdered around midnight. The medical rxaminer will be able to give us an exact time soon." He let his words sit in the silent room a minute, and then added, "For the record, I'd like to know where all of you were at that time."

Hunter started. "I was at a community

meeting at Smokey's until midnight. Lots of people saw me there. Then I went directly to Maggy's and was there until you called."

Logan sent a killing glare towards Hunter.

"Logan?" Peterson asked.

Logan shifted his eyes back to the inspector. "I was with my father at my apartment. You can check with him."

"We will." Peterson turned his focus to Maggy.

She sniffed. Peterson pushed a tissue box on his desk towards her. "I met with Clarence earlier tonight. Then I went to the dock meeting and soon after I got home Mei and then Hunter joined me."

"I'll write up your statements and you can sign them in the morning." Peterson sounded tired but, as always, efficient. He looked at the men. "You guys can go. I want to talk to Maggy."

The men looked at each other and then Peterson. Hunter gave his fuck-you shrug and kissed Maggy gently on the top of her head. "I'll wait outside for you," he said as his lips brushed her hair.

Logan grumbled, and then took his turn kissing the top of her head. "We need to talk," he said.

Maggy fought with her body's determination to cry in front of the cop. She took a tissue and blew her nose. Clarence had been the first person to take her seriously as a musician. Cantankerous as a butler in hell, but also sweet as sugar, he'd opened a door for her in the business. She waved the men away. "I'll get myself home.

You guys can . . . just go."

After the door closed behind them, Peterson's eyes bored into hers. "Maggy, what's going on?"

Part of her wanted to connect with him, but his eyes were so coppish, she reared away. What could she tell him? What would he understand?

"Something you want to tell me?"

"I," she started, but then the tears welled up again. She used all her resolve to stop them. "I wish I had information for you, but I don't. I don't know who the murderer is." She pulled her recycled envelopes from her purse. "Look," she said, handing her garbage over to him.

His eyes widened when she dumped her recycled garbage on his desk, but they became focused as he realized what they contained. He studied each one, hemming and hawing as he read.

"I have lots of questions, but no answers," she said.

"You really think the murders are linked to Brother XII's gold?" He leaned back in his chair and looked into the air as if the answer rested there between them.

"Directly and indirectly, yes."

"Tell me how."

"Why?" she asked.

"I don't understand your question," he said.

"Why do you want my opinion on the murders? Surely your men can tell you more from the evidence."

"Because you are the one living link to all three murders, so that tells me you must know something. Maybe, you don't know you know something, but you do. So I'm asking you, what do you think is going on?"

"I think it all started with Brother XII. He ripped people off, turned their money into gold and hid it." The tears had stopped, and her breathing eased.

"Got it. Go on."

"He had many lovers and one of them, a woman named Rita Whitley, kept a detailed diary of their time together. Her granddaughter passed away recently and left Edgar her estate. The diary was among her things and Edgar read it carefully. He decided that she knew where the famous treasure was buried, last."

"Last?"

"Brother XII trusted no one. He kept burying his gold, then digging it up and burying it somewhere else. He buried it all over Decourcy Island and Valdes Island."

"I see," Peterson said, but he looked perplexed.

Maggy tossed her hair out of her face and cleared her throat, wishing the lump would disappear. "Edgar had a clue, or maybe a bunch of clues, as to where the cult leader buried it, but he needed more information. One of the key clues was a description of a geographical area Edgar couldn't locate, so he hired Jimmy Daniels to find it. Jimmy was a respected investigator who knew how to keep his mouth shut, and a sailor with knowledge of the coast. Edgar figured he was the perfect person to help him."

"And they found it?"

"No. There's more to it. Edgar grew impatient waiting for Jimmy to come up with something and hired a second person to help him look. That's the Decourcy Island fisherman I mentioned to you before. That fisherman turned out to be greedy and dangerous. His threats scared Edgar, and he worried about Jimmy's safety."

"Jimmy's safety?"

"Yeah. You see, he'd told the fisherman two things: first the clue that he was hunting down and second that Jimmy Daniels was also looking for the area."

"So Jimmy knew someone might be after him."

"Edgar warned him. But , according to Edgar, he didn't take the warning seriously. "I think the fisherman caught up with him in the alley and killed him."

"Okay," said Peterson tapping his pen on his desk. "Who killed Edgar?"

"My guess—the fisherman."

"And Clarence?"

"The fisherman." As she said the words she became more certain. "I thought Clarence might have been the killer, but changed my mind after I had a long talk with him. He told me he was in the alley that night. I think the murderer saw him and that's why he's dead. I sent you a text that he was in danger."

"Yes, I got the text, but I didn't really understand."

"I've told you all I know." Her muscles

quivered as she raised her chin. Was it a need to be listened to and respected, or a need to get some sleep? Too washed out to know her own motivations any longer, she shrugged in defeat.

Peterson watched her. "Thank you for being honest," he said. "I find it hard to believe that a legendary treasure buried a hundred years ago could be the cause of three deaths, but I've seen people killed for much less. What worries me . . . " He paused and leaned forward. "Is that you may be next."

Maggy nodded. Beads of sweat formed on her upper lip.

"I don't know if it was the fisherman or some mysterious stranger we haven't identified yet, or for that matter one of your boyfriends, but I'm a pattern person, and the way this pattern reads—you're next. You're the only one who was in the alley that night that's still walking."

She took a deep breath.

"I repeat what I said earlier. You may know something. It may come to you later. Call me if it does, and keep safe. Trust no one."

She released her breath slowly. What else could she know?

"There's something eerie about this whole case." Peterson leaned back with an angry expression.

"Eerie?" she asked, finding her voice.

"Yeah, eerie, like the *Twilight Zone* music should be playing in the background. Like Madame Zee with her whip might appear around a corner, or Brother XII with his ancient texts of wisdom."

She smiled. Someone had been doing his research.

"Eerie, hokey, bull shit. I hate it," said Peterson.

Her smile widened. "Have you found Edgar's grandmother's journal yet?"

"No. We've looked through all his things, but no journal about a cult or Brother XII has been found. Mostly, her journals talk about tea parties. Maybe Edgar was delusional."

"Oh there was a journal," she said wondering why she felt so sure. "It started this whole mess."

"Uh, no. If we want to go spooky-stuff, it started with Brother XII." His sarcastic grin punctuated his sentence.

"Can I look?"

"Not a chance. But I'll let you know if anything turns up."

Her eyes pleaded.

"No. We have professionals going over everything. There's procedure we . . . "

Maggy interrupted him. "Uh huh." Procedure, friggen police procedure. She'd heard enough about that for a lifetime. She needed Rita's journal.

"Ah, get out of here," he said. "And don't leave town." He stared out the window. "Part of me thinks I should put a patrol car on you, but we're always short of officers and you seem to have your own baseball team out there." He smiled.

Maggy turned at his door to stare back at him. What was he doing? He'd just finished

225

warning her that she could be in danger and now he was demanding she stick around like a sheriff in a bad spaghetti western. He wasn't. Nah. He couldn't seriously be . . . "Do you think I'm the murderer?"

"Rose Magnolia Malone, you were the last person seen entering Clarence Snyder's office." Peterson lifted his hands in defense. "That's a fact."

On her way out she slammed the door so hard the walls shook.

CHAPTER 35

*Music expresses that which cannot be put into words
and that which cannot remain silent.*
~ Victor Hugo

As Maggy rushed through the hallway outside Peterson's office, Logan and Hunter looked at her with expectant eyes. But she didn't say a word.

"Maggy." They both called after her, but she ignored them and kept going. She didn't have the energy to deal with them. She needed to sort out the murders.

Her cheeks flushed with rage, she reached the street. Mei stood outside on the curb beneath her red-dragon umbrella. She handed her a coffee, which was cool to the touch, but that didn't matter—the warmth of the gesture flooded her heart.

Mei took one look at her and said, "Got your text. I took a break from work to come down. Let's walk and you can tell me all about it."

As they strolled along, Maggy told her everything that had happened, everything she'd been thinking, everything she'd been worried about. . . right down to her grief and her two-man problem.

Falling for a button down guy looking for a fast roll in the loft to take his mind off his grief was not something she needed right now. There was no denying the hot physical connection between them.

Falling for Hunter was a whole different story.

Mei listened, nodded and murmured "shit" at the appropriate moments, which cheered Maggie considerably. They walked on, towards Granville Island. Mei looked around them furtively, but Maggy didn't bother. She was tired of looking over her shoulder. If the boogey man was going to get her, then so be it. Bring it on. She'd give him a fight.

They arrived at Mei's business, "The Cellar," an art cooperative on the main drag of Granville Island. Two walls of glass faced the streets, allowing the public to see artists making art. There were printmakers, painters and sketchers working. It was a creative space for artists to work, take classes, and sell some of their stuff. Mei lived upstairs in a tiny suite that held all her belongings. She had launched her business five years ago and while she'd never get rich on such a venture it made her and others happy.

Mei turned to her at the door. "Ciao," she said and gave Maggy a quick hug. "Be careful." She made the text-me gesture with her hand, and then disappeared into her world.

Maggy remained motionless for a moment, wishing she could follow her.

On a map, it was a short distance to her place, maybe six hundred meters. Storm clouds brewed on the horizon, but there was plenty of early-morning daylight to help her find her way. Still, her stomach started a flip-flop dance.

The last time she'd had that feeling, Clarence was murdered. And the time before that, Edgar. And before that, Jimmy. Three times now. *Not enjoying this.* The feeling of acid eating her insides was not pleasant, and now she knew with certainty that her body was sending her a warning. *If only it could be more specific.*

It was like being drawn into the nexus of a storm of grief, murder and pure evil and given no direction. The small hairs on the back of her neck rose.

Too many things had happened in a few short days. Her imagination was getting the better of her. Her foot caught on the edge of a wooden plank in the walkway, and she stumbled. *Some strong woman she was. Couldn't even walk in pure daylight.*

Cars and delivery trucks crawled through the narrow streets on Granville Island avoiding the crowds of people milling around, shopping or visiting one of the many fine restaurants or the market. In every direction there were people. *What could possibly go wrong here?* She was basically home. Pulling her coat around herself more tightly, the acid still broiled inside her.

Then she heard music. Her friend Donny was playing classical guitar in the square. It sounded to her at this moment like music sent from heaven. She told herself she could stop to listen. The notes flowed over and through her feeding her soul and easing her grief.

Time to take control. Like a flick of a switch she knew what was going to happen. She would make it happen. She'd face the murderer and he would be the one to go down.

But she needed to see Joe first.

CHAPTER 36

People haven't always been there for me but music
always has. ~ Taylor Swift

Maggy closed the door of the Black Cat carefully, but the sound of it echoed in the quiet space. Joe sat at his usual table, alone with a full shot glass in front of him and a three quarters empty bottle of whiskey.

"Maggy." His melodic, baritone voice, shaking with grief, ripped her insides apart. He stood up. He always knew when she approached, said he liked the smell of her.

"Joe." She walked over to the old man and threw her arms around him. They held each other for a long time, the warmth of their embrace like a shelter in a storm.

He stepped back a little and reached for her

face with his right hand. While he traced her features, she touched the tear running down his face. "I'm so sorry, Joe."

"Sit," he said, and he stumbled into his own chair.

She reached out to help him. "I'm so sorry." What else could she say?

His regal head nodded. "Always figured I'd be first."

"You'll get through this."

He knocked back the shot that sat in front of him and banged the empty glass back down on the table. "Not sure I want to."

"Joe." She stopped. How could she even think about lecturing him? "I'm here for you now—always."

His mouth twitched as he filled his glass. Reaching across the table he put his shaky hand over hers. "Beautiful, inside and out," he said, his words slurring slightly.

"I mean it, Joe. I'm here for you. You can't give up. What do you always tell me—everything will work out?"

Joe leaned back and tilted his head as if he searched the sky, his sightless eyes weeping.

"Joe?"

"I'd like to kill the bastard who murdered him—slow like. Make him feel some of my pain."

This from a pacifist. She squeezed his hand.

"The asshole has no idea how much light he's taken out of this world. Clarence had a temper and he cheated at gin, but he always took care of his friends and family. He was a good man. One of the best."

"Yes, he was."

Joe took a drink coaster with The Black Cat's logo off the top of the table and flicked it into the air. It hit the floor with a dull thud. "Won't be the same without him."

"Nope." A nasty, dry taste in her mouth made it hard to say more.

He poured himself another drink from the bottle.

"Joe, do you know anything? I mean about the murder."

He knocked back the shot. "I found him."

She waited.

"Maggy. Sweet Maggy. You knew, didn't you?" His glassy-eyed stare faced her. "That's why you called."

"No, I just had a bad feeling, a real bad feeling."

He poured another shot. With his unsteady hand the liquor missed the glass and spilled onto the table, where the amber droplets gathered into a puddle. The distinct smell of single-malt whiskey hung in the air.

"What happened, Joe?"

He tilted his head. "I heard a noise out back. It's usually quiet late Sunday night. But I heard a loud bang, and then nothing."

She waited.

"So I headed down stairs to the bar. I called out for Clarence, but he didn't answer. The place was empty. I checked his office. He'd left a full bottle of beer on his desk and he had music playing.

Figured he couldn't be far. But I was getting this bad feeling. Ya know? In my gut."

"Yeah, I know, Joe." Oh boy, did she know.

"So I went to check the back door, and it wasn't closed. It was about six inches ajar. That's when I remembered that Clarence often took extra food outside late at night for the homeless in the alley. So I think, he's just outside. I figure he'll know what the noise is about." Joe shook his head. "But my gut still burned. I shoulda listened to it and called someone."

The paleness of his face worried her. Maybe she shouldn't put him through this. Peterson probably made him go over it a million times already. "Joe?"

He shook his head. "I'm okay. You gotta know. I walked down the stairs. I could smell his aftershave. I went towards the smell. And I found him. Clarence lay a few yards away from the bottom of the stairs, dead. He had a stake in his chest. Cops say the same kind as the other victims."

Nothing could be more horrifying than finding someone you loved murdered. She reached over for his hand and a small smile spread across his face when their hands touched. "I screamed for help. Sheldon, the young homeless guy with the two personalities, came running from the street. He went for help."

Maggy squeezed his hand again. "Together, we'll get through this."

"Yeah," he said, but his voice was not convincing. "If only I had eyes that worked. I might have been able to see who killed him."

"Did you smell or hear anything that might help?"

He shook his tear-stained face. "Regular smells, rotting garbage, urine and cigarette smoke. I could hear a car with a bad muffler going down the road, and a rat munching his dinner. That's all."

"Did Peterson say if he found any clues?"

"That man likes to listen, not talk. Said he'd do everything he could to find the person who murdered Clarence. He was kind actually. Imagine that, a kind cop."

"He's a good cop." What else could she say?

"Can you hear them?" he asked.

She stopped to listen. The faint sounds of motion came from the alley. "They must still be working the crime scene."

"Don't think I'll ever step in that alley again." His voice shook.

"Me either." She laughed and then a strangled sound came out of her throat. Not a good time for laughing. "Look, Joe, about tonight."

"We'll be open and I'm counting on you."

"No one would blame you if you closed for a couple of days."

"We can't afford to lose the money. Besides, I'm not changing anything because of a murderer. Clarence wouldn't want that. He'd be seriously pissed-off at me if I closed the Black Cat."

She nodded. Then caught herself. His strength inspired her. "I called in sick at the dental office and told Mrs. Randolph I couldn't walk the dog today. I need a break from my day stuff, but I'll come back here tonight. We'll do it for Clarence."

"That's my Maggy. I know I can always count on you."

"Maybe you should get some sleep, Joe."

"That could take a long time." He leaned back and took another whisky shot.

CHAPTER 37

Music was my refuge. I could crawl into the space
between the notes and curl my back to loneliness.
~ Maya Angelou

The door of Maggy's houseboat stood open. *I closed it this morning. I'm sure I did. Shit . . . what now? But a murderer wouldn't leave the door open.* Maggy pushed on the door, took a step back and watched it open wide.

Hunter lay stretched out her couch reading a *Pacific Yachting* magazine. He looked up. "I didn't think you'd mind."

"How did you get in?"

"You leave your extra key above the door. It's not exactly hard to find." Large dark circles surrounded his eyes. It made her feel good to know that someone else was having a shitty week. He stood, walked over to her and gently touched her face. Then he kissed her softly on the cheek. "I'm worried about you." Her pulse quickened. The guy was more potent than a hundred percent alcohol.

"I'm okay," she said, walking past him. She threw her purse on the kitchen table and sat down. "I'm not in any mood to hear about patrol schedules."

"I know," he said.

"I have to find the journal Edgar talked about. It has to tell us something."

Silence filled the room for a minute, companionable silence; the kind married couples live in. Each lost in their own thoughts and yet together. Married. . . couples? Did she really just think that? Her shoulders relaxed. Being with Hunter felt like sliding into a warm bath, but then he'd look at her and the water would boil.

"The wind's good," he said, walking over to the window.

That was his way of saying it was time to go sailing. "Uh, Hunter, I don't think so."

"I'm guessing Peterson isn't letting you look at Edgar's things. He'll want to go through them with a certified, Mounty's, magnifying glass. You're obviously not doing your day jobs today, so let's go sailing." He turned towards her and raised his hands like a lawyer about to rest his case. "It's the best way, I know of, to clear your head. Get the big picture."

"You're crazy." Three murders, creepy psychic feelings, and a bad guy on the loose. She couldn't sail off and play on the ocean. Could she?

"Not so much," he said. He gave her one of those killer looks that made her mind stop working.

A smile spread on her face despite her worries. She did love to sail. It brought her almost as much peace as music. Her wind chime tinkled. It was a good twelve knot wind out there. "Ah hell. Let's do it. On the way over I'll fill you in on Joe."

***

Hunter owned a thirty-seven foot Hunter sailboat, which he kept in perfect condition. It was his pride and joy and handled the local waters with ease. With the main sail set, and the jib half furled, they took a port tack out into English Bay. The drizzle eased, and sunshine peeked through gray clouds. The wind held at twelve knots with a light chop. The occasional white cap broke the horizon. Perfect conditions for a leisurely afternoon sail.

The fresh, sea breeze in Maggy's face revived her. There's wind on land, and wind on sea. Different animals in her book. The sea breeze brings with it the cleansing power of the ocean. It's like Gaea feeding you strength through her lungs.

Breathing it in deeply, she let her thoughts run through her mind and out the other side. Nothing seemed so important anymore. Just breathing. The wind and the sea embraced her and all that mattered was being alive. The porousness of life swallowed her whole.

Hunter understood. He always did. She could tell by the dancing gleam in his Irish blue eyes.

The boat slid up and down the ocean swells as they entered the bay. Watching the horizon, she smiled at Hunter, a sailors acknowledgment. All was right in their world.

The scenery took her breath away for the millionth time. She once told Mei, who detested boats, that when you were out on the water you really saw the beauty of the west coast—a place where ocean meets mountain and sky. Its grand scale made her feel small and human; grateful to be a living part of the vast landscape.

Over two hundred years ago Captain George Vancouver sailed into this bay from the Pacific, and wrote about the lush green forests and majestic mountains that rimmed the land to the north and south. The rugged beauty of the west coast now littered with human communities, still held its grand beauty.

Five minutes of sailing washed away all her complaints about Vancouver's weather. The lightening of her heart made her almost giddy. She closed her eyes for a moment and drank in the smell of the sea, the rolling of the ocean beneath the hull, and the thwapping of the sail flapping.

They passed a large coal freighter flying a flag from Liberia, and another barge filled with sulphur hailing from Panama. Two commercial salmon trawlers came in, and a small yacht with an American flag.

They were the only sailboat in sight, and yet the now fifteen knot wind was so fine.

About thirty minutes into the sail, Hunter handed her the helm and went below. He returned with a steaming cup of hot chocolate, the perfect drink for the nippy November day. It smelled of cocoa and Baileys. He took over the wheel and she sat beside him. Everything about the trip had been wonderful.

She could feel the pregnancy of this moment.

Hunter stepped closer. His salty, man-smell flooded her senses. His denim blue eyes held hers captive while he ever so gently moved a stray tendril of hair away from her face with his calloused fingertips. The tenderness in his eyes and his touch sent fireworks through her system, short circuiting her brain. This couldn't happen.

"Maggy, there's something I want to talk to you about." The seriousness of his tone stilled her heart. She'd seen him business-like at the neighbourhood meetings at the Scuttlebutt, but when they were alone, his voice melted to a gentle, almost caressing tone. So this new seriousness sounded like a canon going off. She looked up at the sky and said a silent prayer.

Hunter took in a deep breath and turned the wheel slightly gaining more wind in the main. The canvas flapped sharply as it caught the extra air. The bow lifted and the hull gained speed. "It's about us," he said.

She knew it. Damn. Now? "Hunter, I'm really messed up right now."

"I know. But . . . "

"But what?" A seagull dove into the water and surfaced with a small fish. Why couldn't' she be a sea bird? But then she could be the fish. Odd things you think about at crisis points in your life.

"I hate seeing you this way." He took his

eyes off the horizon for a moment and met hers. They brimmed with emotion, unspoken feelings that she had sensed, but thought she could ignore. Her life being complicated and all.

"Shit happens. I'm a big girl. I'll get through it." She wiped her running nose with her sleeve. "I appreciate you taking me out. I do feel better out here." Her voice sounded tinny to her own ear, false, out of character. She kept her eye on the waves, hoping her words would be enough for him.

"I want to take you in my arms."

"Uh," was all she managed to say, her throat suddenly thick and awkward. Hunter was more to her than a friend, but . . .

"Comfort you," he continued. His voice was low and raw.

Oh hell.

"Keep you safe."

Damn, damn damn. The boat rose to take another swell.

"Maggy, I . . . care for you."

Shit. They rode down the wave. "Hunter not now."

Hardening the sheets, he waited for her to say more.

But she had run out of words. Since the moment she met Hunter, he'd assumed a special place in her life, a friend who was fun to hang out with, a confidant to complain to when things got rough, a neighbor who was a few yards away. And yeah, she knew the feelings between them were growing, but she wasn't ready. "After Adriano I promised myself to stay clear of heavy relationships until . . . "

"You had healed."

His understanding didn't make this any easier. "I care for you, Hunter, but my heart is still raw and I'd fuck it up. I need to feel more whole first. You deserve the best."

They rode the waves up and down. "Maggy, I'll wait as long as it takes. But you know we all have bruised hearts. You've had the wind knocked out of you, but don't give up on love. I think we could really be something."

"Not now."

His chin firmed. "Is it Logan?"

The sadness in his voice pierced her heart. She didn't want to hurt Hunter. What she felt for him was complicated, confusing and above all sticky. The one thing she knew for sure was that she didn't want to lose him. She swallowed. "I like Logan, but it's not that."

"What is it then?" A glint of hope steadied in his eyes. They bounced off a small wave.

"I guess you could say I don't want to ruin our friendship."

"Fuck." His voice hit a new low. "I hate it when girls say that."

"I'm no girl, Hunter. I'm Maggy, and I have strong feelings for you. But right now I don't want to complicate my life by acting on them. I don't want to make a mistake with you—not you—if that makes any sense."

"Okay. Let's leave it for now. But I want to make one thing clear. I do not consider you a friend. From the moment I laid eyes on you, I knew you would mean more to me than that. I'll be here always, through whatever. But be clear, I consider you much more than a friend."

His words softened her heart and she felt free in some inexplicable way, as if he'd rubbed away some of the pain that clung to her and wouldn't let go after her marriage fell apart. He could give so freely of himself, so selflessly. But she still wasn't ready to start a relationship. "Hunter."

"Yeah."

She placed her hand on his arm. "You rock."

His somber face broke into a wide smile. "And you're damned fine too."

The intimacy of their moment was broken by a big wave hitting them across the bow. Thank God.

He rubbed the back of his neck. "Ready to come about?" he asked, issuing the standard warning given by the captain before tacking in the opposite position.

"Ready," she said taking her position by the jib sheets to do her part.

"Helm's a lee," he said.

She adjusted the lines holding the jib and felt the wind take hold on the starboard tack. The boat glided in its new direction picking up more speed and distancing them from shore.

"But you're ready to be with Logan," he said when the sails were secured.

"It's not complicated being with him. I'm risking nothing."

"I wonder."

"What?"

"Haven't you considered the possibility that he could be the murderer?"

"Logan?" Dread slithered through her veins. "No, no. . . he couldn't be."

Hunter shrugged. "You know the story of Cain and Abel. It happens."

She pushed back the darkness threatening to take her heart. "I don't think he could hurt anyone. He's not like that." But did she really know the man? He said he loved his brother, but hate can live beside love. Her marriage had taught her that.

She pushed her hair back under her ball cap. If only she could recapture that first feeling of freedom when the ocean breeze met her face.

They sailed for another thirty minutes without speaking. The waves and wind took over their silence, enveloping them in a soulful rhythm.

As the sun began to set they sailed back into the marina. Hunter helped her out of the boat.

She kissed his cheek. His skin tasted salty. "I do have feelings for you," she said.

"I know," he said. "Maybe someday."

"Someday," she repeated. Warmth grew inside her as if part of her believed it would happen. But someday was not today.

Not when a murderer was after her.

CHAPTER 38

If I were not a physicist, I would probably be a musician.
I often think in music. I live my daydreams in music. I
see my life in terms of music. ~ Albert Einstein

After her last set at The Black Cat, Maggy drove home, her body on auto-pilot while her brain scrambled to make sense of it all. Part of her desperately wanted to buy into Mei's cozy view of the universe, the idea that everything happens for a reason. She wanted to believe that there was a purpose to everything that happened to her. But she couldn't reconcile murder fitting into her life. Was she supposed to learn something from Jimmy's death?

The door of Maggy's float home hung ajar, again. So much for a normal life. The porch light had been turned on. How neat. A murderer wouldn't leave a light on, would he? Hunter? Nah, they had already said enough to each other for one day. Mei should be in bed. Who then? Her newly acquired sixth sense would tell her if she was stepping into danger, wouldn't it? *Oh frig it.*

She pushed open the door, ready to face whatever with a kick-you-in-the-balls attitude. But there was no need for the bravado. It was Logan sitting at her kitchen table looking at nautical maps. He turned his head towards her. "I've been waiting for you."

A simple sentence, but its sexual implications made her wobbly, like someone took a few vertebrae out of her spine and put them back in the wrong order. "Hi," she said.

"I need your eyes. I've gone over the Gabriola shoreline again and again, but no harbor, spit or cave hollers, 'Brother XII was here'." Frustration edged his low voice, giving it a halting quality.

She walked over and threw her arms around him. They held each other for a few quiet minutes while the houseboat moved gently up and down. Small waves rippled below them, but they remained rooted in each other.

With a long sigh, Maggy pushed away from him.

His smile started on the right side of his mouth and spread across his whole face making her lower belly quiver. Deadly. The man was deadly handsome.

"I don't think the answer's on the chart," she said, taking off her jacket.

Watching her intently he nodded. His eyes

had darkened.

"It's in the journal," she said.

"But we don't have the journal. I'm trying to develop the only clue we have."

"A ten-mile-long island in the Salish Sea, riddled with sheer two-hundred foot cliffs that drop into the sea, and a few harbors?"

He smiled. "Do you have a better idea?"

She rubbed her hands to warm them. Maybe, she should try reading tea leaves or something. She had no idea, none, so she shrugged.

"Were you with Hunter today?"

She blinked. How could he know? "Yeah." She stared at him. "So?"

"He could be the murderer." Logan's matter-of-fact voice, lingered in the air like a bitter after-taste.

"Look, I hardly know you. I'll spend my time with whomever I want. Hunter's a good friend." She'd leave out the rest. Explaining her relationship with Hunter to Mei or even herself was impossible, so she wouldn't even try to explain it to Logan.

Her home heaved upwards on a wave. The wind had picked up, signaling another fall storm.

"Think about it," he said.

She tilted her head. "Hunter's a good man."

"Even good men kill."

Maggie exhaled slowly trying to contain a jolt of anger that made her want to tell him to fuck off. "Why would Hunter kill Jimmy?" Logan's accusation made no sense. It was testosteroney-crap. She thought he was better than that.

"Because he loves you."

"Excuse me?"

He held up his hand, so she wouldn't say more. "Listen, if Hunter learned that Jimmy had a third of the Black Cat Blues Bar and was about to sell it. . ." He put one finger in the air. "And if he thought that meant you would lose your singing gig. . . " He put a second finger in the air. "He might get mad enough to talk to Jimmy, and then he might lose his temper and kill him."

So he knows about Jimmy owning a piece of the Black Cat. "No way."

"Hunter has a record of violence. I picked that piece of information up from your Scuttlebutt Café." He put three friggen fingers in the air.

"I didn't say Hunter was an angel. But he's no murderer. And why would he kill the others?"

The wind whistled through the marina, rigging clanged and the houseboat began to rock. It was going to be a long, stormy night.

"You have to put your feelings for him aside." He reached over for her hand, but she pulled it back. "I figure he may have killed Jimmy in a fit of passion. Edgar and Clarence must have figured it out, or maybe they saw him, so he had to kill them. Remember, the murder weapon was a marlin spike. How many people do you know besides Hunter who walks around with a marlin spike in their pocket?"

True, all too true. But it couldn't be Hunter. He may, uh, care for her, but to kill a man so she could sing? Nah. "Hunter thinks you're the murderer."

Logan's eyes shot wide. "Me?"

"You're inheriting a third of the Black Cat. It may be run down, but the earth underneath it is worth a lot of money. Or you could have a dark secret from your childhood, a reason for hating Jimmy that festered through your life until now. You told me you were worried he'd leave your business."

"And I'd use a marlin spike?"

"You have a boat. I'm sure you've used them. Or maybe the spike was in the alley."

"You don't believe any of this." He reached for her hand again.

This time she let him touch her. A warm glow flowed through her body. The hot chemistry between them always simmered just below the surface, like a pot of water ready to boil. She shook her head. "No, Logan, I don't believe you're a murderer, but I don't believe Hunter is either."

His other hand came onto the table to touch her. A chess game: fingers for pawns, looks for knights and she didn't want to think about his next move. With a quick inhalation, she pulled back and gave him as serious a stare as she could muster. "We have to talk, not touch." Her words echoed in the small cabin as well as in her heart.

"I thought that's what we were doing?" His mischievous smile failed to hide his intentions.

"How long have you known you'd inherit the Black Cat?"

He closed his eyes leaned back, as if hit by an ice cold blast from a water gun. "To be honest Maggy, I don't care about the Black Cat."

"It's worth a lot of money."

"Yeah, the realtor offered me one and a half million."

"And you need that money?"

He opened his eyes. "I could use it, but you'd lose your job and the city would lose the best blues bar on the west coast."

"This is not about me right now. Do you need that money?"

He squirmed in his seat.

"What would you do with that kind of money if you had it?"

"I'd. . ." He paused. "I could possibly put my family back together again."

Shit. Double shit. "You mean your wife would come back to you if you had money?"

"Yeah, she's that kind of woman. You know the kind who dreams of a really big house with heating in the damned floor on a fancy street, bigger and better than anything I could ever afford." His voice sounded robotic, as if he was discussing the bottom line of a spreadsheet for a lemonade stand, not his marriage. He sure as hell wasn't talking about love.

"So do it," Maggy said, pushing away a strand of hair that had fallen across her face. "Do it. At least something good will come out of Jimmy's death."

Logan stood up and walked around the table. He took her by the hands and pulled her to her feet.

She took a quick breath.

"I can't," he said.

"It's just money," she said.

As he pulled her close to him, she could

smell his fancy cologne and feel his muscular chest. Her softness melted into his hardness. A dangerous, dangerous zone.

"You want me to sell it?" He spoke softly into her ear. The light push of his breath against her skin sent shivers through her body.

"It would solve your problems."

He kissed her neck. The float home, now caught in the full tempest of the storm, swayed, and her wind chime tinkled. "I don't want to hurt you," he murmured.

Nuzzling into him she answered, "I want you to be happy."

He ran his hand down her back pulling her closer into his embrace. His erection pushed against her and she moaned. His lips brushed hers, soft and needy, yet experienced enough to go slow.

"I want you," he said.

Her tongue licked his lower lip. "I need to know. . . "

"I won't sell the Black Cat," he answered, nibbling her lower lip.

She moaned deeper in her throat. It was what she wanted to hear, but she wanted more. "I thought we weren't going to—," she stopped for breath, "—get involved."

"Right." He kissed her gently and then deepened his kiss, his tongue exploring and inviting. He pulled back just long enough to say, "Not involved." His hand slid under her blouse and undid her bra. "Just playing."

His large hand caressed her breast and his fingertips played with her nipple as he entered her mouth for a deep, demanding kiss. Their tongues danced a tango of desire.

As he stroked her, thoughts of saying no slipped slowly out of her mind. The man was married and wanted to be married. This would be a no-strings-attached romp. She could just. . . He grabbed her behind and pulled her closer to his hardness. Oooooooh. She wanted him.

Taking a quick step back, she threw off her blouse and bra. He took off his shirt. And undid his belt.

"Let me," she said, reaching for him. She stroked his length with a firm hand. His eyes darkened and he groaned. But he stopped her hand a second later. "Not so fast." He swept the charts off the table, and pulled her onto it.

Maggy giggled. The table? Really, the table?

He leaned over her and licked her breast sending currents of desire through her body, pooling in her lower belly. She could handle the table. He held her hands above her head and played with her nipples, nibbling and licking and nibbling again. Yup, the table's good.

"Tell me you want me to make love to you," he said.

"Let's just call it sex. Condoms?" she asked as her knee rubbed him between his legs.

"Uh. . ." He wasn't sounding so wordy now. "One." He was croaking.

"I have a jungle pack upstairs. You can pick your color."

He undid her fly and pulled on her jeans. "We'll save them for later." Slipping his finger inside her panties, he grazed over her center. "I want you."

"Yes, I want to have sex with you."

"You're so beautiful." He kissed her deeply as his fingers stroked her clit. It felt so damn good. Six months was way too many. She wanted him. Now. Oh God, did she want him. His fingers pushed inside her, while his thumb played outside. She flooded with moisture.

"Now, please. . ."

He moved back. His khakis fell to the floor, followed by his shorts. His erection was mighty impressive.

Leaning back over her, he licked the inside of her thigh. She groaned. Such exquisite torture. His other hand reached up for her center and played as he continued to lick and kiss her inner thigh higher and higher.

She wreathed in exquisite pleasure and expectation.

He licked her sex and inserted two fingers inside her.

"Logan. . ." she panted.

Rhythmically he moved his fingers and his tongue. She grabbed his hair. To hell with worrying about what is right or good or proper. To hell with thinking about dead men or ex-husbands. There was just him and her and now.

All she needed was this and now. Her body took over. All she could feel was her burning need. Red, hot desire flamed through her, wanting release.

His tongue teased her until she fell apart, into a million pieces of ecstasy.

"Now," he murmured.

He entered her, hard and strong.

***

Logan felt like a buck in heat, all cock and no brains, but that was okay for tonight. He pushed into her and felt her warmth envelop him. Hotter than hell, sweeter than heaven and wilder than anything he had ever experienced.

Afterwards, they lay entwined on her bed in the loft of the float home, rocking in the wind, holding each other, while the storm raged outside.

How could he, a thirty-eight-year old man feel so new at sex, so overwhelmed?

As her hand stroked lower and lower on his stomach he stopped thinking. Jungle pack?

CHAPTER 39

*After silence, that which comes nearest to expressing the
inexpressible is music.*
~Aldous Huxley

Sunlight peaked through Maggy's venetian blinds. Her body was well sated, but her mind—not so much and her heart not at all. It had been a long night of good, really good, sex. The noise of the wind and waves had passed, and the boat house rested.

He'd left the bed, and she could smell coffee. A man who could make coffee! Oh yes, maybe she could hang out with this guy.

They had to talk. She'd tried to mention that fact several times in the middle of the night, but they couldn't keep their hands off each other. Every attempt at discussion led to another tumble. And another.

On her last trip to the head, she found she could barely walk. It had been quite a night. She ran a hand through her hair.

The sharp smell of toast burning made her move.

Shit! She couldn't have the fire alarm start. The whole dock would be in her living room in. . .

The alarm went off with a shrill and deafening noise that would raise the dead.

"Shit." She jumped out of bed and pulled on her silk housecoat. "Logan, pull the battery out." She slid down the ladder. He was trying to dismantle the alarm, but it wouldn't open. Just her luck. Hell, everyone would come to her aid.

Fires on the dock pose a great danger because there's so much gas around. So when a fire happens everyone runs to help. And everyone was hyper-vigilant right now because of their problem with the Rat. *Shit. Shit. Double shit.* The whole dock would be at her doorstep in seconds. And yes everyone, including Hunter, would know how she spent her time during the storm. *Sweet baby Jesus.*

Logan gave the alarm a good yank and it came crashing to the floor, just as the pounding started on the door.

Hunter burst into the room with Elena running up behind him barefoot. Others were heading in. *Shit shit shit.* So much for a private affair.

Hunter's steely-blue eyes gave her a look that could fry a fish, and then gave Logan one of raw anger. He threw his arms in the air. "What the hell, Maggy?"

She shrugged. What else could she do? The others were arriving fast. They looked at the two of them and their burnt toast that now sat in the sink doused in water.

A few laughed; most just nodded their heads, gave her a side-grin and left.

That took ten minutes. Her whole world knew about her and Logan now. All because of a piece of toast. Damn it.

She had bad luck when it came to men. The look Hunter gave her sat at the base of her spine heavy and uncomfortable. She didn't want to hurt him, but she had. This would complicate their relationship further. "Hunter."

He looked at her with those eyes, so blue they looked like you could dive into them and he shook his head. "Don't say anything." Then he left.

"Coffee?" offered Logan when the last person left. He smiled weakly as he pulled his pants on. Yeah, all the neighbors had a good look at her new lover's impressive apparatus, as well. Lord, love a duck.

Maggy started laughing, even though her heart ached. "I think I earned it." She ran a hand through her hair.

"Oh yeah."

"Logan, this is crazy. We aren't meant to be together. I think the god of toast has sent us a message." She smiled. "We're complete opposites. You're all neat, tidy and organized. And I'm. . ."

"Wild. I love it. And you can't deny the sex is great."

"But life is about more than that."

"Tell me something I don't know."

CHAPTER 40

The only truth is music. ~ Jack Kerouac

I t was a good thing Maggy didn't judge a man by the way he made toast. Logan's second attempt wasn't much better than his first, but the alarm was no longer functioning so they ate blackened toast without the neighbors. Silence infected their space like worms at a picnic slithering into forbidden places.

"I'm sorry," Logan said, breaking the storm of quiet. "I suck at toast."

"Really," Maggy said, lifting her eyebrows. His eyes widened.

"You really think this is about toast?" she asked.

"Is this one of those man-woman moments I don't get? I'm a logical man Maggy. Just talk to me; help me understand."

Sitting back crunching on her crust she rolled her eyes. "It's not rocket science, Logan. Last night was wonderful. But the timing sucks. Add to that I like my privacy and in the last fifteen minutes our relationship was telegraphed through my whole community. Almost everyone I care about is chatting about who I'm fucking." She watched his eyes for a response to her words but he looked catatonic.

"Talk about being naked," she continued. "I feel exposed in more ways than one. I don't know yet how I feel about us. Sex is one thing, but there's more going on here and it's all going too fast for me. I don't want to be burned again."

"You're not toast." His eyes twinkled.

She glared at him.

"I wasn't trying to be flippant. My point is that you're a beautiful woman. What happened last night was great. . ."

She raised her brows. *Great? It was mind blowing sex fuelled by an animal chemistry that couldn't be denied.*

"I can't believe that it was only for one night. Give us a chance."

Could she open her heart up to him? Love and be loved? That would take time and a whole lot of trust. She crunched into her toast. Besides, she had vowed to herself that she wouldn't get involved with anyone right after Adriano. "Logan, you have to look at the big picture."

"Yeah, I've been thinking about the Black Cat."

She raised her brow. When the hell did he have time to do that? "And?" she asked.

"I don't know the music world, but I know business. I figure you and your friend Joe can manage the music side and I can handle the books and stuff. The third guy, whoever he is, seems to want to be silent, so he can stay that way." His chocolate-brown eyes gleamed. Did he really believe that running the Black Cat could be as easy as choosing a play list?

Maggy looked at her fingernails. Like the rest of her life, they needed work. "I don't know, Logan. Lovers don't make good business partners."

He tilted his head and looked down at her. "Why not?"

"'Cause I don't think. . ." She paused. How could she tell him what she was really thinking without hurting him? "I don't think we can be as. . ." she searched for the word.

"Honest with each other?"

That would do. She nodded.

Logan ran a hand through her bed-tangled hair. "I'd like to think we'd be more honest."

Oh how she wanted to believe that one. "I'd hope so too, Logan, but. . ."

"But that's not your experience." He pulled her back into his arms. Her body quivered in his embrace. It felt like she'd never left, their bodies entwined so damn perfectly.

"Hell, Logan."

He kissed her gently on the lips, but with a yearning that transmitted his intent right through her body.

"Seriously, Logan."

He licked her long, swan neck, his breath tickling her skin.

"Logan."

"We can do it, Maggy. I know we can do it."

They stopped talking. He picked her up and laid her gently onto the sun-streaked sofa.

It would be a sweet dream to not only sing at the Black Cat, but to run it. She didn't have the contacts—not yet—anyway, but she could make them she wanted to make them. It was like a dream come true—except for the fact that it had come on the back of three murders. And all that blood. She pushed Logan away. "I can't."

"What the hell?" He panted, lifting his head from her breast.

"I know we have something. . ."

"Something?"

"Something sexy. But I haven't had time to get over losing Clarence, and you haven't buried your brother. The ink probably hasn't dried on your divorce papers. The timing is so wrong. If we do have something real, something that's meant to last, it can wait. And the fate of the Black Cat has to be separate from that."

"Wait?" His eyes were large, ringed with incredulity. "Wait?"

"There's too much in my head, not to mention my heart. I need time."

He rolled over onto the floor with a loud grunt.

"Where do you suppose the diary is?" she asked.

Logan threw a pillow at the wall and growled again. It was amazing how much feeling the man could convey with a pillow.

CHAPTER 41

The only escape from the miseries of life are music and cats. . ." ~ Albert Schweitzer

Gilbert Harrison's calico cat, Sly, stretched on his lap, purring louder with each stroke of his hand. Most days, the warmth of the feline's body comforted Gilbert, but not today. He picked up the cat and dropped her to the floor. Her paws thudded when she landed. She rotated her head to give his master a narrowed cat-eyed glare. Meowing her annoyance with a vengeance, she raised her tail straight into the air and strutted to the other side of the cabin.

"Fuck you, too," Gilbert said.

He picked up his vibrating cell phone. It was his mother. Could the day get any worse?

"Where the hell are you?" Her scratchy voice bit into him like rancid acid.

"Taking some time off, Ma," he said.

"Time off? In my day no one took time off. Son, aren't there some fish to catch?"

He looked at the ceiling of his boat cabin. *You're such a fucking fool. You shouldn't have answered her call.*

His mother knew the answer to her question about fish, so why did she always need to ask it? "Ma, there's no opening right now. I'm seeing some guys in Vancouver about a job I can fit in between fishing."

"Well," she started, and then her voice broke into a smoker's cough. "That sounds good."

So why didn't she believe him? He could tell by her voice that she didn't. Guess he'd given her this line too many times. Still, why couldn't she give him the fucking benefit of the doubt like other mothers? "Ma." "I've got a pile of bills that need to be paid, Gilbert. I'm countin' on you."

"I'll be home soon." As soon as he found the gold, that is. But he wouldn't tell her that. He'd never tell her that. She might wonder why he stopped fishing and all the bills were paid on time, but he figured he'd say he won a small lottery. Everyone dreamed of that and believed it could happen.

She clicked off without a goodbye and he poured himself a cup of strong Orange Pekoe tea. There had to be some way he could get to Maggy Malone. She knew something. He was sure of it.

The way she leaned into Jimmy Daniel's body at the end.

"Hey, Gilbert." He recognized the woman's voice. Smokey, the café owner who was a Canuck's fan. She knocked again.

Opening the door wide, he motioned her to come in giving her his widest smile. She liked him. He always knew when a woman liked him. He could see it their eyes. Wait. An epiphany hit. She could be his way to get close to the target. His smile grew wider.

"Smokey, great to see you. You're looking good this morning."

"Good, eh?" she scoffed. But a blush rose in her age spotted skin. "It's our turn to patrol the docks."

"You sure about that? I got a hot pot of tea. I'd love to see you sit back on my boat, while I serve you a cup."

The muscles in her face relaxed for a moment, as if he'd just offered her a trip to a summer cottage, then her jaw tightened. "Thanks, but we got work to do."

Grabbing his jacket, he nodded. *Domineering bitch*. There's more than one way to skin a cat. He'd have to get her to talk while they walked.

Sly gave him an evil cat eye from her perch on top of the bed.

Sorry, Sly. Gilbert broke out in laughter— wild and unbridled.

Smokey's brows rose.

He leaned forward and kissed her hard on the lips, grabbing her fat ass with his hands and pulling her into him.

She dropped her clipboard.

CHAPTER 42

Music is . . . A higher revelation than all Wisdom &
Philosophy ~Ludwig van Beethoven

Peterson looked at the thirteen, neatly packed boxes of stuff Rita had left behind when she went to the pearly gates. A young constable he called Dudley, had stacked them into neat piles in the corner of his office. His real name was Colton Conners, but no one called him that unless they had to. Dudley fit better. He stared at the boxes as if they contained the Holy Grail and then looked at his boss.

"Sir, I didn't find the journal you're looking for."

Peterson expected that. Solving murders

never got easier. And Maggie Malone's link to Brother XII smelled of shit. "What did you find?"

Dudley coughed. "Well," he said, "stuff, lots and lots of stuff. I catalogued it all here." He handed him a stack of papers neatly typed and stapled. "I created a database on Excel."

"Of course you did."

"For example here," continued the young man, "in what I call box 1, there's a pair of thirty-year-old oven mitts with stripes on them, a small box with valuable ruby earrings, two envelopes filled with faded photographs and a shoebox full of photographic negatives of people."

Peterson cocked an eyebrow.

"But I've also sorted the items under categories: jewelry, mementos, and photos."

Dudley handed him his notes and Peterson scanned them. *Very thorough.* There were exactly 551 negatives. An impressive digital catalogue, but he knew from experience such detail didn't always catch the bad guys.

"Each box holds mementoes, some valuable, some not," the young constable added in a serious tone that would have fit well at a Christie's auction. "Items the old woman treasured."

"The journals?" He flipped through the pages skimming for the word.

"No, sir. At least not the journal you're looking for. I found a journal of her married life which talked about baking pies and raising her sons, and a journal from her young childhood which talked about her doll collection. No journal mentioned her life with Brother XII."

"Interesting," the inspector mused. Dudley must have spent hours reading through the woman's notes about her domestic life. Thorough. He could get used to having him around. He grimaced. *On the other hand, the guy's OCD crap would drive me nuts.*

"Sir?"

"A woman who's in the habit of writing about her life, doesn't stop and pick it up again. Especially in those days. I bet Rita wrote diaries her whole life. The question is, where is the journal with Brother XII in it?"

A jingle played on his desk computer indicating a Skype message. Peterson pushed buttons and his receptionist's face appeared on the screen, a big, gruff guy who drove a restored classic 1973 silver Thunderbird.

"Sir, Mr. John is ready to talk to you. He's anchored off Vancouver Island, near Ladysmith."

Finally. He'd been trying to reach the Decourcy fisherman for hours, leaving messages all over his islands to get his attention. He'd even tried hailing him on the marine radio. His pulse quickened as the video feed brought him a picture of a middle aged man with warm brown eyes and chubby cheeks. He wore a gray, wool sweater and a navy-blue toque.

"Hello. I'm Inspector Peterson."

"Heard you were looking for me," the man answered. His slow cadence had a melodic tone. He had the distinct accent of coastal First Nations people.

"Mr. John. I'm looking for the man that Edgar Whitley hired a little while back."

The fisherman broke into a rumbling laughter that sounded like waves rolling on shore. "That would be me. He was looking for Brother XII, ya know."

"That's what I heard."

The man laughed again. Had to like that laugh, genuine and deep. "Well, not really anyone's brother. Ya know, that cult guy took everyone's money and ran."

"I've heard that."

"Edgar wanted me to look for an area where the con man might have buried the treasure." He pushed up his hat. "It's not the first time I've had someone ask me where the gold might be hidden."

"Did you look?"

"Oh yeah. He was paying me well enough. I looked."

"And?"

"The coast is large and varied." John leaned back in his chair. "I didn't find a place that fit his description perfectly, but I found three that were close. I let him know."

"And?"

"That was it. But he seemed spooked the last time I talked to him. Like he was scared of me or something."

"Mr. John, we have it on record that he said you threatened him."

"Me? Why would I do that?"

"Gold?" Peterson said.

"Nah. That gold legend's a pile of shit. I'll go looking for a rainbow if someone's gonna pay me to do it, but Brother XII's gold is not out there. My people have lived in these parts since long before Brother XII. We know what goes on and I can tell you there's no gold left here." He snickered. "But it hasn't stopped people from lookin'."

Peterson tapped his pen on his desk. "Gold pulls all sorts of people out from under the rocks."

John nodded. "You know the story, eh? One guy who thought he'd found the treasure. He got to the bottom of one of Brother XII's burial sites and found a message from the brother: 'For fools and traitors—Nothing.'" John broke into his hearty laughter again. "The cult-guy got away with the gold, I tell ya, and he laughed at everyone he left behind."

Pain nudged between Peterson's eyes. "So you didn't follow Jimmy Daniels?"

"Nah. Edgar told me he thought that guy was close, but I didn't care. I don't' believe any of the shit. I was just working for a few extra bucks. Nothing against the law in that." The softness in his eyes hardened. "I'm not your man, Inspector."

Peterson massaged his temple. The room fell silent for a minute.

"Mr. John, did you happen to mention your business with Edgar Whitley to anyone?"

"Oh yeah, lots. We have a good time laughing at the bar about the gold diggers. There's a new sucker every season—no end to the line-up of fools hunting for the almighty dollar. They hear the story and they gotta look for themselves."

Peterson smiled. Maybe there was a lead here after all. "Could you name the people you told?"

Mr. John's laughter rolled through cyber-space and echoed into his office. "'Bout, half the country." He leaned forward with a big smile on his chubby face. "No way could I give you all their names."

"And I bet they all have marlin spikes."

The old fisherman narrowed his eyes. "Yeah, of course."

"Thank you, Mr. John. Constable Conners will take your complete statement. If it's thorough enough, I probably won't have to bother you again."

The man nodded. "Sure." The man's tone

spoke volumes. Without words he said he thought the whole exercise was stupid. Another example of white-man's law.

***

An hour later Dudley returned to take his seat on the other side of his boss's desk. "What?" Peterson asked.

"Is there anything you want me to do?" There was an eagerness mixed with urgency in the young man's voice that grated on his nerves like an out of tune violin. What did this guy eat for breakfast? The muscles in the young man's face tensed in the growing silence. He was ready for action, keen to look under the carpet of evil.

Peterson winced. His headache was hell and he'd been looking under that carpet too long, to be keen about it.

"Sir?" the constable said.

Tapping his desk with his broken pencil, Peterson stared at the Escher print on his wall, taking a moment of comfort in its endless, intertwined patterns. "I'm missing something," he said at last.

Dudley's eyes widened.

"It all comes down to motive. Why was Jimmy Daniels killed?"

"Number One: Brother XII's gold." Dudley pointed to the white board where they'd listed four possibilities.

"Could be. And then our suspects are everyone who knew Jimmy was involved in Edgar Whitley's search. We now know that includes almost all the fishermen on the west coast of Canada." Peterson rubbed the spot between his eyes.

"Two: Ownership of The Black Cat Blues Bar?" said Dudley.

"Yes, another possibility. The suspects are: Clarence, Joe, Maggy Malone, the third partner, and Logan Daniels."

"Three: Old jealousies?" The constable bit the side of his lip. "That's new."

"I added that one this morning. Brothers don't always get along." Only one suspect for that motive.

"And four, the last one, is: Unknown."

"Someone out there may have a motive we don't know about yet. I figure a good looking stud like Jimmy Daniels must have bruised a few hearts along the way."

Dudley blinked.

Could the man be that unworldly? "It happens." Peterson assured him. He looked back at the Escher print. "Some women want more from a man than he's ready to give." His eyes followed a stairway up and around, up and around. . . to nowhere.

"I want you to go through those boxes again,

and see if you can find anything tying her to Brother XII. I'm going to talk to Maggy Malone. She's the one common denominator in all of this."

When Dudley left the room with a box in hand, Peterson pulled out his cell and sent a text to Maggy: "No sign of the journal in Edgar's things. Any idea where it could be? Come see me. Now."

CHAPTER 43

Everything in the universe has a rhythm, everything dances. ~Maya Angelou

Maggy got the inspector's text. He hadn't found the journal and worse, she had to go visit him again. Wait. Would he know if she got his text? She had nothing to tell him, anyway. She clicked off her phone. She'd plead ignorance. *Yeah, like that's going to help with a cop.*

A deep sense of foreboding slithered through her blood and kept trying to get into her head. But it only made her angry. Where the hell was the murderer? She had better things to do with her life than play hide and seek with the devil. She wanted to face the bastard, once and for all.

Logan had phoned that he needed to hang with his dad and meet relatives coming in from all over the country. The funeral had been planned for tomorrow and a celebration of life the following day. Maggy thought she'd go to the celebration. It seemed the least she could do for the man who'd died in her arms.

Having taken a personal leave of three days from the dentist office she still had two free. Mei left last night to visit her grandfather in Maple Ridge who had pneumonia and needed help. Hunter was busy organizing Rat hunts. She really needed space from him right now anyway. Napoleon, the dog she walked, had been put in quarantine for some weird virus. Joe said he wanted to be alone to, "sort through stuff." She'd see him later tonight at the club. So Maggy was alone with her thoughts, the crappy, dark feeling and her anger. Great. . . just great.

She picked up her guitar and tunes scrolled through her mind, but none seemed to fit her mood. She put it down and picked up her iPad. She googled Brother XII. Ever since Jimmy cast his feral gaze on her at the bar, she had been having weird prescient feelings. The idea that it could have something to do with the old cult leader nagged her. A silly thought, but she would never know the truth unless she looked into it.

Maybe the brother and his black magic had somehow connected to her feelings and everything that was happening. Stranger things had happened in Vancouver.

First, she read articles about the growth of theosophical groups in the early twentieth century and how their esoteric beliefs in the relationship between man and the divine fuelled Brother XII's sermons and books.

She read document after document. They all told the basically the same stories about the cult leader, with different embellishments. Facts were few. Later in his life, after meeting theosophists, Edward Arthur Wilson became the cult leader Brother XII. He claimed he had a connection to a spiritual guide on another plane and talked about visions that included ancient Egyptian symbols.

Yeah right.

She rotated her shoulders, trying to ease her tension. Mei and her belief in the I Ching had taught her not to be skeptical of everything. What if some of the spiritual stuff was true? According to Wikiwit Theosophy went way back to three hundred years before Christ. Could all those people who believed in it, century after century, be wrong? What if spirits were playing with her? A chill crawled up her spine.

She rolled her head around and tried to shake out that thought. The hokey stuff gave her a headache. Maybe she'd become the butt of a nasty, karmic joke. The Greek concept of warring gods toying with humanity suddenly felt close and personal. She imagined a handsome, naked god standing above her and proclaiming, "Let's shower her with dead bodies." Laughing at her own black humor felt good.

Someone knocked on her door. Maggy jumped. She pulled her silk robe around her body and went to the security window. It was Smokey with a man she didn't know. But any friend of Smokey's should be okay.

When the door partly opened, Smokey breezed in. The man followed. Maggy took a step back and motioned for them to sit down.

"I need to talk to you Maggy," said Smokey, taking off her Canucks toque and not sitting. "This here's Gil. He's been docked at the marina for the last week and he's had a good view of your houseboat. Says he's seen some interesting things."

The man nodded Something about him made her want to gag. Maybe it was his rotting fish smell. Maggy tried to breathe through her mouth. In his forties, the guy wore loose, grubby jeans, a yellow rain jacket that looked as if it had seen a century of storms, and fisherman rubber boots. Brown hair with gray streaks hung out the bottom of his toque and he had a mole near his upper lip. But what bothered her even more than his smell was the way his eyes slunk away when she looked directly at him. Talk about rotting fish in Vancouver. She rotated her shoulders again.

"So what did you see?" Maggy asked.

"Some guy's been hangin' around your place. Dressed all in black." His voice was stone cold and utilitarian, like the girders under a bridge, capable of holding together sentences but not emotion. Maggy's creep-sense blared. Why did she dislike this guy so much? It would be nice if Smokey had a regular man. It might improve her temperament. If ever a woman needed a good screw it was Smokey.

"Tell her the rest," commanded Smokey more with her steely eyes than her words.

"Last night." He stopped and looked around the room.

Why the infatuation with my décor?
"Yeah—" she said.

"Durin' the storm, he was outside peering in your window."

Maggy looked at the window he pointed to. The venetian blinds weren't new, but they did give her privacy. The guy in black wouldn't be able to see much.

"Was he there for very long?"

"'Bout ten minutes, that I saw." His smile revealed a chipped, side tooth and tobacco stained teeth. Some people shouldn't smile. "The guy circled the house, looked again, then left."

She had thought someone was lurking outside. Her scalp tingled. "Can you tell me anything more about him?"

Gil frowned for a moment. "Sorry. I looked, cuz I thought he might be the Rat, but then I figured he was just a Peeping Tom, so I went back to watching the hockey game." He grimaced. "Figure a good looking woman like you has lots of men watching her."

"Good game," said Smokey.

The Canucks must have won. "Tall, short, anything?" Maggy asked.

"Medium, smaller than me, wore a raincoat."

Not a lot of help. "Wait. How did you know he wasn't the Rat?" There had to be something that distinguished the guy.

A slow smile spread across Gil's whiskered face. "Just a feelin', I guess." He scratched his chin. Was that dried egg stuck in his hair?

"I mean," continued Gil, " he wasn't planting any bombs, or starting fires. He wasn't even taking pictures. He was just looking. Stupid thing to do in the rain if you ask me, and I wouldn't have bothered saying anything except. . ." He stopped.

"Except I told him to," said Smokey. "I thought you should know. That murderer of yours has done a hat trick already and I don't want him taking you out with one of his marlins."

"Is this place safe?" asked Gilbert.

"Uh-huh," Maggy answered, still stuck with the image of a bloodied marlin spike.

"Windows secure?"

Did she want to have this conversation? She hesitated.

"I know a lot about security. I help people fix up their places when I'm not fishing. I could take a look around." His eyes scanned the room like a professional.

Maggy tried to remember where Logan had flung her thong. "Uh, I have a security advisor," she said. Boy did that sound odd. She had an advisor? But it was true, sort of. Logan was in the security business.

The fisherman's hooded eyes caught hers. He grumbled. What was with men grumbling today?

Another knock on the door. And when did her place become Grand Central Station?

Peterson strode into the room with his cop gait. Guess she'd forgotten to fully close it. The fall wind gusted in after him. A freaking circus. Would life ever get normal?

"Maggy." The gruffness in his voice made her want to change her name.

"Inspector Peterson, let me introduce you

to. . ." She turned towards Gil, but he'd slunk back, clearly not wanting to take part in a "meet and greet" with a cop. Interesting. He probably sold more than fish on his boat. That certainly wasn't uncommon on the coast.

"Not now. I need to talk to you. Alone." Peterson's words echoed as if they were in a tomb.

Smokey harrumphed and glared at the cop as she turned towards the door. Her man friend followed her out like a stray puppy who had found a new food source. Just plain weird, that one. And his smell. She waved them good-bye.

Maggy turned to Peterson and balled her fists. "They were my guests and you dismissed them like fleas on a dog's back. That's just not right. People who make other people feel small really piss me off."

He chuckled and looked down his nose. "I'm sorry if I interrupted your social life, but I need to find a murderer. And you didn't answer my text."

"You don't have time to be human?" She couldn't resist.

The corner of his mouth twitched.

"What do you want?" she asked.

"Has Logan talked to you at all about his brother?"

"Some."

"Did they have a good relationship?"

She let out a long, slow breath. Was she being asked to tattle on her lover? The last thing she wanted to do was say something that would make him look guilty.

"Ms. Malone."

"Considering my options, sir."

A slow grin softened his features. "The clock is ticking."

"I need a coffee," she said stretching. Her home had become a revolving doorway of people coming in and out, and the pain growing between her eyes told her she'd forgotten her mid-morning caffeine hit.

His square jaw hardened, and his eyes stared her down. "Maggy."

She wasn't going to let him win, totally, so she talked as she headed over to the kitchen counter and pulled out her coffee machine. "The Daniels boys were close from beginning to end. Logan's grieving hard. I don't think there's any point looking further there."

"Clarence. How do you feel about Clarence?"

Out of the blue? This guy had interesting interrogation techniques. "Aw… ful," she said in an unsteady voice that broke half-way. "And I haven't had the time to sit down and properly sort out my feelings and pay him proper respect. There's too much blood in the way."

"Do you feel in danger?"

"Shit, yeah." The on button switched to red and she waited, smelling the coffee as it brewed. The aroma comforted her, but did nothing for her queasy gut.

"Where's Logan?"

"With family."

"Hunter?"

"Looking for the Rat. They both check on me with texts and calls. Why?"

Peterson's mouth turned down.

"I want you to come into my office with me. We're going to go over your first statement of what happened the night of Jimmy's murder. I want to see if you remember something you left out, like a smell, or a shadow. Anything. It's the details that will lead us to the killer."

"The police station? Again?"

"Maggy." He looked down his nose. Not good.

"I haven't had my coffee." She ran a hand through her tangled mane. She needed some time for herself. "Or my morning shower."

Peterson did his cop shrug.

She glared at him.

"Put it in a travel mug."

CHAPTER 44

Did you know that our soul is composed of harmony?
~Leonardo Da Vinci

Gilbert slammed the cabin door of his boat. Pretending he cared about Smokey and the dock Rat pissed him off, big time. The crazy hippies on this dock deserved fires. They weren't normal, for Christ's sake, not like people further north, or on the islands. They were city assholes who liked their coffee with foam and their food green.

He'd spent two hours walking around the docks checking on boats with Smokey. He needed her for now, so he'd kept a smile plastered on his face. She ranted on about who should be the starting goalie in the next Canucks game. There was only one choice: Alberto. Anything else was suicide, but he let her rant and said nothing. Bile rose in his throat.

Finally, when he couldn't take the hockey banter any longer, he said, "Smokey," in as soft a voice as he could muster. "I need a break."

"A break?" She lifted her eyebrow.

"Yeah. I got an aching hip, an old injury from my time in Afghanistan." It was the truth.

Her eyes softened. "Okay. Thanks for coming this far."

"Not a problem. We got to keep each other safe, after all."

She nodded and a smile warmed her weathered face. Then she cupped him, and he stepped back out of her reach. "Later," he said. The woman knew how to get her point across, but he had had enough of her for one day.

Smokey headed over to the Blue Heron Marina. He waved to her, and then went back to the Shady Lane dock with the houseboats. It was a perfect time to check out Maggy's place. She'd left with the cop in an unmarked car ten minutes ago.

He needed to see the chart rolled up on her kitchen table. It could be a treasure map with an "x" marked on it. Limping to stay in character, he moved down the old wooden dock.

When he got to her houseboat he tried the door. Locked. He felt above it and found the key. After he looked in every direction and felt confident no one was watching him, he opened the door and went inside.

It smelled of Maggy, sweet and saucy. What a bitch. He knew her kind. They teased men. Hell, even the way she walked hardened him. He didn't want to have to hurt her, but he would if she got in his way. He sat at her kitchen table and opened the roll of charts.

On top lay a chart numbered 3310-Sheet 4, Porlier Pass to Departure Bay. Large area. Most of the chart showed Gabriola Island. Hmmm. Close to Decourcy Island where Brother XII had his commune. It was possible he took the gold there.

He scanned the chart and the ones beneath. They were all connected to Gabriola. But none of them had an x marking the spot.

And the cop had Maggy. What if she remembered something? What if she actually saw him the night he killed Jimmy?

Could he kill a woman? Hell, at this point what difference did it make? One murder, two. . . man or woman. His ship was headed straight to hell anyway. No saving his fucked-up soul.

But then he had known he had no chance of living a righteous life after Afghanistan. The image of the carnage he'd wreaked drifted into his head. His throat tightened. *Fuck it.* I'm going to live my life.

Before he danced with Satan he'd have fun. Live the high life. All he needed was the gold. He'd show them. He'd show them all. No one would look down on him again. He would have everything he wanted. Scratching his beard he released the edges of the chart and it rolled back up.

He searched the kitchen and living room. Nothing. Climbing the ladder to her loft he scanned the lower floor. He checked it all, every nook and cranny.

In the loft, the bed was covered in a mess of blankets, tangled sheets and pillows that spoke of a busy night. On the left side table sat a bunch of stuff. Kleenex and a box of condoms. Then something black on the floor caught his eye. It was a leather wallet.

Opening it he found Logan's driver's license, credit cards and one picture. He pulled it out. A cute little girl missing a front tooth with a wide smile. He turned it over "Hugs and kisses, Daddy, love Sasha," was printed on the back. "November." Taken this month. He flipped to the other side. Under her cherub face was the school name: St. Mary's Elementary, and below that her home address. Bingo. Taking a deep breath, he stared into her bright little eyes. Did he have the balls?

He put the picture back into the wallet and put the wallet in his pocket. Then he turned the bedroom upside down. Nothing. It was getting late and he had things to do.

The time had come to take action, no matter the cost. They knew something he didn't. He was sure of it. And now he had a way to get Logan to tell him the location of the gold.

CHAPTER 45

The truest expression of a people is in its dance and music. ~ Agnes de Mile

When Maggy opened the door of her houseboat a weird, musky smell hit her first, then a faint vibration of something truly nasty, like a psychic echo. Ye gads, she was really beginning to lose it. Smells, echoes, what next? Chanting monkeys? Time to take it in stride. She slammed the door behind her and rushed to get ready for her dinner date, the first in six months.

***

Maggy and Logan met at Giovanni's, an Italian restaurant known for fine cuisine and intimate seating. After they sat down Logan leaned over and said, "Can you pay for dinner tonight."

She raised a brow.

"I lost my wallet." His face reddened. "I think it's at your place. We'll settle up later."

"No problem," she said. She couldn't afford this dinner, but that was the least of her worries right now.

The menus arrived and, soon after, Tuscany bread with aged, fig-flavored, balsamic vinegar and olive oil. Candlelight dinners for two were supposed to be romantic, but it felt like a crowded table. The friggen ghosts of the murder victims hovered in her head, and she supposed by the drawn look on Logan's face that, he felt their presence too.

"Dead people really kill the ambience, eh?"

"I keep thinking about the marlin spike." His voice caught on "spike."

She reached for his hand, cool to the touch. If only she could turn back the clock a week, to the time before the murders. Then maybe she'd be more ready for a romantic dinner. Even the expensive wine Logan ordered tasted off.

They spoke of their days. Maggy gave him a rundown of her chat with the inspector. Logan told her about spending time with his family, swapping stories about Jimmy. The air grew heavier with loss as each story reminded her of how a young man had been taken in his prime. She ran a hand through her hair. "I wish I could do something to ease your pain."

He shook his head and then looked at her with tenderness. "Talking helps," he said. "And being with you makes me feel more alive than I have felt in years. It's a good thing, you and me, a very good thing."

She nodded. What else could she do?

Their meal had been *bene*, in a distinctly Italian way, rich in flavors that reminded her of Tuscany sunshine. They lingered over tiramisu and coffee.

"The highlight of my day," Logan said, "was being with Sasha, my little girl. She just turned five and is the one perfect thing in my world. My little angel.

"Was she close to Jimmy?"

"Oh yeah. She loved him with all her heart. He'd get down on the floor and play games with her for hours. She doesn't really get death. She told me. . ." The emotion in his voice brought him to a stop. "She said. . ." Logan stopped again and took a deep breath. "'Uncle Jimmy wants us to be happy, always. He's waiting for us in heaven.'" Tears welled in his eyes.

"She's a smart little girl."

His face relaxed. "She lost another tooth this week. When she smiles she looks so darn cute."

"Proud papa."

Logan reached for her hand on the table and was about to say something when his cell phone rang. "I'll just take this. It says 'unknown' but could be someone in the family. I've been giving everyone my number today." He shook his head as if sharing his number was as difficult as baring his soul to the universe.

Maggy put her spoon into the delicate mocha colored pudding and lifted a mouthful.

"What!" Logan's eyes widened. The color drained from his face. Maggy put down her spoon.

"Who took her? When?" Sweat formed on his brow. He stood up.

"What man?" His chin trembled. "He took her from her home? How could that happen?"

Holding onto the edge of his chair he listened to the caller. "Have you phoned the police?" Anger rolled into his voice.

"Me? What have I. . .Oh shit." He dropped the cell phone. As it fell to the table, a woman's voice rattled on.

Maggy grabbed the phone. Logan took it back from her and shook his head.

"I'll take care of it," he said and clicked it off.

He looked at Maggy. His face was deathly white. His eyes bulged, nostrils flared, and she could see tremors take his body. His cell phone made another noise.

"A text." He read it out loud: "I have Sasha. Where is the gold?"

Logan's face sunk. "The murderer's got Sasha." His voice caught. "Sasha." He put his head in his hands.

"So tell him," Maggy said.

Logan lifted his head. "How do I know he won't hurt her anyway?"

"Just—tell him."

"That I know nothing? I have to do what's best for Sasha." Logan looked away from her and breathed out slowly. "I'll phone Peterson."

"Not the police." Maggy's heart sank into her personal cesspool of bad cop memories.

"They know how to deal with kidnappers," he said firmly.

"Yeah, maybe." *But they don't care about Sasha the way you do.* How could she tell him that without upsetting him more, that policemen are only human, and they're bound by protocols made in offices not hearts?

Logan sat down and punched buttons on his cell. Maggy drank down the rest of her hot coffee, feeling it burn her throat all the way down. There had to be another way.

Logan stated fact after fact like a shopping list. Sweat beaded on his brow and the rancid smell of his fear hung in the air.

"Yeah, yeah, okay," Logan said and ended

the call.

"I'm meeting Peterson at his office. We're going to go over all the options." He must have seen her apprehension in her face. "Maggy. I heard what you said, but I want his help. "There's got to. . ." He choked on his words. "There's got to be a way for me to save my baby."

The image of a child's body with a marlin spike in it crossed her mind like a whip from hell, and her chest froze. How could she make him listen to her? "The guy's not going to like you bringing in the police."

Logan glared at her. "Like I care."

She opened her mouth and closed it.

"Aren't you coming?" He stood, doing up his jacket

She swallowed. "No." She couldn't stand by and watch a child be murdered. All over gold. This had to stop. Somehow the whole mess had something to do with her. As silly as it sounded to her reasoning mind, she had become the vortex of this evil. She had known this right from the beginning; felt it in her bones. Just as she now knew she would be the one to make it stop. A strange determination rose like anger within her, empowering her with purpose. "I'll catch up with you later. I have something to do."

He winced and stared at her for a few seconds. Then he turned and ran out of the restaurant.

Maggy sat alone. If only she had the information the murderer wanted, a bargaining chip in this horrid game of death. Where the hell was the journal? What had Peterson said? They'd searched Rita's boxes for hours. So if it wasn't there, where could it be?

Feeling the answer lay just beyond her fingertips she replayed every moment she'd spent with Edgar. There had to be something he said that would lead her to the book. He'd talked about Rita's life, about Brother XII, about the islands. . . Nothing. He'd said nothing. Okay, if he didn't say anything that would help her, maybe he did something to. . . . lead her to a clue. What? What? She played his actions over in her mind. Just as Peterson said from the beginning, she knew something; she just had to figure out what it was. Again she went over every movement of his body, every bead of sweat that rolled down his wiry neck.

Then it hit her. Sweet baby Jesus. Was that it?

The very first time she saw Edgar he stood in the library stacks in the reference section. He had his hand on the books. Could he have left it there? Wouldn't it be found in the library stacks? She ran a hand through her hair.

Her chances were slim to none. But her intuition said she "had it." She went back over everything he said, and then again everything he did, and the only thing that stood out in her mind was the image of him when she first saw him in the library, and she knew what she had to do.

She paid the bill and ran for her car.

CHAPTER 46

Music is the resonance of the soul. ~ Maggy Malone

The library was open late, one of the new initiatives of the city to make the community more livable. Sometimes politicians did good things.

Maggy went directly to where Edgar had stood looking at the shelves. There were rows of books, tomes of knowledge rarely looked at. She pulled one so that it tipped forward. Nothing. Did the same for the next, and the next and the next. She looked at every book on the shelf. Nothing.

Would he leave the journal inside a book? She started the same row again and shook out every book. When she was half way down the line, a pile of papers fell out. She picked up the papers from the floor. Notebook pages with beautiful handwriting.

Rita's journal? Could it be?

Grabbing the pages, she walked over to the nearest table. The same one she had sat at with Edgar. She opened the papers and started reading. There were a lot of pages to go through.

She sent a text to Joe: "The murderer has taken a kid—won't be coming tonight—replace me." She clicked send and went back to reading.

Joe responded: "Be careful."

The lights in the library flickered just as she read the first details of Brother XII's black magic rituals. Closing time.

She gathered her papers and headed for home, racing through the city traffic like a desperate woman trying to outrun a murderer. The weather had turned nasty, the way it does before a big storm comes in. The roads were slick from rain.

Once home she took Rita's journal out again and combed through the last details. She wouldn't call Logan unless she had something definite. The sound of rain on her roof, which usually made her feel cozy inside, sounded threatening. Time slowed. *Focus, Maggy, focus.*

She poured through page after page of old-fashioned prose detailing the local plants and animals. If she heard the word "sublime" one more time she thought she would retch. She pushed through it all. Towards the end an image of the location began to form in her head. At first it wasn't distinct, but it became clearer and clearer. Little details here and there came together to create a picture in her mind.

She started the last page. Her phone buzzed.

A text from an 'unknown'. She clicked it open: "I've got Sasha. Tell me what you know or she dies." He signed it M. Spike. Not funny.

Sweet baby Jesus, she needed to do this right. She wrote, "You're the murderer?" and pressed send, wanting to stall him while she conjured up some kind of plan.

"What do you think?"

Her throat constricted.

"You're not responding Maggy. That makes me nervous. When I get nervous. . . THINGS HAPPEN."

"Relax," she wrote. "I have what you want."

"TELL ME. . ."

The tiny hairs on the back of her neck rose. So much depended on her doing this right. She swallowed and punched her response. "I'll take you there."

"You know where it is?"

"I know everything. I know the general location and the details for finding it when we get there."

"TELL ME OR…"

"I don't trust you."

"You want Sasha?" She could almost hear him laugh.

"It's on an island."

"I got a boat."

"Where?"

Her door burst open and banged against the wall. A strong gust of wind blew in the rain. Gilbert stood there with a cell in his right hand, looking like the devil himself.

"Let's go," he said in a voice as cold as the grave.

"I. . ." Things weren't going the way she'd planned. She hadn't had time to hide the notes or text Logan. If she left now. . .he'd kill them both.

"Maggy, get your jacket, and bring the charts you need."

She stood and faced the asshole. Her heart lodged in her throat. Her body trembled, but she ignored it. "I have to go to the bathroom, and then I'll be ready. Is Sasha okay?"

"She's still breathing." He grabbed her arm roughly and took her cell phone. His fingers dug into her. He threw her cell phone on the floor and stomped on it, hard. The sound was like another nail being hammered into her coffin. "Be quick," he said.

In the head Maggy took out her lipstick and wrote on the mirror, "Drumbeg-Smokey's guy." What were the chances Logan would come to her place? What were the chances he or anyone else would look in her bathroom and get the message before she and Sasha were sent to the bottom of the Pacific Ocean?

Something inside her said she still had a chance. Funny how hope was the last thing to leave. But as long as she was breathing, she'd fight the bastard.

"Ready," she said, when she came back out into the living area.

"If you left him a message he's not going to get it in time." His wicked laugh bounced between the walls of the room. Bastard.

CHAPTER 47

Life hurts. . . but there is always music.
~ Maggy Malone

*F*ucked up—*my life's so fucked up.*
Logan raced to the police station. He
had to get Sasha back. Had to make
things right. He ran an amber light, then another.
The rain fell hard, making visibility poor and the
roads slick. When he ran his third light his luck ran
out. A blue pickup sideswiped him. He felt the hit,
felt the car lose control. . . knew he had to ride it
out.

His car spun. Taking his foot off the brake
he tried to straighten his path. Gripping the steering
wheel with all his might, the car spun once, twice,
and then a third time, stopping abruptly against a
telephone pole. His body wrenched forward, then

whipped back as the air bag engaged.

A guy in green work overalls and a slicker pried his door open and helped him out crawl out. At least he was conscious. Rain poured down. Logan stood up slowly, his heart pumped in his ears and his mind buzzed. Couldn't he do anything right? He looked over at the pickup. An angry lady with black hair waved a fist in the air and strode his way. "What the fuck, mister. You ran a red."

"Sasha," he mumbled.

There must have been something in his eyes that made her stop. "What?" she screeched.

"My daughter. A murderer's holding my daughter. I got to get to. . . "

The woman blinked and took a step back. "You should call the police mister."

Logan licked fluid off his lip and tasted blood.

The man in overalls said, "An ambulance is on its way. The police will come."

There would be so many questions about the fucking accident. By the time he got out of this mess. . . Shit. There was no telling what the murderer would do. Should he phone Peterson?

Fuck it. He punched the top of his car. Now his hand and his head hurt. Sirens approached. The lady with the black hair talked to the man in overalls. Probably trying to get them to stay and make a statement. He knew he was in the wrong. But it didn't matter. Nothing mattered but Sasha.

Logan walked slowly towards the sidewalk. Once there, he picked up his pace. A couple hundred meters from the wreckage he began to run towards Maggy's. Together they'd work this all out. She may have been right about the police. Calling them was a knee jerk reaction. She understood the world better. He could trust her.

Law abiding citizens call the cops, but this murderer was ruthless, and to fight him, to beat him, he needed to be more creative, needed to do whatever he had to do to get Sasha back. That's what Maggy tried to tell him. It took a car accident to get it through his thick skull. Maggy understood. He phoned her as he ran. She didn't answer.

When he got to Maggy's, her place was empty. Fuck.

He pulled out his cell. No messages. It rang. It was Peterson.

"Peterson," he said, "Sorry, I had a car accident. I'll be awhile. Can you, uh." He clicked off. Why lie? Better to just work under the radar. That's what Maggy tried to tell him. His head ached. His body trembled.

Maggy? It wasn't like her to leave no message or text. He didn't know her that well yet, but he knew she took care of the people close to her. Nothing seemed out of place. Guitars, music sheets, half-empty coffee cups.

Blood flowed freely into his mouth now. He went to the head to check it out and he saw her message. "Drumbeg Park!" Fuckin hell. He should have guessed it. The Garry oaks and petroglyphs that Edgar Whitley was looking for were there. Drumbeg Park on Gabriola Island. Everything about the location made sense now.

Wait. Why would she go on her own? Why

leave a cryptic message in lipstick. Fuck. He went back to the main room. On the table lay an old, leather-bound book, and on the floor Maggy's smashed cell phone. She wouldn't have contacted the murderer on her own, would she? How could she?

Running onto the dock with the journal and charts, he ran straight into Hunter talking to Smokey under an umbrella. They must be doing a patrol.

They turned to look at him. Smokey's jaw dropped. Hunter just stared.

"You're face is bleeding, lover boy," Smokey said.

"Maggy's in trouble. I need a boat—fast." He gulped air. "She said it was your guy."

"Gilbert?" The color in Smokey's face drained.

"Does he have a boat?"

"A fishing boat – a trawler. I saw it leave about twenty minutes ago. I thought he was crazy going out before the storm."

Hunter didn't ask any questions. With his head, he motioned Logan to follow. They ran together over to the next marina and leaped into a Zodiac with two 75 horsepower outboard motors. Hunter reached under the console and pulled out a hidden key.

"Where are they heading?" he asked.

"Gabriola with the murderer and my daughter Sasha." Logan opened up the chart.

Hunter started the engines, shaking his head and muttering. "Murder's been stalking Maggy worse than a fucking albatross."

Smokey caught up to them huffing and puffing. "Here," she said, handing Hunter a gun. "I've been carrying it on patrols." She stopped to take a breath, and spoke in a halting manner. "Be careful. There's a wicked Southeaster brewing."

CHAPTER 48

Music is my life. ~ Maggy Malone

Gilbert's fishing boat smelled worse than he did: a disgusting mixture of fish entrails, fried spam and cat feces. Maggy breathed through her mouth, so as not to gag. In the corner sat sweet little Sasha, with duct tape on her mouth, her eyes wide with fear and plump cheeks wet with tears. A thick wad of gray duct tape bound her wrists. Her feet were tied with rope to one of the table legs.

The fisherman shoved her onto a chair.

"Take the tape off her mouth," Maggy demanded.

Gilbert pulled a gun from behind his back and aimed it between Maggy's eyes. "When we're out at sea, you can take the tape off her mouth and hands, but the rope stays. I'm not losing her overboard." His voice remained steady and low, all business and practicality, as if he were talking about transporting a case of oranges. He clicked off the safety on his gun and fingered the trigger.

She nodded.

"So where are we headed?"

"Drumbeg Park, Gabriola Island," she said.

"Drumbeg?" His body jolted as if he'd been hit with a blast of cold air. "And you know where to look when we get there?"

"Yes."

Without another word he left them in the putrid smelling cabin and went topside. When he closed the cabin door, she heard a lock click into place. She rushed over to Sasha.

"My name is Maggy. I know your dad."

The little girl's swollen red eyes pleaded with her.

"I'll do everything I can to get us safely away from. . . from the bad fisherman."

Maggy dabbed at Sasha's tears with a tissue. They flowed freely and her nose ran. Had Maggy made the right decision contacting Gil, or had she put the child in more danger? The little girl's body trembled. Maggy took off her own jacket and put it around Sasha as best she could.

Sasha tilted her head in response. She had curly brown hair, freckles and a button nose. An extraordinarily beautiful child. A picture of innocence. Maggy held her.

Sasha stopped crying and relaxed into her embrace. Maggy sang. She didn't know what else to do. She chose her favorite song from childhood, "Hush-a-bye, don't you cry. . ."

The diesel engine roared to life adding its nauseous gas to the mix of horrid smells below, and a rumbling noise echoed through the tiny cabin. A mangy, calico cat appeared out of the shadows, stretched and walked up to them. She jumped onto the table beside Sasha and nudged her shoulder. Then she lay down and closed her eyes.

The engine slipped into gear and the boat began to make way. Maggy stroked Sasha's cheek. The little girl's eyes had dried, but fear showed in the tightness of her face.

As Maggy stroked Sasha's hair, she said, "I'm going to take the tape off, honey. I'll do it fast, but it's going to hurt.

Wide-eyed, Sasha nodded.

Maggy ripped the tape. Sasha let out a little scream.

"Sorry, there was no easy way."

"I want my daddy."

Maggy could hardly hear her above the drone of the engine, and the sound of the waves hitting the hull. She tried to answer her, but her words were lost in the noise. Sasha nuzzled into her.

"Bang." A wave hit the boat hard. I shuddered off-course. Dishes rattled, and a pot on the stove slid across the top to the far side, caught by a safety bar. The hanging light swung back and forth. Wind whistled through the rigging. It must be a Southeaster.

Another wave hit, hard. The boat shook and creaked. The engine droned. The diesel smell made her nauseous. Then another wave. . . and another. The boat bobbed and weaved like a floating cork in the high winds crossing the Salish Sea. Part of her wished she could see the water. She'd never experienced this kind of heavy weather in a boat.

They were below. If the boat capsized she'd need to get them out. If Gilbert got washed off the deck they might only have a few minutes. People become trapped below when a boat goes over and they drown, but not right away. It would take time for all the air to escape. Time enough to contemplate death. She shuddered.

As the boat rocked like a bucking bronco, Maggy searched through the side lockers until she found life jackets. A wave slammed the starboard side and her body smashed against the stove.

She made Sasha put on one of the jackets and then put the other on herself.

We'll die of hypothermia within fifteen minutes in these waters and no one can reach you that fast after a Mayday call in these conditions. Still, she had to prepare them for a rescue. Sometimes she hated the sailor in her.

Another big wave hit and Sasha heaved. "Daddy," she cried. "I want my daddy." Her small voice, amidst the sound of the waves and howling wind, pierced Maggy's heart. She had to do something.

Her stomach rolled and her head spun like an old LP record. She lived on the sea, and loved to sail, but she'd never go out in weather like this. It was suicidal. Another sign that the murderer was insane.

She grabbed a roll of paper towel and threw sheets of it on Sasha's vomit. Checking the locker under the sink she found a bucket and put it under Sasha's head. "It's going to be all right," she said, hoping the little girl could hear her. She stroked Sasha's hair. "It's going to be alright. Your Daddy will find us."

If only she believed that. Maggy didn't believe in being saved by a knight in shining armor, never had. She had to take care of the rescue. There had to be a way.

Another wave crashed into the side. Maggy bent over the bucket.

CHAPTER 49

Singing heals my wounds. Maggy Malone

"Thanks, Smokey, over." Hunter switched off the marine radio.

"He's got a diesel engine on his fishing boat. He'd make eight knots in good conditions. Less in these conditions."

Logan nodded. Normally he had no trouble being at sea. He would become slightly nauseous at the most; but he'd never been out in this kind of weather. The storm was picking up quickly.

Chanel 16 on the boat radio spit out the end of a weather warning: "Conditions Environment Canada—changing to gale force winds. . ."

Shit. It felt even worse than that. Way worse. He kept his eye on the horizon to steady his senses and breathed deeply.

He used the radio to hail Smokey. Told her to let Peterson know where they were heading. Hunter, on the helm, nodded his head in approval. It wouldn't hurt to have backup when they got there. Maggy may hate the police, but he wanted all the help he could get.

Hunter powered through the waves, throttle fully open, heading straight for Silva Bay, the southernmost point on Gabriola Island.

Logan scanned the rising seas. The wind hit them full force on their port beam, pushing them hard to the northwest. The engines worked hard to keep the boat on course. Five foot waves splashed over their port side. "Greenies," sea people call them. Trouble from the deep.

No boats were on the water. Not even a ferry. No seaplanes in the air. Logan turned up the volume on channel 16, the emergency station monitored by all boats. Just audible above the sound of the wind and the thrashing waves, it crackled, "Marine forecast, issued by Environment Canada at 8:00 for today tonight and next day. The next scheduled forecast will be issued at 3:30 p.m. Visibility poor. Strait of Georgia, north of Nanaimo: strong gale warning in effect. Winds southeast forty to forty-seven knots increasing to southeast fifty knots. Storm warning by next morning. Chop two meters."

"How do you think the fishing boat's going to handle this?" Logan shouted.

Hunter didn't answer, which said more than he wanted to hear.

"Entrance Island," the marine emergency station announced, "winds at forty-seven knots and a two-point-five meter chop."

Shit. They were heading for a full out storm. No one goes out on the Pacific Ocean in conditions like this—unless they have to.

But fishermen don't get to choose their weather. Hopefully the man would know what he was doing and keep Sasha and Maggy safe.

As the wind picked up, dense streaks of foam formed along the top of the black water in the direction of the wind. The waves grew so high they started to crest and topple over, tumbling and rolling over, and over, creating a hell of a bumpy ride. Spray messed with their visibility. On a good day a boat like this could make fifty knots and make the crossing in an hour, but the elements were against them.

Hunter held the helm firmly, his jaw clenched, navigating through the tumultuous sea as best he could. He would steer their craft through a trough between six foot waves for as long as he could, and then let the boat rise over a big wave and down the other side. Then he would get back into another trough. Spray drenched them. The cold wind and even colder ocean water chilled him to the bone.

Logan held on to the side of the hull and prayed. He hadn't done that since he was ten when his dog was run over. But he didn't know what else to do. *God, help us. God help us all. I'll do anything, anything. Please, help us.*

What else could he say? Did he deserve

redemption? Maybe not. He prayed for grace. If he had paid more attention to people and worried less about business he would be a more deserving man. Maybe all this had happened because he'd fucked up his life. He hadn't kept track of his brother, or at least not close enough. He hadn't put his family first in his life.

But Sasha, sweet Sasha, deserved to be saved even if he didn't. And hell, he wanted a chance with Maggy.

Hunter might be an asshole, but he was a damn good man to have at your side when the seas got rough. Despite the worst conditions imaginable, they made way towards Gabriola and stayed afloat.

Please, God, I know you save the wicked, the lost and the lonely. I'm all those things. Forgive me for my rotten ways and my crooked soul. Lend me a hand.

Another greenie crested the side of the boat. . .and another. Logan held on with all his might, fighting the water that threatened to wash him overboard. A strange sense of peace filled him from inside, a resignation that he would die, but maybe not today... *As long as there is life there is hope.*

The life jackets were probably stored in the aft locker, but he wouldn't risk moving around. Besides, if they were swept overboard they would die of hypothermia. No one would be able to get to them in time. Unless he had a full survival suit on, he'd be a goner. The lockers weren't large enough to hold full suits. Stay put and hold on.

Logan had no choices left. He had to trust

that. . . Trust? How could he trust a God who had let his brother be murdered, who'd let his marriage fall apart, who'd let his innocent daughter be kidnapped? He exhaled slowly.

Another greenie. It hit the radio washing the receiver off the stand. Shit. All they needed was a broken radio.

Yeah, he had to trust that this time things would work out.

The sound of the wind imprinted itself on his heart. Could any boat withstand this force for long? The energy of the storm kept building.

Hunter looked crazed, like a wild pirate daring the elements. But the guy could make any facial expression he wanted as long as he got them there.

Another greenie, and the wind tossed them aside like a child's toy boat in the bath tub. In a gust of wind coupled with the smash of a wave, Hunter lost his grip on the steering wheel. Logan kept his left hand on the side of the boat and used his right to grab Hunter's arm, keeping him in the boat. Logan's gut clenched. Hunter gripped the side of the wheel again and righted himself.

As the vessel turned southeast into the wind, Hunter regained control of the helm. Logan released him. Too close. Hunter had almost gone overboard and Logan couldn't make this trip alone.

Hunter pulled hard on the wheel, returning the boat to its heading, as the wind howled around them. Logan didn't need to look at the chart to know that Hunter was heading for the Commodore Channel. Two small islands to the southeast of

Gabriola, Acorn and Gaviola islands, would break the weather, and they'd be able to cruise through the passage to Drumbeg Park. They were only making half the pace they would in good conditions, but they moved forward.

Logan kept the image of Sasha and Maggy safe in his mind. His stomach rolled with the waves. The spray made it hard to see, but as they crested the next wave he finally glimpsed land.

It seemed impossible, but the wind picked up even more. If only the damn radio hadn't stopped working. Hell what did he need a radio for? There were no longer gale-force winds. They were in the thick of a storm now. The waves had long, overhanging crests and rose nine feet. Dense, streaks of foam gave the sea a white appearance. The tumbling of the waves made it look heavy. Visibility worsened. Could they make land?

Hunter kept his eyes steady on the horizon with the throttle fully open. His never stopped to look back or look at a chart. The man motored by instinct.

The waves continued to bounce them in every direction, until they made the entrance of the channel. Hunter used the GPS on his cell phone to navigate through the treacherous Gabriola shoals. Wind bursts whipped through them, carrying the boat shuddering to the south. It felt as if an angry Poseidon was trying to blow them back out to sea.

And then they were on the inside, between Gaviola and Acorn Islands. He'd sailed through here many times and knew the slim passage well. It had been two hours of hell, fighting the wind and the sea. But it was over now. Here they were protected. The wind still blew hard, but the force of the waves broke on the small islands. The swells grew smaller. Logan breathed fully for the first time since he'd jumped into the boat. Sea water drenched his body.

Hunter knew these waters as well as he did. They'd follow this passage through the flat top islands and then head north to hug the shores of Gabriola. They would pass by Breakwater Island and then navigate around Rogers Reef. Once they were clear of that they'd either risk motoring into the storm and head straight for Drumbeg Park or take shelter at Kendrick Island until the wind died down. What they did would depend on how much worse the storm became, and how crazy Hunter was at the helm. He was ready to risk it all.

Maggy had written Drumbeg on the mirror, but the murderer could have taken them anywhere, especially in this storm. He could be anchored somewhere safe, or . . . Shit. there was no way of knowing what the asshole would do. Who could get into the head of a man who'd killed three people?

The motors droned on. Still—no sign of the fishing boat or any other boat on the horizon.

CHAPTER 50

Music is my universe, ~Maggy Malone

Maggy held Sasha in her arms as the fishing boat crashed into wave after wave and plummeted down their sides. The only thing worse than being in a storm at sea, was being below deck, in a storm at sea They were tossed in every direction, like running shoes in a washing machine. The boat shuddered in the sheer force of the wind. All the time, the diesel motor droned. Its nauseous fumes enveloped them in a toxic swill, making it hard to breathe.

"It's going to be okay," she'd say each time they were tossed, hoping the little girl believed her. The fear of capsizing grew and held her mind captive. Vivid images of sea wrecks drowned her thoughts. When she stopped vomiting her stomach clenched into a knot and stayed that way. Her head throbbed, her mouth dried, but she held it together. Her biggest worry was that Gilbert would be washed off the deck and the boat would be without a captain and at mercy of the sea.

After what felt like an eternity the motion of the boat calmed. The engine droned through the chuck with a smooth precision, no longer tossing as it met every wave. She stroked Sasha's hair. Did she dare hope?

The motor chugged on. After about twenty minutes they came to a stop. Where were they? Through the porthole, she could see land about two-hundred meters to the port side. No dock in sight, but there were big steel rings attached to a twenty-foot wall of sandstone sculpted by the sea. It must be the side of a cliff. Would he moor here and wait out the storm? She tried to swallow, but her throat was dry.

The boat slowed. The clanking of an anchor chain mixed with the whistling of the wind. The boat motored a little further and then stopped. He had set anchor.

Gilbert's heavy footsteps went up to the bow, and then to the stern. No point trying to escape. Sasha's muscles relaxed and color returned to her face. They'd made it to a safe harbor, and after that horrible storm Maggy couldn't help but feel some elation. They'd weathered the worst Mother Nature could throw at them.

But there was still the threat of the marlin spike.

The cabin door burst open and Gilbert appeared in a soaking wet slicker with a scowl so nasty it would chill Jack the Ripper. "We have to wait out the storm," he said.

"She's been sick. Do you think we could. . ."

Scowling he grabbed the bucket they had used and returned topside to toss it. When he returned, and threw it on the floor.

"Aren't we going to Drumbeg Park?" Her voice sounded shakier than she wanted it to.

"We're less than a nautical mile away. I've anchored behind Kendrick Island. When the storm eases we'll make the crossing in my runabout."

"That close?" she asked trying to gauge his mental state by his reactions.

"Half a mile. But we'd never make it in these conditions. We're on the edge of Gabriola Passage which is running eight knots right now. The storm'll ease off, and then we'll be able to make way. The water gets wild even at the edges of the passage and, depending on the tide, can be impassable. But I know these waters. I can get around it."

None of this was news to her. "A small skiff?"

"I can't take this big boat into the shallow bay. We'd hit bottom. The small boat with a small motor will run us ashore at the point, then you'll lead the way to the gold."

"You could go alone."

"No. You said you know the details. We'll find it together."

"But Sasha?"

"She stays here."

"Oh." She didn't like the sound of that at all. Small boat, fast current, a child left alone. . .

Sasha started crying. "I want my daddy." She gave Gilbert a fierce look. "He's. . . he's going to kill you for being so mean. He's bigger than you."

Gilbert laughed, and then laughed harder. Deep ugly laughs that rolled through the room like a battering ram, knocking down what little hope Maggy had been trying to build. No doubt about it. He thought he had them cold.

Sasha cried harder and Maggy stroked her head wet with sweat. There had to be some way out of this.

Gilbert stopped laughing. "Shut her up." He stomped over to the cabin door. Sasha began to sob. He turned back towards them. "If you don't shut her up, I will." The door slammed behind him.

The storm raged all night. Tucked behind the island they could hear the waves pounding the shores, but they were safe. The fisherman didn't return. He must have chosen to stay up in his pilot room away from his next victims. With Sasha snuggled against her, Maggy wondered if anyone back home got her message, and what they would do if they did.

CHAPTER 51

I always sang. My first memories are of me singing with my mom. ~Maggy Malone

One of the motors sputtered. Hunter yelled over the roar of the weather, "Check the gas."

Hanging on to the hull with one hand, Logan opened the aft locker. The gauge on the gas tank neared zero. He opened the cap. He couldn't see anything in it. Hunter looked back at him and Logan shook his head.

He searched the lockers nearby for an extra fuel tank. None. Hunter looked back at him again and shook his head. A greenie on the port side slammed the boat and the door of the locker shut.

Logan moved forward, as the boat rolled down the side of another dark, frothy swell. The engines groaned under the strain. Hunter looked back, and gave him a thumb down sign.

He turned the boat starboard heading into Silva Bay. They couldn't make Drumbeg Park without gas. They were in trouble. Taking a boat into a storm is dangerous; taking a boat without fuel into a storm is suicidal. There were no boats out on the water to see them. They had no radio. They would soon be at the mercy of the wind and the waves. They did have two paddles, but they would be as useful as toothpicks in these conditions.

The waters calmed as they drew closer to the marina. Logan held his breath hoping they could make it. The gas lasted until they saw the docks, 500 meters away. Then they paddled.

Logan jumped onto the dock and secured the boat. Hunter leaped out.

The docks were about half full, with boats bobbing up and down in the storm. There weren't many live-aboards at this marina. Most of the boats belonged to people who were warm in their homes. There were no lights.

Where the docks ended, an old hotel stood. There were no lights on there either. The storm must have cut their power.

Logan yelled through the noise of the storm, "It's going to take time to get gas."

"Sooner we start, the sooner we get it." Hunter yelled back and started running.

Logan caught up. "It's not that far on land to Drumbeg Park. Maybe six miles."

"You want to hike in this?" The docks beneath their feet pitched with the waves

Logan caught Hunter's arm. "I have to."

Hunter's jaw clenched.

"Our best chance," Logan said, panting, "is to split up. You find someone to get some gas, phone the police and head out on the water. I'll go by land. One of us will make it." He left out, "hopefully in time."

"How? No, don't tell me. Just do it." Hunter punched Logan's arm lightly, then he was off at a full sprint on the slick, wet, wooden dock towards the hotel.

Logan followed him up to the land, and then veered over to the parking lot. Without street lights, darkness flooded the area. The cars were large black shadows within the darkness, like smudges in a film. He found a pickup first. No keys. He could try out each car or take the time to hot-wire this one. It looked sturdy—decision made.

With a pocket knife he started on the wires and the engine caught within minutes. The old truck rattled up the bumpy, sodden dirt lane to the main road. Wind whistled through the hundred-foot fir trees. Broken branches littered the ground. No one was in sight.

He turned left onto the road and headed for the Drumbeg Park road, which he knew lay five minutes away in a car. Finally he had hope. He could make it. He had to make it. Sasha and Maggy needed him. The normally smooth pavement, had become riddled with broken branches. Widow makers, the loggers called them, large enough to take your life if they fell on your head. The truck took bump after bump as he floored the gas pedal.

Shit. Logan slammed on the brakes and stopped within an inch of a five-foot-wide tree trunk lying across the road. The truck skidded to the right and hit the tree on its passenger side. He slammed his fist on the steering wheel. So close.

The adrenaline surging through his body made him want to run. He got out of the car and walked the length of the tree both ways. There was no way to drive around it.

Now half-way to Drumbeg Park, he'd have to hike the rest of the way. His eye caught a shape in the back of the truck. No. Could it be? Hell yeah. It was a bicycle.

He grabbed the bike and pulled it over the trunk of the tree. Once on the other side he hopped on and peddled with all his energy, and then some, feeling the clock ticking against his heart.

Driving over the branches had been hard, but cycling proved harder. He zig-zagged as best he could around the broken branches with a strong wind hitting him at the side. The bike veered left and right as it took the bumps. Sweat poured from his body. His muscles tensed under the pressure. He pushed forward.

***

Hunter banged on the wharfinger's office door. He was just about ready to break in and search for gas-pump keys when the light of a flashlight appeared from behind him.

"What the fuck you up to?" said a gruff voice.

Turning he saw a man dressed in rain gear from head to foot. Under his sou'ester his face looked weathered. "I'm chasing a murderer who's kidnapped a little girl. I need help," said Hunter. "Gas and cops for starters."

CHAPTER 52

I think in notes and beats and harmonies.
~ Maggy Malone

In the fishing boat, Maggy gave up trying to sleep. Thoughts and memories flowed through her mind. So many things she wanted to do in her life. This couldn't be the end.

Still, morbid thoughts bit into her like rats feasting on dead meat. She swallowed. It was not the time to let herself wallow in darkness. She had others to think about. So she thought about Logan. Together with Joe they could manage the Black Cat and she could really get her singing career going. Good friends and an on-going gig—what more could she want? There was Hunter. . .

Her body shivered, her adrenaline rush still pumped on high.

Sasha had cried herself into a restless sleep.

She'd cough every so often, a horrible throaty cough.

The night refused to end.

But then she wasn't sure she wanted it to.

It was still dark, but the water had calmed a little. Gilbert entered the cabin with ropes in his hands.

"What are you going to do?" asked Maggy.

"Relax. I don't kill girls." He flashed a wicked smile. "Unless I have to." He moved over to Sasha. "I'm going to tie her up and then you and I are going to go get the gold."

No time left. No cavalry. No luck. A metallic taste filled her mouth and her heart raced. "What then?" she asked.

"Then we bring the gold back to the boat and I drop the two of you off somewhere safe."

That sounded way better than anything she had imagined. But could she trust a murderer? It would be so much easier for him to kill them. And he was good at killing.

Sasha woke up. Her eyes filled with tears. She hadn't missed a word. He wrapped a rope around her tiny waist and tied her to the chair. Then he secured her hands. "I don't kill women," he muttered. "Or children. It's not right." Sweat poured down his face, its acrid smell saturated the air.

"What if I refuse to help you?" said Maggy.

"Then I'll make an exception this time. I'll kill you." He looked at her with empty eyes. "And the wee one."

Maggy gritted her teeth. No way in hell would she let that happen.

CHAPTER 53

When the music plays the din of the world fades. Hey, I
rhymed that one. ~ Maggy Malone

Logan made it to the Drumbeg Provincial Park turnoff and headed down the hill to the beach. Almost there. He followed the one clue Maggy had left him, and only that. There were fewer branches on this road. He gained speed. He was almost there.

***

Hunter was back in the Zodiac with the engines topped up. The storm had eased, and his route to the park was protected by the flat top islands. It would be rough, but nothing like what he'd come through already. With luck he'd be there in thirty minutes. The police were coming by road from the other end of the island and should be there about the same time. He shook his head. He couldn't believe he was working with the RCMP. The fucking Mounties! He turned the ignition key.

"Hang on, Maggy, hang on." The wind took his words, as the boat flew through the three-foot chop. Could he make it in time?

CHAPTER 54

Music is my lover. ~ Maggy Malone

Logan ditched his bicycle at the beach and started running. As he broke through the trees, the anchor light at the top of the mast of the fish boat in the distance came into view bobbing with the action of the waves. *They made it*. But had they made land? The flashing light from the buoy marking Rygars Reef, lit the black sky in an eerie staccato of darkness and light.

He ran forward, scanning the area. As he passed the last of the Garry oaks on the path he could see the open beach and a meadow. Two figures stood close together over a hole. The larger figure held a shovel.

Logan crept closer. The man was focused on

digging. Maggy stood beside him with her arms folded across her chest. No sign of Sasha. The air in his lungs escaped. No Sasha.

Picking up a big branch, a real widow-maker, he said his last silent prayer. Coming up from behind the fisherman, he narrowed the distance between them. The sounds of the violent storm in the distance hid his approach.

The man couldn't see him unless he turned. *Please don't turn.* He lifted the branch high over his head. It must weigh twenty, fucking pounds. He brought it down slicing the air. But just before it made contact, the asshole turned and jumped out of range. The murderer's eyes flashed in the night, so cold they made Logan hesitate.

Then he swung the branch like a baseball bat at the man's midsection with all the hatred his heart held. The man stepped out of the way and pulled on the branch as it missed him. It fell to the ground. Logan lunged at him. *No fucking mercy.*

They tumbled onto the ground.

***

Maggy's heart logdged in her throat. Logan looked younger and more agile than Gilbert, but Gilbert was meaner than a grizzly with an abscessed tooth. She screamed, but her voice disappeared in the wind. Lot of good that was going to do. She looked at Logan's branch, hesitated, then picked it up.

The men pummeled each other, pounding, groaning and swearing. Nasty. They were fighting to the death and they both knew it. Desperation and rage filled the air around them.

She wanted to swing the branch and connect with Gilbert's head, but they were moving around so much she could hit Logan by mistake. She waited for her chance.

Maggy gasped for air. She could do this. *Concentrate. Wait for the right moment. Focus.* She'd hit that bastard as hard as she could. Now. No. Logan rolled on top. Shit.

A shot rang out. Turning she saw Hunter coming along the beach with a gun in his hand.

The noise startled the men on the ground, and for an instant they fell apart. Just long enough. Maggy brought the stick down on Gilbert's head and heard a loud crack as it met the bones of his skull.

Gilbert at the last moment saw it coming, but it was too late. He tried to move out of its way, but the wood caught the right side of his head. A horrible crunching echoed in her ears. Blood spurted in all directions. She screamed.

Sirens blared in the distance. The cavalry was on its way. But too late for her. She'd already killed him.

Hunter came to her but she prevented him from holding her. She had to take it all in. Logan slowly got up. The wind howled. A confusion of images and sounds enveloped her. Her mind stayed focused on the blood pouring from the fisherman's head. She'd killed him.

Hunter bent down and checked Gilbert's pulse. Logan tried to put his arm around her, but she pushed him away. Her body started shaking uncontrollably.

Hunter shook his head, no. As in no pulse. But she knew that already. Deep down in her soul, she knew that. She had killed him.

"Where's Sasha?" yelled Logan.

Maggy pointed towards the fishing boat, and then her world went black. As she sank into the comforting darkness, the image of Brother XII greeted her. Lifting one brow, he nodded his head, as if welcoming her to another world. A world she didn't ask to enter. Gentle hands guided her body carefully to the ground.

CHAPTER 55

"Love. . . Sing. . . Live." ~ Maggy Malone

L ogan's heart raced. Sasha?
The police and ambulance sirens stopped close to them. They'd be down in a couple minutes with a million questions. Logan looked at Hunter. He nodded towards the chuck.

Logan looked towards Kendrick Island. The light of the mast of Gilbert's fishing boat bobbed in the waves. It was moving. "Oh fuck."

"Take the Zodiac. I'll handle things here," said Hunter.

"Sa—sha." Logan's chest tightened.

"The light's moving, man. Gilbert's boat anchor isn't holding."

The storm had released the anchor's grip.

The wind was pushing the boat towards. . . Oh shit. He knew that area. It couldn't be worse. Dark swirling water created by the strong current. He had to get to the boat before the eight-knot current from the Gabriola Passage sucked it into its narrow rocky strait.

Logan didn't need to say any of that out loud. They both knew how dangerous these waters were and what was at stake.

He looked at Maggy, lying semi-conscious on the ground.

"Go," said Hunter.

He leaned over Maggy. She babbled about "the brother." Paramedics were heading their way with a stretcher. He'd have to trust that they would take care of her. Logan turned and ran for the Zodiac.

The shouts from the police were lost in the wind. He didn't have time to explain his actions. Hunter would take care of that, and Maggy. He had to get Sasha.

As he turned the key, the Zodiac's motors came to life and he pulled out into the bay. The storm waves were running at three feet and the boat bounced between them. It didn't matter how wet or cold he got. All that mattered was Sasha. His gut clenched.

As he approached Kendrick Island, the fishing boat blew closer and closer to the strait. It took ten minutes to get within a few feet of it and by that time it was out in the open being pulled towards the Gabriola Passage by the eight knot current.

He brought the Zodiac alongside and cut the

motor. He jumped on board the vessel with a tow rope in his hand. Once aboard he secured the rope. The wind howled through the rigging, and the deck pitched on the waves. He edged along to the cabin door. It was locked.

He kicked it open. Sasha was tied up and crying. Her eyes wide. Her body trembling. He ran to her, and undid the ropes. The boat sped up on the current. It rose out of the water and gained momentum, as if the motor was running. Throwing the ropes aside he pulled Sasha towards him for a big hug.

"Daddy," she cried.

"Hang onto my hand. We've got to get out of here." He would not chance starting the diesel motor. Fishing boats motors were notorious for their idiosyncrasies. They'd have to get back to the Zodiac.

Above deck the wind had picked up. He hadn't made it in time. They had entered the passage. The water was running fast.

"Hang on to the side of the boat here." He placed her hands where he thought she'd be most secure. "Hang on honey. With all your might." He spoke into her ear. "I'll slip into the boat, and when I motion to you, I want you to jump into my arms."

"I can't."

"You have to."

"Daddy, I'm scared."

"I'm scared too honey. But that's what we have to do."

"No," she cried. "Can't we just stay in this boat? It's bigger."

The current was speeding them along. They couldn't wait any longer. Logan slid into the Zodiac.

"I can't." yelled Sasha.

He motioned again and with every fiber in his body willed her to jump.

She stood trembling and for a moment he thought she'd never find the courage to take the leap. Then her quivering jaw firmed and she jumped. He almost fell over when she arrived in his arms.

Sitting her in the passenger seat, he released the rope tying them to the fishing boat and started the motors. At first it was as if they weren't working. The boat didn't seem to move. The current held them. The fishing boat sped away into the depths of the passage. He prayed his engines would keep them out.

He opened the throttle fully and slowly they began to make headway. He hoped their gas would last long enough to get out of the deadly current that was trying to push them back. After ten minutes they popped out of the current, and the Zodiac leaped ahead. They headed back to the bay where Maggy and the others waited.

CHAPTER 56

Rita's Journal

I'll never forget the last time we made love. We sailed on the *Lady Royal* under a full moon through a narrow passage. The wind and current flowed with us, and it felt like we were gliding on air. After anchoring in a beautiful bay, he helped me into a little row boat.

On the way to the shore, Eddie showed me a group of ancient carvings clustered together on a sandstone boulder. One looked like a fish, another like a hunter with a spear. We wandered along a path, past some Garry oak trees and came upon a meadow near the water. That is where he put down the blanket and we made love.

Always a passionate lover, Eddie was even more attentive that night. I felt as if I had entered the world of the spirits with him. Afterwards we lay in each other's arms and talked in soft voices.

He told me where he had hidden his gold. "I buried it up there by the arbutus with the lovers heart carved into it. I put your name in the heart."

"You're always burying it and digging it up again," I said not wanting to be duped by his charm yet again.

He didn't answer me.

"Well, why are you telling me this now?"

"There are men who wish to harm me. If I should disappear, I want you to know where it is. I don't want you to be desperate for money. Whatever they say about me, remember that what we have is real."

I wanted to believe him. Oh how I wanted to believe him.

CHAPTER 57

Always listen to the music. ~ Maggy Malone

When the RCMP called her down to the scene of the crime the next morning, Maggy didn't know what to expect.

Hundred-foot fir trees dominated the entrance of Drumbeg Park, where First Nations people had gathered for centuries to fish. She never felt alone in magical places like this; she felt part of something larger, not set in time, or even in place. As she walked with Logan and Sasha along the edge of the bay they passed the grove of Garry oaks Rita had talked about in her journal. Following the path, they came to the meadow marked by the sprawling arbutus tree where Brother XII had carved Rita's name.

She looked around. Hard to believe it was the same place she'd been last night. A shiver stole up her spine. The sun shone, illuminating a magnificent view. To the northeast stood the snow-capped, coastal mountains. Mount Baker in the middle. To the south, only a stone's throw away, lay Valdes Island. Closer still was Kendrick Island, the tiny land mass that had protected them in the storm. Straight across from where she stood, the channel opened up and she could see the long waterway that extended down the eastern side of Vancouver Island. It was a breath-taking view, ruggedly beautiful and peaceful.

Sasha clung to her father's hand as they approached the area where Maggy had killed Gilbert. It had been cordoned off by police tape. A constable lifted the tape for them and they approached the hole in the ground. Hunter stood there. His blue eyes, soft and comforting, greeted her like a warm hug. A few feet away a group of three men, two in uniform and one not, stood talking in a circle.

The hole Gilbert had started to dig was now about six feet deep, and beside it was a pile of dirt and a wooden box. They stood together looking at it—the box. All this for a box. Maggy took a deep breath and let it out slowly.

"Gold?" asked Logan.

A man in a dark-blue trench coat turned towards them. It was Peterson. "Depends how you look at it," he said. "All I see is a box. Stopping the murderer—that was the gold." He walked towards them.

So Gravel Voice is a philosopher-cop.

He gave Maggy a weathered smile. "Open the treasure chest. You deserve the first look."

If there had been a lock, the police had removed it. All she had to do was open it. Maggy crouched and with great care lifted its lid. The rusty hinges groaned as it fell open.

The box was mostly empty. But on the bottom lay a single scroll of paper. Carefully, she lifted it out and read: "Only fools love gold." It was signed by Brother XII in a fancy, scrolling hand. Maggy started laughing.

She let the paper fall back into the box and stood up.

"Maybe Brother XII was a wise man after all," said Hunter.

CHAPTER 58

Sometimes I hit the wrong note, but I get it right
eventually. I trust the music to make it right.
~ Maggy Malone

"What do you want?" Hunter entered her houseboat with one long stride, his face tight, and his voice heavy. "I've been giving you space and time, only because you asked me to."

"I. . . can't get Gilbert's face out of my mind. His smell . . . his . . ."

"Death." Hunter's eyes held hers. "Maggy, the guy was a scumbag. He killed three men. He deserved to die."

She sighed. "I just wish it didn't have to be me."

"Maggy, sometimes life happens and we

don't always get a choice."

She shook her head and tears welled in her eyes. "We always have a choice."

Hunter waited a few seconds and then said, "There's no point beating yourself up about it."

"Don't tell me I'm going to get over it, because I won't."

"No, Maggy, you won't." He moved closer to her. "It's only been a couple days. Gil's death has left a shadow on your heart. You won't ever forget what happened that night, but you can . . ." He reached for her, but she moved back. "You can learn to live with it."

Maggy wrapped her arms around herself. "I'm not going to let him ruin the rest of my life. I will manage."

"You're the strongest and bravest woman I know."

She looked at a spot on the wall and tried not to let the avalanche of emotion brewing inside her leak out. "I called you over to talk to you about something else." She ran a hand through her tangled hair. There was no easy way to do this.

"What?" he said in an intimate tone.

Her eyes slid down the wall and fixed on her sink. "Um... It's my garburator."

"Your garburator?" His brows rose.

"It's stuck." She swallowed her nerves. "It's too full and . . ."

He shook his head. "Maggy." The heat of his body, only a foot away from hers, flowed over her like a tropical wave. His Irish-blue eyes met hers with hurricane force. "You don't have a garburator."

"Still, it's stuck. And I can't seem to . . ."

"Sweet Maggy." A playful smile crossed his lips. He touched her face gently with his calloused fingertips, sending a primal need for him rippling through her body. She swallowed again. She touched his chest with the palm of her hand, flooding her senses with him. "Hunter, everything's messed up."

"The garburator again?" He laughed, but it sounded hollow.

"I don't want to end things between us."

"That won't happen. Ever." A mischievous smile crossed his lips. "You want me to look at your . . . sink?" He took a strand of her hair and pulled it through his fingers as if he was handling strands of pure gold.

She lifted her chin. Nothing was easy about this. "You mean a lot to me."

"I know," he said, stepping closer. His breath touched her face as he spoke. "Honey, your real problem isn't your plumbing. It's your electrical panel."

"You think I'm crossing wires?"

"Overheating circuits can cause serious trouble." His voice, steady and low, stirred her in ways she really didn't want.

"Like sparks."

He nodded. "And fire."

"Any suggestions?"

"I could have a look." His whole hand was in her hair now, pulling her head towards him. His lips were inches from hers. "Make sure everything's connected the way it should be." His mouth stopped so close to hers. She could smell coffee on his breath. "Then test it."

She gulped for air. "I bet you could." She pushed on his chest, giving them more space. At least a respectable quarter inch more. How could she tell him?

"Maggy." The way he said her name made her heart ache. He wanted her. And she . . . ...

"Hunter, I'm not ready for you."

His eyes narrowed.

"And I have a relationship with Logan."

"The garbage again."

She clenched her jaw. Was there any way to say all that was in her heart without giving him false hope? It wasn't right. One man, one woman—that's the way it was supposed to be. But she wasn't ready to be with Hunter. He was so intense. Their relationship would swallow her whole. Logan was fun and easy. Sex and laughter. That was enough for her for now.

"I'm not ready to love. And the truth is, I may never be ready to love again."

"You've made your decision." His eyes hardened and her throat constricted.

A stubborn tear flowed down her cheek. "We're going to run the Black Cat together, and he's advancing me wages so I can help my mother out." She swallowed. "We . . . have fun together. It's not love. It's not commitment. I'm not ready for that with anyone."

Their eyes locked, the silence between them heavy and volatile.

After a couple seconds, he said, "I'll always be here for you."

"Hunter."

Without another word he turned and walked away. Her heart sank like a rock into a bottomless pit as he closed the door behind him.

CHAPTER 59

Let the Music in. ~Maggy Malone

When Maggy opened the back door of the bar the cold wind off the sea hit her hard, just as it did the night Jimmy died. The rain had stopped, but the skies were still gray and the air damper than a dungeon cellar. She walked down the narrow steps with Logan behind her. She could hear the team working below. Sounds of ladders moving and people talking greeted them.

"What's going on?" asked Logan.

"Come see." She took him by the hand and led him to where Jimmy had died. Two men and three women were painting on the brick wall beside the spot. A couple of them turned and smiled. The smell of fresh paint dominated the narrow space.

"What's this?" he asked.

"Mei organized a group of art students to paint a mural for Jimmy. It's going to be a picture of the *Emerald Empress* on the sea, with the mountains in the background."

"Like my photograph."

She waited, giving him time.

His eyes widened as he studied the brush strokes. "How did you . . . "

"The guy who owns the building agreed that a mural would help make the alley feel okay again. He liked the picture I showed him and gave me the green light. When the students heard the story they offered to do it for free. They said they could showcase their work. The newspaper's going to do a feature on them."

One of the painters, in a blue bandana turned towards them. Mei flashed her lopsided grin. "It's good karma." She dipped her brush into the paint can and turned back to the mural.

Maggy touched Logan's hand. "It all just came together." As Joe said it would.

Moving closer to her, Logan put his arm around her shoulders. The sun peeked out between the dark clouds and flooded the alley with light. They stood there, in the place where Jimmy had died, and watched its transformation.

THE END

A Note from Jo-Ann

Dear Readers,

"Every time a reader leaves a review an aspiring writer gets a new pencil."[iii] It may sound like a cheesy-line, but it's true. Reviews help readers find books. Please take a few minutes and write a review. Don't be intimidated by the task. All you need to do is string a few words together. If you're stuck, I'll give two examples: 1) I loved Black Cat Blues and can't wait to read Carson's next book. Or 2) Black Cat Blues is filled with danger and a touch of the paranormal. I enjoyed it. The best places to post reviews are Amazon and Goodreads. Word of mouth and written reviews are pure gold for budding writers, like me.

You can learn about my latest publications from my newsletter. Want to connect? My home on the Internet is my website (www.Jo-Ann Carson.com) which contains all my social media links.

To send me a personal note, you can email me at **connect@jo-anncarson.com**. I'd love to hear your thoughts on the story.

On the next few pages you'll find information about the other books in the Mata Hari series, and my Vancouver Blues series. As a bonus feature, I have added the first chapter of the next novel in the series, *Ancient Danger*.

Thank you for reading my story.

Hugs

Jo-Ann

Smokey's Killer Salmon Chowder

Smokey's Killer Salmon Chowder

This is a recipe that I learned when I lived up on the Haida Gwaii, a remote and pristine wilderness area of Canada, often referred to as the northern Galapagos Islands. In my book, *Black Cat Blues* it's served at the local restaurant on Granville Island called The Scuttlebutt.

Ingredients:

a few tblsp. oil
1 medium cooking onion
2-4 medium potatoes, peeled and diced
1 can (or equivalent) lima beans
2 fresh carrots thinly sliced
2 stalks celery
4 cooked sliced bacon strips
4 cups milk
6 tablespoons flour
1 lb. can of salmon (or equivalent fresh)

Instructions:

1. In a large, deep skillet sauté sliced onion in oil until it's soft. Add previously cooked and drained bacon that has been cut into half inch pieces.
2. Add flour and stir until it cooks. Add water (about ½ cup) and stir until it thickens.
3. Boil 4 cups of water. Add the roux created in #2 and stir.
4. Add potatoes, beans, carrots, celery and the fluid from the canned salmon.
5. Add more water if it's too thick.
6. Cook twenty minutes or so, until the potatoes are cooked. Season with salt and pepper.
7. Add salmon (that you have flaked with a fork). Always add fish at the very end, because you don't want to overcook it. This salmon is already cooked. You are just heating it up.
8. Add milk.
9. Bring to a boil, then reduce the heat. Serve.
10. I garnish it with shredded cheese (mozzarella is fun, cheddar is yummy – experiment).
11. Enjoy!

Suggested Book Club Questions for Discussion:

1. Why is it important that Maggy sings the blues?
2. Why Vancouver? What is it about the setting on Granville Island that enhances the story?
3. Does the use of the legend of Brother XII deepen the story for you, or does it make it seem silly, like a pirate's treasure hunt?
4. What do you think of Maggy?
5. Which main male character do you like best? Logan or Hunter? Why?
6. What do you think of the murderer?
7. Which secondary character do you find the most intriguing and why? (Mei, Edgar, Jimmy, Smokey, Peterson)
8. What were the main themes running through the book and how well do you think the author handled them? (i.e., ideas about life/death, quest for gold, love)
9. Did the climax work for you? (You can take this however you like, but I will let you know that romance writers refer to the climax of the story as the black moment, because they like to have lots of climaxes<grin>, and then there is the climax to the suspense story as well.)
10. If you could rewrite the ending what would you have happen?
11. For writers: Find an example of where the

visceral description of an event worked, and find an example of where more could be put in.

12. For writers: How many hooks are there in the first paragraph and what kind are they?

13. What do you imagine will happen with the cast of characters in the second book?

Brother XII
Research Bibliography

Books:
MacIsaac, Ron, Clark, Don, and Lillard, Charles.
The Devil of Decourcy Island: The Brother XII.
Porcepic Books. 1989
Peterson, Jan. *Harbour City Nanaimo in Transition*,
1920-1267. Heritage House. 2006.
Internet:
Pearl, Luke. "Will the Real Madame Zee Please
Rap Three Times."
http://www.harpercollins.ca/author/authorExtra.asp
x?authorID=60000868&isbn13=9780002005135&d
isplayType=bookinterview, August 18, 2012
Ruttan, Stephen. Greater Victoria Library, "Brother
XII." http://gvpl.ca/using-the-library/our-
collection/local-history/tales-from-the-
vault/brother-xii/, August 19, 2012
Randsco Scott and Rachel. "Blue Heron Park to
Pirate's Cove Marine Park on DeCourcy Island."
http://randsco.com/?p=604&more=1&c=1, August
19, 2012
Wagner Thomas, "Brother 12, aka Edward Arthur
Wilson."
http://www3.telus.net/cowbay/island/brother12/inde
x.html, Aug. 13, 2012.
http://en.wikipedia.org/wiki/Brother_XII, Aug. 13,
2012.

Ain't Misbehavin'
Chapter One

Maggy Malone gritted her teeth as she scanned the grisly scene in The Tuscan Trattoria. Sirens and flashing lights closed in on the small restaurant. The screams of patrons shredded the tranquility of the night. She swallowed. Another dead person. Inspector Peterson from the Vancouver Police Department strode through the front door took one look around and found her. He headed in her direction. Of course it would be him. She grunted. His eyes cut through the distance between them like razor blades, bringing the memory of the last time she dealt with him back to her with the clout and clarity of a hammer blow between the eyes. He stopped a foot in front of her and nailed her with his cop glare. "Why do men get murdered around you?"

"I wish I knew," she said. Her heart raced. Ten feet away, a man's face lay motionless in his plate of spaghetti. Her quiet, Friday dinner had turned into a nightmare.

Joe, her mentor, sat across from her at the white-linen-covered table, holding his glass of merlot in the air. Of all the places they could be . . .why did they end up here? Now? His head swayed to the classical guitar music—"Speak Softly

Love," better known as the "Godfather theme,"—
but his jaw firmed in a way she'd only seen once
before. Her chest tightened. This excitement would
be hard on his heart.

Two constables in uniform threaded yellow
tape across half the restaurant where they sat. More
sirens blared through the night. The ambulance
should be next.

Inspector Peterson motioned for her to get
up. She walked with him a few feet away from Joe,
making every effort to look normal, even though
her legs felt like wobbly bands of rubber.

"Tell me why you're here." His gravelly
voice brought back many memories. She knew from
experience that its quality ranged depending on his
mood. It came from somewhere deep in his personal
abyss, and sounded so rough it made the tiny hairs
on the back of her neck stand up and take notice.

A strand of long blond hair clung to his
black dress shirt. Some lucky lady had been leaning
on his broad, cop shoulders. Maybe that's what had
made him so cranky. He smelled of expensive
French cologne and cigarettes, a scent she
remembered too well. When Maggy didn't answer
right away he grumbled to get her attention and
gave her his full-powered-cop glare.

"I needed to be alone with Joe," she said.
Murder hadn't been on the menu. She chose The
Tuscan Trattoria to get away from their friends. She
loved the place, built in the old grocery warehouse
in Gastown, it had an urban-kitschy atmosphere,
with old, red-brick walls, rustic, wood ceilings,
antiques and artifacts.

The detective nodded. "Why?"

"To talk some sense into him." She frowned. "He needs to take the meds his doctor prescribes, but he won't because he says they make him feel tired all the time, and they're expensive. So, instead he knocks back an herbal concoction three times a day some pretty lady talked him into. It makes him a little crazy. Meanwhile his health isn't improving." She looked over at Joe again. He held his glass of wine in the air, swirled it like a pro and dipped his nose inside the edge to smell its bouquet. But he didn't drink it. Instead he repeated the process.

Peterson's persistent glare brought her eyes back to his like a tractor beam. His six feet towered over her five-foot-four, which made her straighten her back and jut out her chin, as if that somehow equaled the playing field. A jagged purple scar ran across his square jaw.

"I remember Joe," he said. "Clarence's cousin, and now one of the owners of the Black Cat Blues Bar where you sing."

She nodded.

His hazel eyes drifted over to Joe and back to her face, not softening even a smidgen. Cops. "So you're out with him on a Friday night. What did you do with your other men?"

She exhaled slowly. Men—in the plural. Talk about being judgmental. There had been two men in her life when she last met the detective, but she had chosen one shortly afterwards. Not that it was his, or anyone else's, business. "I'm here with Joe." She shook her blond curls out of her face.

Curly, long and wild it had a nasty habit of getting in her way, but men loved it and it had become as much her trademark as Dolly Parton's girls.

Peterson took out his notebook. "So what did you see, Ms. Malone?"

Having been married to a cop for seven years she knew what he wanted. Facts--lots and lots of facts. The people in blue believed, without a shadow of a doubt, that sorting facts into neat columns on white boards could reveal the truth. She admired the simplicity of their plan, but she could never render life into tidy columns. The universe held too many surprises and nothing in her life had ever been logical or lineal. She took a deep breath of the garlic and basil laced air and sighed.

"We got here about seven—that would be an hour ago. Most of the tables were full, and a steady stream of people flowed in and out. The wait-staff hustled."

She hesitated a moment, letting the images of people sift through her mind like musical notes. "A baseball team with blue shirts that read, "Vancouver Hitters," sat near the back." She pointed towards the kitchen. "They'd be in their early twenties. They had a burping contest."

"Burping," Peterson muttered as he scribbled.

"About half an hour ago, eight women in their thirties ushered in a lady dressed like a Steam Punk heroine with red-shadowed eyes and a funky black hat. I figured it was a stagette. They sat near the front and made the bride-to-be hand out condoms to every man who passed. When the screaming started, they were the first group to scurry out the entrance."

He nodded, as if red-eyed Victorian vixens were a common sight. Maybe they were in his life.

"A couple in their eighties wearing matching blue jogging suits sat at the table between us and *the man* . . ." She wanted to talk about the victim with respect. ". . .the man with his face . . . in his dinner. They were there when we came and left just before it happened."

Peterson's pen raced across his notepad. His mouth twitched, as if he needed to say something, but wouldn't let himself.

"The man sat alone. On the far side of him, about twelve people celebrated a birthday. I know that, because every so often a person in their group would stand up and give a toast. Some slurred. There was lots of happy chatter."

When she stopped talking he looked up from his notepad. "And?"

"Inspector, I don't know what else I can tell you. It seemed like a normal night in Gastown." *If that makes any sense.*

The oldest part of Vancouver, Gastown got its name from Gassy Jack the wild frontier man who opened the first saloon on the edge of the Canadian wilderness. Over the years, it had become well known as a place for both debauchery and commerce. Now considered the hippest neighborhood in the city, the hood had transformed itself. The old warehouses had been converted to upscale condos, nightclubs and art studios. Meanwhile the homeless wandered the streets outside. Gastown had changed its outward appearance over the last two centuries more times than a busy whore at midnight, but some things never changed. It was, and always had been, a place where the word "normal" didn't apply.

He tapped his pen on his paper. "Gastown—normal."

Maggy ran a hand through her hair. "I didn't see anything unusual. No one stuck out."

Peterson twisted his mouth, as if he had difficulty digesting something she'd said.

She smiled as best she could. "We sat over there." She pointed. "Where Joe is now, two tables away from the . . ..um . . .victim. Do you wanna know what I ate?"

"Just get to the murder, Ms. Malone." His eyes held steady and his voice flattened out like concrete on a prairie highway, pushing her forward to a place with no horizon, a place she didn't want to go.

"It happened behind me." Her voice caught on her last word. It had been easy to talk about the crowd. Easy to make jokes about their behavior. She cleared her throat. Violent death would never be easy for her to talk about. "First, the big group sang "'Happy Birthday,'" loud enough and out of tune enough, to make you want to cover your ears. Then the lights went out." She swallowed.

"Then I heard a shot . . .then another. Two, close together. The whole room shook with the sound. It rattled everything, even my bones. A blast of warm air hit the back of my neck and then the lights kicked in." Maggy crossed her arms across her chest and took a deep breath, seeing the whole event again in her head. She slowed down.

"A woman screamed. A loud, break-the-windows screech like in the old black-and-white movies. Then another screamed and another. By the time I turned around, people were huddled around the man's table. I couldn't see a thing."

His eyes narrowed. "But you saw something."

She swallowed. "Two waitresses got people to back away from the table. The man's head, or what was left of it, lay in the middle of his plate of spaghetti. Bright red Bolognese sauce had splattered all over the table and floor."

"What happened next?"

"Rick, the manager, ran in and checked his pulse. It all happened so quickly..." She tried to remember every detail. "A couple of the waiters came in and did the same. They shook their heads. Then I heard the sirens. Then you came."

Peterson kept writing in his notebook, his body tensing with every new piece of information she fed him about the murder. She didn't bother trying to read his face. She knew from experience he kept his emotions hidden behind his shiny badge. He'd tell her only what he wanted her to know, and that would be a sterilized version of the truth. A cop version.

While the good inspector had intriguing complexities, she didn't want to explore them. He brought back too many bad memories. How the hell did he end up in her life again? Not to mention another murder? She'd put the past behind her and refocused on her career.

Anticipating his next move with dread, her fingers fidgeted. She clasped them together.

"You have any connection to the deceased?" he asked.

And there it was. She swallowed. No point denying the truth. He'd find out later. "Inspector, I . . ."

When she didn't finish her sentence, the pupils of his eyes hardened into small pin-point dots.

She shook hair out of her face again and glanced quickly in Joe's direction. "Don't know him personally, but . . ."

He lifted his left eyebrow.

"I'm pretty sure he's the guy they call the Naked Alderman." And her best friend Mei Chang's lover, but she didn't say that. She exhaled slowly. "Kyler Ravensworth."

An unwanted tremble entered her voice. Dead bodies did that to her, and this one was too close to home. His death would break Mei's heart. Next her limbs would tremble uncontrollably. She'd been this close to murder before and didn't want to go back.

Peterson thumped his pencil on his notepad. "The guy who wanted a community garden on every block?"

She nodded. "Yeah. He got called 'the naked alderman' because he always took part in the annual naked ride in town. He liked to say he had nothing to hide." She remembered laughing the first time she heard him say that, but it didn't seem so funny now. The image of him on the local TV news flickered through her mind: young, healthy and virile, a handsome civic minded man in the prime of his life.

Peterson nodded and jotted more notes.

Flashes lit up the room sporadically as a police officer took pictures of the scene. They reflected off the ornate Tiffany lamp that hung from the ceiling with the name Tuscany's on it, creating a macabre kaleidoscope of colored lights. While the detective wrote, she took in the changing scene.

In the opposite corner of the room sat the ghost table set for two, vacant as always. According to local legend, the ghost liked his space. To sit at his table would bring bad luck. Scores of stories about what happened to people when they dared to sit at *the table* had circulated ever since the restaurant opened fifty years ago. A cold shudder snaked up her spine. She didn't need to be thinking about ghosts now.

The trattoria's saucy mix of relics from the past and present usually charmed her, but tonight, with the flashing lights, and spilled spaghetti sauce, it made her blood run cold.

The ambulance attendants waited while the medical examiner studied the body. After a second look at the deceased, Maggy turned back to Peterson. Her knees weakened. The last dead man she'd seen . . . No. She didn't want to think about that. Nausea rose in her stomach.

"Take a deep breath in and let it out slowly," Peterson said. His attention shifted to someone behind her.

"Can I take Joe home now?" she asked. The old man continued to swirl his wine and sniff the edge of the glass.

"Does he know anything more than you?"

"Don't think so." That was sort of true.

"I know where to reach you. Thank you for your help, Ms. Malone." He said this as he brushed past her to join a group of policemen in uniform. He gave her no good bye, just a nod and a stirring of air, scented with his cologne, as he passed.

Maggy walked over to Joe. "Ready to go?"

"Sure, Maggy." His thin lips spread into a soft smile that slid straight into her heart. Hmmm. She couldn't let him win with his damned charm. There had to be a way to get the stubborn old goat to take his meds.

"I'll get you back to the Black Cat," he said. Logan would be angry at her for being gone so long. No doubt about that. She'd left him to do all the work at the bar.

Maggy waited as Joe slowly rose. He leaned on his white cane to steady himself. She knew better than to offer assistance. He'd get all huffy. Once he stood, she looped her arm in his.

Outside, the fresh, salty breeze off the strait mingled with the sweet smell of cherry blossoms. She inhaled the freshness of the spring evening and squeezed Joe's thin arm.

He leaned his head towards hers. "Did you tell him what the ghost said?"

About Jo-Ann Carson

Jo-Ann Carson has lived most of her life on islands off the west coast of Canada, surrounded by snow covered mountains, lush rain forests and pristine beaches.

Growing up, she dreamed of traveling the world like James Bond, searching for relics like Indiana Jones, and finding true love, so it's no surprise that in her Mata Hari Series she combines elements of adventure, danger and steamy romance.

In her Vancouver Blues Series she slides into the realm of Urban Noir and explores the dark side of the city. These books are mainstream suspense with strong romantic elements and are very-Vancouver.

[i] Quote from Brother XII's book, *The Three Truths*, taken from

Ron MacIsaac, Don Clark and Charles Lillard's book *The Devil of Decourcy Island The Brother XII* ,Porcepic Books, Victoria, 1989, p. 24.

[ii] Wilhelm Baynes, The I Ching, Princeton University Press, New Jersey, 1967, p. 629.

[iii] Bobby Adair, *Ebola K*